A Woman's Game

The Sequel

Paula McCoy - Pinderhughes

Published by Crispin Publishing

Designed by Vince Pannullo
Printed in the United States of America by RJ Communications.

ISBN: 978-0-578-18701-3

DEDICATION

To my parents who made me believe that my aspirations would only be limited by the limitations I place on myself. To my readers who continuously make the trip exciting and to the two most important men in my life…thank you for sharing your intellect, love and laughter.

As Sonya and her guest turned and released from their easy embrace, an unfamiliar car pulled into the already crowded driveway. Ary and Marcus' attention turned from the front door to the idling engine behind them. For a brief moment, both siblings had experienced feelings of relief and a resurgence of lost emotion and forgiveness. But now, they wondered if it were only temporary.

CHAPTER 1

SONYA had once again found solace in painting as she stood facing the expanse of her backyard, filled with trees whose leaves were transitioning to their fall wardrobe of burnt oranges, muted yellows and radiant ambers. Her mind painted the images before her brushes stroked the canvas. So much time she thought, so much of life had passed her by. Now it was time to catch up to herself, where she would have been, where she *should* have been at this stage in her life. She'd come to accept the love Matthew had for her ex-husband. A love she herself once shared. Now, she felt, it was okay if she wasn't quite sure if or how she could still love or care for Bruce. No, all that mattered right now was a heart filled with peace and forgiveness, if not for herself emotionally, then surely for her sanity.

As she mixed the colors from her palette, she recalled the moment she'd made the decision to call Matthew and invite him to Brookstone. It was shortly after she and her strong willed daughter had their final argument after returning home from the hospital. Ary stood at the front door, stoically watching as her mother broke down in tears, crying for all that she'd gone through, all that her family had endured, purposely hesitating before walking over to comfort her. She'd summoned the courage to tell Sonya to look inside herself, at her own grief and misery that she herself helped to create before judging others. It was at that very moment Sonya realized she'd hit rock bottom, with no one else to blame but herself. She knew then that she'd have to do or say something to hold what little was left of a family in despair. After all, this is what she'd done from the time she'd become Mrs. Alexander.

Once Ary had disappeared behind the looming front door, Sonya went into the den and opened the drawer of the desk Bruce had left the envelope containing information on where he would be living his new life in San Diego more than twelve years ago. She had only opened it once before, crumbling its contents and tossing the pages on the floor where they laid for years. Eventually, as time passed, she filed them away and labeled the package '*The beginning of the end of my life,*' a life and lifestyle she'd known for eighteen years. But on this day, she would open it once more to retrieve a phone number, hoping it hadn't changed. After dialing the 619 area code, she paused and quickly hung up. *Whose voice would she hear? What would she say if Bruce answered? Could she muster the strength needed to actually talk to the man who, in her mind for so many years, had stolen her husband, partner, and indeed her life?* She sat down in the henna colored, tufted leather office chair, held the receiver of the phone in her hand, the same phone Bruce had used so many times while conducting business and possibly the same phone he'd used to plan out the rest of his life with Matthew. She dialed *67 to block her number from showing and dialed 619 again. This time she continued with the last seven numbers. It rang once, twice and then, "*Hey, Matthew here.*"

Strangely, the tenor of his voice, those few simple words, calmed her fears. Her heart slowed its pace. The tight grip of her fingers clutching the phone loosened, and her thoughts suddenly unscrambled. "Matthew, it's Sonya Alexander and I'd like to apologize."

CHAPTER 2

THE door to the recently polished car swung open and the tall, handsome driver slowly emerged. His Forzieri, handmade Italian brown leather shoes touched down softly against the cobblestoned driveway that led the way to the massive home. He paused for a moment, stopping to gauge the reaction of the reunited family.

"What are you doing here?!" Ary shouted through her quivering voice. "Why can't you let us heal?"

Bruce took a step forward, slightly distancing himself from the short-lived, yet unexpectedly comfortable position next to his ex-wife, and away from the horrified stare of his daughter.

Marcus wrapped his arms around his distraught sister as she buried her head deep into his shoulder. "It's okay Ary. It's fine."

Bewildered, Bruce confided, "I had no idea you were in New York."

Stepping closer to reassure him, Sonya curved her soft hands around his arm and whispered, "I invited him to come. You were the surprise."

CHAPTER 3

AS he drove along the crowded highway to her childhood home, his cell phone rang, interrupting the velvety jazz infiltrating the interior of his BMW 6 Series Grand Coupe. Ary's name and number displayed on the orange highlighted instrument panel, resembling more of a twenty-first century spacecraft than a luxury automobile.

"Hey," he said, his voice revealing a tone of machismo deference. "I'll be there as soon as I can. I got off at the wrong exit earlier and I swear Ary, I think I heard my GPS snoring," he finished, hoping to elicit some much needed laughter between the two of them. "Can't wait to see you."

"Dwayne," she said, with consternation, all the while ignoring his last statement and attempt at humor. "I have to insist that you turn around."

"What?" he asked, profoundly astonished. "Are you kidding me?"

"Please don't come here," she begged. "Please don't come to my mother's house. Just do as I ask and head back to the city."

Dwayne quickly exited the expressway, awkwardly pulling to the side of the service road, barely escaping the onslaught of fast moving cars. He could feel the heat of anger stirring in his body, hairs rising on the back of his neck, shoulders tensing, his face grimacing, all while his fingers locked their already tightened grip around the smooth leathered steering wheel.

I can't let her do this to me again. I won't, he promised.

CHAPTER 4

WHAT felt like having sat for an hour by the roadside was in actuality a mere ten minutes. Dwayne's heart raced, seemingly outpacing the unending flow of traffic. Brushing a hand over his freshly cut hair, once, then twice, he leaned his aching head against the forgiving headrest. *How could this be happening?* he wondered.

He'd already convinced himself that she was worth the fight, but at what price was he willing to pay to find happiness with a woman whose very existence seemed to dwell on heartache, pain and suffering?

"Should I go? Should I turn around? Is she in trouble?" he questioned his already weary brain. "How much shit is a man expected to take from his woman, I mean *a* woman?" Instead of an answer, he asked Siri for directions to the nearest bar, unaware that the morning sun had only recently secured its place high in the shimmering blue sky.

CHAPTER 5

"WHY didn't you call me?" Bruce inquired. "Sonya, is it okay? Is this too much?"

Sonya walked down the steps of the spacious porch, passing her stunned children to meet Matthew where he stood fixed near his rental car. "Matthew," she called, reaching for his hand, a tacit cue to Bruce that it was indeed okay. "Thank you for coming. I wasn't sure you'd accept my hasty invitation, but I thought it was important to ask you here, now, while my heart is in a good place."

Before he could take another step, Ary turned once again to her mother and asked, "*You* invited him here? Today?" her voice swelling to a familiar crescendo. "To be with *our* family?"

As he looked down on the still frail matriarch, his eyes swelled with tears and the rhythm of his heart beat with years of restrained emotion. *Could this be the beginning of acceptance, forgiveness, even friendship*? he thought. *Would Bruce be able to fully love him despite the guilt he'd always known existed, but what he'd relentlessly denied? How will this play out between himself, Marcus and Ary?* His mind filled with questions. This is the way he'd wished it could have been so many years ago but dared not insist or interfere with Bruce's life before him.

"Come inside Matthew. Let's get to know one another over some of my favorite imported teas."

Sonya, with her arm enfolded through his, walked past Ary and Marcus, stopping momentarily to collect Bruce, whose emotions, like his children, ran somewhere between shock, incredulity and a strange sense of relief. As the three of them disappeared behind the front door, Ary turned to question her brother.

"How is this happening? You must have known something?

How is it that you happen to come on the very day that Daddy and Matthew appear? And all at nearly the same damn time!"

"Okay now, here we go," he cautioned, taking a few steps away from his probing sister. "First of all, I'm just as shocked as you are, maybe even more. I just didn't verbalize it as vociferously as you did. Secondly, I called mama to ask if it were okay for me to come and talk things out with her and she said yes, never mentioning that she'd contacted Matthew for an overdue pow-wow, come-to-Jesus, kum-ba-ya, meet 'n greet! So slow your role big sis and stop with the accusations."

"Then why, Marcus?! She knew I was coming. I called early this morning to let her know I was on my way. I wanted to talk about everything that was happening with me and my job."

"What's happening with your job? I thought you were kicking ass over there, being the Ary Alexander that we all know and *most* of the time love," he joked, trying to coax a smile from her troubled expression.

"This is definitely *not* the time to make jokes, Marcus. And nothing is happening with my job. It's been resolved. What we have to determine now is do we go in and face all three of them or speak to mama separately to find out how all this came about."

"Well, I'm not sure how *you* plan to handle this," he answered, "but right now, *I'm* going in. I could use some food and some premium alcohol to go along with mama's *'imported teas.'*" Marcus kissed his sister on her forehead and made his way up the steps.

"Marcus," she called, halting him before his hand reached the door handle. "I'm not ready."

"I understand sis," he nodded, not fully believing his own words. "I'm sure they will too."

And with that, Marcus walked into the next chapter of the Alexander's lives.

CHAPTER 6

ARY stared at her childhood home a few minutes longer before walking back to her car. For a split second she wondered if now *she* would be the topic of conversation instead of her parents and Matthew's newfound relationship. Was *she* being unreasonable and immature? After all, Marcus found it within himself to face them, why couldn't she? Ultimately, it proved too much. She had just gone through enough drama in her life with bringing down the Senior Vice President of one of the fastest growing oil firms in the country, causing the breakup and firing of the company's CEO and his long-time lover, responsible for exposing her true identity and that of the brother she'd fought so hard to keep hidden. No, this would have to wait. *Let them work out their issues,* she thought. "I'll call you later mama," she whispered softly, sliding into the security of her waiting car.

CHAPTER 7

STOPPING for a red light on Route 110 and checking her iPhone for messages, the one person she was hoping to hear from sat 25 feet outside her passenger seat window, ordering breakfast in the very same diner she'd assumed Marcus was going to for coffee and a salad while she lingered in the hospital waiting room hoping for answers to the cause of her mother's sudden illness. Having resigned himself to the early hour, Dwayne consoled himself with coffee instead of scotch. His mind was overloaded with confusion, while his heart attempted in vain to make sense of it all.

"Will that be all?" asked a waitress whose face revealed the many years of repeating a rote phrase over and over before placing the check on the table and ending her shift.

"Ah, yes, I guess so. Hey, before you go, can you tell me what time the nearest bar around here opens or am I shit out of luck? I've asked Siri but I'd rather rely on the advice of someone who might actually know."

"Toppin' off a long night or just gettin' started?" she laughed, with a tired grin.

"Not sure to be quite honest," he answered, taking the last sip of his second cup of black coffee. "And I know it's still early, but I'm more than an hour away from home and I could use some help forgetting about a situation."

"Well, young man, in that case, I'd suggest 'The Silver Oak' about four miles down the road. It's open 24 hours and the crowd is pretty respectable."

"Even at this hour huh? Well Lilly," he confirmed, straining to look at the cursive name sewn into her uniform, "Thanks for the suggestion. I just may have to pay '*The Silver Oak*' an early visit."

Dwayne reached in his wallet and pulled out a fifty dollar bill. "Keep the change Lilly. That's for the good service, *and* the bar tip."

"Thanks. And listen, not meaning to pry, but I've seen and heard just about everything in this place, and if it's what I think it is, follow your gut. It'll tell you if she, or he, I'm not one to judge, is worth it. Just follow your gut."

"My gut?" he mumbled, placing his wallet back in his sports coat pocket and pushing his chair back from the table. "My gut hasn't exactly been on its 'A' game lately. And did you say '*he*'? Yeah, I don't think so." They shared a quick laugh as she winked and strolled off to deliver checks to the last of her customers whose stories she had most certainly heard before.

CHAPTER 8

ARY made a right turn onto the entrance ramp of the Long Island Expressway and reflected on her last conversation with Dwayne. *I hope he's not too upset*, she thought. *He knows my family comes first. I made that very clear from the beginning. And my career comes second, which is something I'm sure he…* "Oh my God," she blurted out. "Dwayne's job! I forgot about him losing his job because of Joseph. I'll call G to ask what happened—if he's rehired him. NPI was his life before any of this bullshit happened. And although I know he could find another job in the industry, I'm sure he'd prefer to be back there."

She nervously wondered how to broach the subject with her CEO. "Siri, call G Gicardi."

"Mr. Gicardi's office, Connie speaking."

"Hi Connie, it's Ary. Is he available?"

"Hello Ary, just a moment, please."

"Hello Ary, how are you?"

"Hi G, I'm good, thank you. I apologize for interrupting your morning but I needed to ask you a question."

"No need for apologies. What's up? You haven't changed your mind about returning to the firm have you?" he asked, chuckling.

"Oh no, it's not that at all. I, I was just concerned about Dwayne Hargis, I wasn't sure if you'd been in contact with him about returning to NPI or whether he'd taken a position at another firm or…"

"Well," G interrupted. "Funny you should ask. I did speak to him about coming back and I was hoping that he would, but

I'm not sure if he's made up his mind yet. And I fully get that. He went through hell with Joseph. A hell I wasn't made aware of, but I'm sure took a tremendous toll on him. So for now, my answer is, I don't know. But if *you* happen to see or speak with him, please reinforce how much we need and *want* him back at NPI. You know I think of you both as family."

"Thank you G. I appreciate that and I'll tell him."

Her concern grew even stronger. *What if he still blames me for all of this? I tried to fix it, though he may not yet fully understand my unorthodox ways of going about things.* Ary's car swerved from the left towards the middle lane as her curiosity grew even deeper. Only the blaring horn of an irritated driver forced her back to reality and her car into its original lane.

"Oh God! I'm sorry, I'm sorry," she screamed, throwing up a peace sign. After righting herself safely back in her lane, she gathered her thoughts. *I really don't need any more drama in my life right now, including road rage or another unplanned hospital stay. I should probably call him when I get home or better yet invite him over for dinner tonight so I can at least try and explain it all. I at least owe him that, along with telling him why he couldn't meet me at mama's house.*

But instead of driving towards the Throgs Neck Bridge through the Bronx and over the George Washington Bridge to New Jersey, she took the Midtown tunnel into Manhattan and drove past NPI. She'd hoped to see Robert standing outside the building for a mid-morning smoke as he'd done so many times before. She rounded the block through heavy traffic twice, with no sign of him. Disappointed, she headed across town toward the West Side Highway, taking her over the bridge into Fort Lee. But before going directly home, she stopped at the Whole Foods market to pick up the ingredients for an Italian themed meal. Chicken breasts, gourmet tomato sauce, grated parmesan, mozzarella, bread crumbs, eggs, seasonings and fresh vegetables were piled into her handheld basket. After checking out, she walked to her car and placed the groceries in the back seat before heading over to her favorite wine store just a few stores away in the neat little urban-inspired strip mall.

Walking through the door of the tiny shop, whose walls were adorned with beautiful images of Sicily with her black sand beaches and the erupting volcanoes of Mount Etna, Ary greeted the owner. "Hey Dino, how are you?"

Dino, who was old enough to be her grandfather was busy reconciling the ledger at the register. He looked up over his glasses to see who had called his name. "If it isn't one of my favorite customers, and one of prettiest," he added, in heavily accented Sicilian. Ary, who considered herself a feminist, always let him slide with his less than politically correct remarks. Most times, after a long day at work, she actually enjoyed his less than 21st century feminist compliments and the small talk that usually followed.

"Dino, I need a special wine for a special dinner guest. What do you suggest?"

Pounding both hands on the counter, and wearing a serious smile, he leaned over towards her and asked, "How special is this dinner guest, amore mio? Twenty-five, fifty or one-hundred dollars special?" his sly grin on full display.

"Well, let's see. I'm attempting to make parmigiana di pollo, *a la truce* tonight," she added, laughing, "and I think a special wine will help the food and the conversation go down a bit more smoothly for both of us," she finished.

"Okay, I see," he winked. "Non preoccuparti, not to worry, it's a common request. I'll be right back. And while I'm gone bella signora, feel free to ring up a couple customers for me. With your looks, I'm sure you can do much better than my son, Enzo, here. " Ary smiled as she always did, while Enzo shook his head.

"This is what I go through all day long," he confessed, releasing an energetic laugh. "You ladies keep him young and happy, and it's a good thing, especially since my mama passed away, so I let him slide. And besides, he's a hellava dad and a damn good businessman. He's taught me everything I know. Mio padre e' il mio ero, he's my hero," he told her, looking towards the door his father disappeared through.

"I can tell," she said.

Dino returned with a bottle of *Sagrantino di Montefalco 'Collepiano' 2007* and a sample serving for Ary to taste before making a decision. "I only open certain wines for my best customers, my bella customers. This one, I know you'll love."

"Oh Dino!" she exclaimed, after taking a generous sip. "It's perfect. Sei il migliore, you're the best," using the little Italian she knew. "But will I be able to pay my rent this month after paying for this?" she joked, as Dino instructed Enzo to place an unopened duplicate bottle in a gold foil bag and tie it with a satin bow.

"Less than $70, amore. And believe me, this wine, along with your delicious Italian 'parmigiana di pollo truce,' will sooth even the fiercest tiger," he finished, placing his hands over his heart.

"Thanks guys," she said, topping off the rest and handing the small glass to Enzo. "I can always count on you in my times of dire need."

Making her way home and into the elevator, carefully holding onto her packages, she rehearsed the impending conversation with Dwayne in her head, ending with, "All I can do is try," she agonized, letting out a deep breath, unaware her last thoughts had spilled out verbally. The only other elevator passenger turned towards her and agreed, "It's all any of us can do." Ary smiled, somewhat embarrassed and quickly wished him a good afternoon as he exited through the closing doors on the 20th floor.

CHAPTER 9

DWAYNE found his way to *The Silver Oak* and sat at the bar among a few other men who looked as though they all had memories that needed washing away. Although initially hesitant after looking around and not seeing anyone who could even remotely pass for a person of color, after a few glasses of Jack Daniel's, it no longer mattered. *This has got to stop,* he thought, after downing his third glass in one swig and clearing his throat of the temporary sting. *My focus right now needs to be on whether I want to go back to NPI. What the fuck will I be facing? Does it even make sense to work in an environment where your girl is working and then have to face whatever bullshit the two of us might be dealing with on a daily or weekly basis? I don't know man, I just don't know.*

After more than an hour of self-assessment, Dwayne's attention was interrupted by a young woman sitting alone at one of the rustic tables near a corner of the bar. Dressed in a tan, custom fitted blazer, a matching tan linen chambray blouse, indigo skinny jeans, and nude flats, the attractive woman seemed unbothered by the fact that she was the only female in the establishment. She multi-tasked from her iPad to her iPhone, to the glass of merlot sitting in front of her and ignored the men at the bar who took, what they thought, were discreet glances in her direction. Dwayne cautiously looked over his left shoulder to gain a better view. He asked the bartender what she was drinking and requested that he send over a refresher.

Glancing up at the bartender, who was now standing at her seat, she shook her head a polite '*no*,' refusing the offer, then returned to working on her iPad. After a couple of minutes, she turned to look at the curious men, deducing that the drink was either from the desperate one staring at her as though she was a bowl of rich, chocolate ice cream, or the handsome, unruffled, younger one looking in her direction, trying hard to shield his disappointment. With his ego bruised for the second time today, he chalked this day up as a total fail. And to save himself any further feelings of embarrassment, concluded, that it was probably still too early in the day to try and engage any respectable lady in conversation.

After a few minutes more, she rose from her seat, walked over to the bar, squeezed in between Dwayne and an empty stool and said to the bartender, "I didn't really care for the Merlot, but please tell the gentleman who generously offered to refresh my drink that the lady would prefer the Cabernet Sauvignon." Hoping that the 'gentleman' was Dwayne, she returned to her table.

CHAPTER 10

DWAYNE watched the attractive stranger walk away and asked the bartender for a glass of top shelf Cabernet Sauvignon. Pushing away from the bar, with drink in hand, he strode over in his now confident swagger, stood at her table and said, "Let me properly introduce myself," feeling the initial sting of rejection fading with every word. "I'm Dwayne Hargis, the guy who was trying hard to be hip, cool and unobtrusive at this early hour," he finished, flashing his irresistible smile. Her dark brown eyes took a moment to explore his handsome face before responding and offering him her delicate hand. "Nice to meet you Dwayne, I'm Deidra Scott. And if what you're holding is a Cabernet Sauvignon, please, have a seat." Dwayne was intrigued without yet knowing why.

"I hope this one fares better than the Merlot," he volunteered, setting the glass directly in front of her.

Taking a small sip, she breathed deeply and closed her eyes. "Much better. Now, I'm sure you're wondering why a lady would be in a bar at this time of day?"

"Well, it might have crossed my mind," he snickered. "But then again, considering all things equal, you could ask why a highly regarded, good-looking guy, such as yours truly," he said, pointing to himself, "would be in here as well."

"Okay then. Confident *and* handsome, and still able to pull together a coherent sentence after more than a few shots of what looked like whiskey," she laughed.

"So you were watching me, watching you? Impressive." he laughed. "Now, I don't generally send over a $40 glass of wine to just any ordinary lady sitting alone in a bar. And being as though I'm not really familiar with the area, you'll surely forgive me for not knowing that Long Island had such beautiful, wine conversant connoisseurs."

"Oh, you're good," she acknowledged, returning a flirtatious smile. "And charming too," she continued. "So, Mr. Charming, what brings you to Brookstone?"

"Well, I was trying to be the good Boy Scout I was brought up to be and help a damsel in distress," he laughed. "Seriously though, I was on my way to help console a friend in town. But it turns out, they no longer needed comforting. And being that I live in the city, and didn't feel like tackling heavy westbound traffic, I decided to bide my time in this recommended, reputable establishment. And of course I was also hoping to find a beautiful lady willing to engage me in conversation. And as I'm sure you'll agree, dreams ever so often, do come true."

"Oh really?" she asked, offering a slight smile. "Consoling a friend? A boy scout? Mr. Hargis you sound almost too good to be true."

"Believe me, I'm not," he laughed. "Honestly, I was on my way to visit a person who I consider very dear to me who called, just as I was near her place, and told me, out of the clear blue, with no explanation, to turn around, not to come. So I ended up here instead."

"I see," she said, intrigued. "Well, this is one of the few bars in town where you can actually come and drown your heartache at any ungodly hour and not be judged," she confessed.

"You sound like you may have had to do that in excess of just one occasion."

"I come here to take my mind off of what I go through and witness almost on a daily basis."

All sorts of thoughts rushed through his mind. *What does she go through on a daily basis that requires the aid of mind numbing beverages?*

"May I ask what it is you witness that requires spending an afternoon in a bar?"

"I'm a trauma center nurse, with crazy hours. I come here just to wind down after a night or early morning of helping to save someone's life. And sometimes before going home, it helps to clear my mind of everything I've seen and don't wish to remember in the emergency room," she explained.

"Wow, that's deep. And I thought my job was stressful. Yours is stressful *and* consequential. I respect that."

Now she was even more curious about him. They sat and talked for over an hour, sharing stories about work, hobbies and life. She admitted her penchant for collecting art and the fact that she often bought pieces without considering the cost, only to have to work overtime just to pay for it. He confessed to his love of fashion, not something he readily admitted to. "People might just start referring to me as a metrosexual," he laughed. "And I can't have that—I have to keep up my reputation as a solid, five-day-a-week, gym fanatic, he-man, working on my six-pack—not my designer suit and shoe collection." They both laughed long and hard.

"Listen Dwayne, I've enjoyed talking and laughing with you, but I have to go. I'm meeting someone this evening and I want to try and sneak in a quick nap before I do."

He didn't want the conversation to end or lose the chance to get to know her better.

"Deidra, you mentioned your love of art. I'm also an admirer of art, granted I'm sure nowhere near as knowledgeable as you. And seeing as though I'm not ready to get on the long road back home, and you need to get home to take a nap, I could really use your suggestion on finding a nearby museum," he smiled. "And don't misunderstand me, although I *definitely* consider you a work of art standing right before my very eyes, and someone who I'd like to get to know, the fact remains that I'm as lost as a stray kitten out here on the Island."

She stared at him with a feminine intensity, wondering what he was actually suggesting. "You *are* a charmer, Dwayne Hargis. But the museums around here don't open until two in the afternoon."

"Well, that's disappointing," he said, displaying his best puppy face.

"Don't look so sad. Okay listen, why don't you follow me to my place and I'll show you some of my pieces before the museums open up."

"Are you sure? I mean, I wouldn't want you to feel uncomfortable or anything…"

"I live in a well-guarded community with quick access to security. So no, I'm not worried about anything wicked happening."

Dwayne walked over to the bartender, paid the tab and followed Deidra out to the parking lot.

CHAPTER 11

I think making this meal will help take my mind off of everything I've gone through today, she thought, making room inside the refrigerator to push the wine towards the back for a better chance at chilling. "Alright Ary," she mused out loud, "You know you'll have to eventually call mama to find out how all of a sudden, Matthew became an accepted member of the Alexander family. But right now, you have to try and convince Dwayne that you're not crazy and that he should spend his evening with you."

But Dwayne was in the throes of a spontaneous tryst after concluding that she obviously had family issues that still required her undivided attention. And having just gone through a miniseries of tribulations with her at the hospital, he wasn't in any hurry to replay that scenario tonight.

CHAPTER 12

DEIDRA'S townhouse was neat and modern. The pumpkin colored Largo Chaise Italian leather sectional with its matching ottoman took up most of the living room space. The end tables were round Ebonized Oak in the shape of African bar stools. Sitting atop the tables were ethnic trinkets from Africa and the Middle East.

The walls were a stark white background to the oddly shaped picture frames holding prints and pricey originals of known and unknown artists in every available space. Dwayne was particularly drawn to an African oil painting with mixed vibrant colors and bold shapes. What he didn't notice was the signature of the artist in the bottom right hand corner of the work. The letters, '*SA*' were written in a beautiful gold cursive type.

"Is there a particular artist that touches your heart," he asked. "Or is it whatever moves your mind and captures your soul?"

"That's a beautiful way to think of it, Dwayne. I'd have to say that it's all three," she admitted, staring at him for a brief moment, wanting to know more about the sensitive man she'd just met. "So okay Picasso, stand over here, next to me and tell me which piece stands out to you over on the far wall."

Dwayne walked closer to her and placed his left hand underneath his chin, thumping his index finger against his nose as he stared at the paintings. "You know, when we first walked in, I was immediately drawn to the oil painting in the center of the wall. The colors remind me of my life right now."

"How so?" she asked, with a curious sincerity.

"Well, things are a bit chaotic with my job right now, and when

I say chaotic, I really mean fucked-up, almost out of a movie kind of fucked-up, excuse my French."

"Sooooo," Deidra quizzed, "Would there also happen to be a lady involved in this 'fucked-up movie,' excuse my English," she laughed.

He sighed, turning directly to face her. "You know what? I'm in the presence of an attractive woman, surrounded by her collection of astonishing artwork, encapsulated in this stylishly modern home. I'm sorry I even brought up my issues. Right now, just looking into your rousing brown eyes makes all of it seem so insignificant."

Deidra felt her knees weakening. She steadied herself but couldn't control the pace of her heartbeat. Her mind pleaded with her to use better judgment—her body overruled.

Dwayne lifted her chin to meet his lips. Hers already anticipated what he might offer. He pressed lightly against her mouth, halting, waiting for a non-verbal cue to continue. Deidra, whose eyes were closed and whose hands were pressed firmly against his chest, playfully tugged at his lips before giving in to his masculine game of seduction. But for an uninvited moment, Dwayne's nights with Ary—her scent, her hair, her body, her sensuous sexuality crept into his mind. His eyes flashed open, reminding him of the sexiness within his grasp. He pulled her in closer, wrapping his arms tightly around her curvaceous waist and wondered, *Am I really gonna let this happen? We've just spent a few hours together and I really don't know anything about her and I'm sure as hell not looking to get into anymore relationships right now.* But before any further thoughts or doubts clouded his mind, he and Deidra had lowered themselves onto her leather pillowed sofa, in an eager embrace and passionately explored one another's exquisitely toned bodies. She whispered seductively in his ear, "When I see something I want, it's impossible to resist." He'd come to the same conclusion.

Her long fingers moved down one button to the next, slowly revealing his chest hairs. Her heart raced faster as his impressive pectorals lay bare for her eyes to feast. Dwayne felt content to let her lead the way while he watched every teasing move. Lowering his shirt down and around his deep, brown, broad shoulders, she leaned back to drink in his inimitable physique before slowly raising her arms above her head. Dwayne, taking the cue, lifted her blouse over her natural curls, watching as it descended to the wooden floor. With skill and precision, he unhooked her pink, satin bra with one hand, eagerly anticipating the swell of beauty peeking from underneath. Leaning in to kiss the hollow of her neck, then gently tugging at her earlobe, his thoughts were now solely focused on making love. The tempting heat of their two bodies outpaced any hesitation he'd had. Time stood still as he pulled her in closer. Deidra found the refuge she wanted in the gentle strength of his muscular arms. With their heartbeats pounding metrically against each other's chest, they gave in to what came naturally.

CHAPTER 13

ARY had left several messages for Dwayne on his cell explaining how she'd wanted to cook him a special *'truce'* meal and that she'd leave her door unlocked at 6:30pm. It was 7:45pm and there had been no word from him. Since they hadn't spoken by phone, she'd hoped that maybe he'd surprise her by just showing up as a sign of accepting her apology.

"Well, who could blame him really?" she asked herself, realizing that her plans and food would be for one. "I really needed you tonight, Dwayne," she continued. "And no one is perfect. You of all people should understand that. My flaws sometime serve as my strengths Dwayne, and I was hoping that I'd be able to let my guard down tonight and reveal to you who I really am—my crazy-ass family, that I adore, my big-girl daddy issues and my god-forsaken determination to reach the mountaintop with every project I take on, and every struggle I face. I wanted to share all of that with you this evening Dwayne, but you either never checked your messages or just decided that you'd had enough of me and my drama. I'm hoping that it's not the latter and that we can maybe start over again without NPI's past hanging over our heads."

She opened a kitchen cabinet reaching for Tupperware when her cell phone rang, startling her. She raced into the living room to retrieve it, whispering a silent prayer that it was Dwayne. The unrecognized number on the display caused her to pause a moment, finally deciding to answer before the fourth and final ring.

"Hey Ary, I just wanted to check in with you to make sure you were alright, especially after what you've just been through."

"Darias?" she asked, cautiously.

"Yeah. Oh, sorry, I'm using my new phone and for some reason all my contact information didn't download and I haven't yet figured out all the new bells and whistles on this thing," he explained, with an easy laugh. "Did I catch you at a bad time?"

"No, no, not at all. I was just putting away my frivolous attempt at a truce dinner for what may very well be, a former friend."

"Wow, I'm sorry to hear that. But on the other hand, I'm impressed that you're cooking!" he admitted. "I'm sure you'd agree that a lot of professional women say they just don't have the time or the inclination to do it anymore. So let me compliment you on your efforts, although it sounds like your attempt at a reconciliatory meal didn't turn out the way you'd envisioned."

Ary lowered her head, tears welling in her eyes. It seemed, she thought, most of her days were filled with sadness and confusion and it would be up to her to change it all.

"Darias?" she started, trying hard to compose herself, "Would you like to go away with me? Somewhere exotic, far away, no cell phones, no meetings, no clients. Just you and me and..."

"I have a friend who owns a luxury resort on Randheli Island in the Maldives," he interrupted. "Not too far from the capital, Malé. We can seclude ourselves on the island and take a private seaplane to the markets, restaurants and shops when you get tired of just being with me," he laughed.

"That sounds wonderful. Oh how I'd love to spend my days and nights with you on a romantic, tropical island, and in my head, I'm already there. But the monsoons? Isn't this the time of year…?"

"Babe, the only monsoons you'll encounter will be the heat and sweat of passionate bodies clashing intimately under the stars on a bed of white sandy beach, if that's something you can imagine as well," he added, playfully.

"I'll make the reservations?" she volunteered.

"No need. That same friend has a private jet. I just have to call him and find out when it'll be available. I'm thinking that in a week or so, we should be walking along the crystal clear waters of the Indian Ocean with not a care in the world, except for how to make our time memorable."

"It sounds perfect. I can't wait."

CHAPTER 14

DWAYNE glanced toward the generous window frame of her townhouse, stealing a glimpse of the magnificent sun which had begun to cast a shadow against the backdrop of a pale blue sky. He didn't know whether to feel guilt or pride about his actions. His ego led him to believe that what had happened was between two consenting adults who were obviously attracted to one another. His thoughts, now free from the irrepressible grip of a casual sexual encounter were telling him to leave as quickly as he could zip up his pants and not get emotionally involved. He knew he'd have to face Ary sooner or later, especially if they were to return to their jobs at NPI. He also didn't need or want the responsibility of dating and caring for more than one woman. That was more in line with his male buddies whom he'd teased in the past, telling them that he'd hate to be around if, or when all the ladies found out about one another. *No,* he thought, *that is definitely not a scene I want a starring role in.*

"Deidra," he began, haltingly, "I want to be honest with you. I find you extremely attractive…"

"But?" she interrupted.

"No buts'," he finished. "What I was gonna say was that I'm in such a state of confusion right now and it involves a woman who has really just gotten under my skin, and not always in a good way. And it wouldn't be fair to you or anyone else to lead you to believe that I could fully commit to a relationship right now. I also don't want you to believe that I'm one of those brothers that would take advantage of a beautiful, intelligent woman whenever the opportunity presented itself. That's not me at all. I feel like we were two adults who found one another extremely attractive and gave in to human emotion. I hope you feel the same way."

Dwayne felt his words and explanation spilling out awkwardly but hoped that the situation would remain civil and that they could possibly develop a friendship.

"Look Dwayne, you are one helluva handsome and *sexy* man, whose kisses by the way, would melt the coldest of hearts. But I feel the same way. I'm also in a relationship with a wonderful man."

Dwayne's initial reaction was shock, but he tried to conceal any stunned expressions.

"Oh, okay. I was *not* expecting to hear that," he admitted. "Then, what just happened here, and why?"

"It's what you said Dwayne, we were two consenting grown people, giving in to physical attraction. No further explanations necessary, right?"

"Uh, no, I guess not," he hesitated, feeling confused and just a little bit used. "Well then, it's getting late and traffic should have eased up. So I think I'll be heading home now."

"Ok," she answered, nonchalantly. "Do you need help in getting out of the development? It can be tricky, especially in the evening."

"No, no. I'm a big boy. I think I'll be able to find my way out."

"Dwayne," she began, before he stopped her.

"Deidra look, let's just leave it at that okay. It's like *you* said, no further explanations necessary. Dwayne straightened the collar of his button-down before putting on his sports jacket. Checking his pockets for his wallet and keys, he was all set to leave, but not before leaning forward to kiss her on the forehead. She backed away.

"Good night, Dwayne," she asserted, "And thank you."

"Thank you? Thank you for what?" he asked, looking both annoyed and puzzled.

"Thank you for reinforcing in me what I thought I'd lost in my relationship. I realize now that I do still love my fiancé and can enter into our upcoming marriage knowing that there is absolutely nothing else out there that I'd be missing. I know that I've chosen the right man."

Fiancé? Marriage? Ouch, he thought, *that shit just stung like hell. And here I am thinking I'd handled my business pretty damn good. Just goes to show that I really don't fucking understand women at all. And as far as this forming into some sort of 'friendship,' fuck it. I just really need to get back to fixin' my own damn life and concentrating on my career.*

Dwayne shook his head and started out the front door, pausing as he walked down the first couple of steps. He turned slightly, looking in her direction. "Could it have been something I said?" he asked out loud, wondering if she'd made it all up. But Deidra had already shut the door. He breathed deeply and picked up his pace, finally settling into the comfort of his car.

CHAPTER 15

IT had been a week since Ary had made her 'truce' meal for Dwayne. She'd neither heard from him nor reached out to find out why he didn't show up. But right now her mind was on her wardrobe for the trip to the Maldives. "So, is this how it was all supposed to turn out?" she asked herself. *Even while my mind is telling me that I definitely need to get the hell away from here, my heart is saying that I'm going with the wrong man,* she thought. *But the right man didn't have the decency to call, come or even accept my apology. So really, how can he be the right man for me? I have to go on living my life and preparing for my return to NPI in a couple of weeks and facing only God knows what with my so-called colleagues, minus the devious two. That's gonna be hard as hell. But we all have bills to pay and I'm not ready to start interviewing for another position someplace else. My biggest apprehension will be facing Dwayne if we don't talk this out before going back. I'd like to wipe the slate clean, get back into the grind and the excitement of once again constructing multi-million dollar deals and the acknowledgment that not only* can *a woman take command of what was once a man's world, but an Ivy League educated, black woman, representing women of color in these here United States,* she laughed. But before she could think another single thought, her cell phone rang. "Ok, ok. I'm coming," she called out, walking over to the bed to pick it up.

"Hey sis."

"Marcus!"

"Hey, how you be? It's been a minute and I thought I'd call just to check up on you."

"It's been more than a minute, Marcus B. Alexander," she scolded. "And I have *not* been fine! One would think that her family would have reached out two weeks later."

"It hasn't been that long but ok. And let me just remind you that *you*, Ariel M. Alexander, were the one who decided not to go inside the house after Matthew showed up and mama invited him in."

"You don't have to remind me of what I did or didn't do, Marcus. And if I chose *not* to be a part of that little family gathering, I'm a grown ass woman who is more than capable of making her own damn decisions."

"No one is disputing how grown you are or what your ass is capable of doing, although I really don't even want to imagine that," he joked, trying to elicit a laugh.

"What? Eww! Go straight to hell, Marcus," she snickered. "You of all people should know why I couldn't go through that door. I had just gone through a nightmarish scenario at my job, thinking that I was unemployed and possibly blacklisted and then I walk up to a *'Brady Bunch'* scene in Brookstone, New York. That shit was just a little bit much to take."

"I know. I get it and really, I'm sorry I haven't been in touch. I've been trying to reconcile all this shit in my own mind too, Ary. It's a lot to absorb. Daddy, Matthew, and mama, finally putting it all behind them, I think. And any future I may or may not have with Caroline being up in the air..."

"Whoa, wait, '*finally* putting it all behind them,' a future with Caroline, or *maybe not*. What does all that mean? I thought you and Caroline had worked out your issues. And I have no plans of discussing any *'Matthew'* details with mama until I get back from the Maldives."

"The Mal-whose?" he asked, teasingly.

"You heard me. I'm going away for a few days to clear my mind. I want to be able to come back fresh and hopefully more open-minded before I talk to or interact with anyone, especially mama. I want to hear her rationale for accepting him into our family all of a sudden."

"All of a sudden?! She's been holding a grudge against him for thirteen years!" he yelled, causing her to temporarily move the phone away from her ear. "I would hope that a decade or longer is plenty time to think about forgiving somebody for 'doing you wrong!' And if that's not enough, I'd hate to know what exemplifies *due-time* in your mind?"

"Alright, calm down soldier. So it may not have been sudden. But why now? Do you think it was her hospitalization that was the catalyst for contacting him? Even Daddy seemed surprised when he showed up, and he used to be the rational one in the family," she laughed.

"Well big sis, had you stayed around long enough to hear the conversation, you'd understand how all of this came about. But before I say another word, the Maldives, huh? What's the deal? And can I ask who you might be trekking across the world with?"

"Okay, okay. Way to deflect little brother. I'll hand you that one. I'm going away with a very dear friend and for now, that's all *you* need to know about him." she shot back. After all I've been through I think I need to refocus my priorities. Hell, I'm still not 100 percent sure about returning to NPI."

"Wait, what? Returning to NPI? What does *that* mean? What the hell happened with your job? I feel like I'm missing out on a *whooole* lot of information," he dragged.

"Alright Marcus…" she started, before he interrupted.

"And this '*dear friend*' sis, would he happen to be the brotha I met at your job, otherwise known as, yo' boss?"

Ary walked out of her bedroom and stood in the narrow hallway, staring into the living room before answering him. Memories suddenly resurfaced of her intimate time with Dwayne.

She pictured herself being lovingly embraced in the security of his arms.

Desperately shaking her head, she tried to erase the tender recollection.

"No mister nosey. It's not 'my brotha boss,' It's someone who was there for me when the shit hit the fan and who really kept me from losing my damn mind during that awful time. But this isn't something I want to rehash right now, Marcus. I have so much to sort through in my head and it feels like it's spinning at ninety miles an hour."

"I know sis, no pressure. But you should at least let someone know where you'll be staying out there in the Indian Ocean. That's a fucking long way from home," he ended, with obvious concern.

"I will. As soon as I know where '*out there*' is," she promised. "I love you Marcus and I'll be in touch soon."

He waited to hear the line release before putting his cell phone down on the small nondescript kitchen table. In truth, he was still struggling with all that had happened to his mother because of his engagement to Caroline and wondered if she'd really forgiven him as she had Matthew and his father, and was she really ready and willing to meet the woman who, he hoped, would soon be her daughter-in-law.

Although the conversation at his childhood home between Bruce, Sonya and Matthew was cordial and seemed genuine on the surface, he questioned whether it would be long lasting. He still hadn't fully forgiven Bruce for all that he'd gone through in his young life—and in his mind, was the principal cause of so much confusion. But for now, for the sake of the family and for the life he'd begun to carve out for himself, he would go along with this newfound understanding, acceptance and relationship between his parents and Matthew.

CHAPTER 16

WITH one stopover in Dubai before continuing on to Malé, the couple decided to take advantage of the desert beauty while the private jet refueled. Darias suggested dinner at the beautiful Al Mahara restaurant located in the famous sail-shaped silhouette, Burj Al Arab Jumeirah hotel. Surrounded inside by a floor to ceiling aquarium and entertained by the colorful sea life swimming alongside their table, helped to not only relax Ary from the twelve-plus hour flight, but also further eased her mind away from her worries back home. After perusing the menu, she decided on the wild sea bass with tender trumpet zucchini. He elected to go with the waiter's suggestion of seared Wagyu beef, braised celery, and potato gnocchi. They cleansed their palates before and after their meal with strawberry and champagne sorbet and a small plate of local fruit. What she didn't know was that he'd booked the dual level one-bedroom suite with sweeping panoramic views of Dubai and the Arabian Gulf.

Feeling satisfied after a delectable meal, Darias suggested they walk around the hotel, finally stopping at the elevator that would lift them up to even more luxury. Surprised, she turned to him and asked, "Why are we waiting here?"

"You'll see," he answered, roguishly.

As the bronze doors opened on the top floor of the hotel, a man dressed in traditional attire introduced himself as their butler for the evening and tomorrow morning and led them a short distance around a picturesque corridor before arriving at the opulent suite.

"You certainly know how to impress a girl," she admitted, gazing seductively into his eyes.

As they entered, the light scent of jasmine filled the air, complementing the majesty that beckoned throughout the space. Their butler inquired whether the Jacuzzi should be prepared, alongside a bottle of imported champagne, or if it were their preference to relax on the exquisite Egyptian cotton bed linens covering the super king-sized bed after their long flight and sumptuous meal.

Ary could only stand in the center of the room, mesmerized, thinking that this was indeed a fairytale, but something she could easily become accustomed. Darias spoke in hushed tones to their personal manservant, then turned to her and asked, "What's your pleasure, a moonlit massage on the private beach or here in the suite?" Still recovering from the transatlantic flight, she opted to stay inside, reasoning that they'd have plenty of time for beach activities once they reached the Maldives.

In the bedroom, candles flickered with golden lights while soft music from local Emirati artists filtered through the hidden speakers creating an atmosphere of romance and tranquility. As the butler disappeared to the lower level of the suite Ary wandered into the massive marbled bathroom where she found, enclosed in mesh wrapping, a maroon colored silk robe. She could hear the Jacuzzi running faintly in the distance. It was time to free herself from the clothing she'd traveled across the world in and luxuriate in temperate waters. Darias had already made his way downstairs and called out her name. Descending the stairs, with her hair pinned into a tousled bun, wistful strands flowing across her shoulders and tipping her center back, she paused on the last step. He gestured for her to join him in what looked more like a miniature infinity pool. *How could this be?* she wondered. It was clearly an engineering feat for a hotel. She tiptoed silently across the floor and stood at the edge of the water, nearest to where he patiently waited. He couldn't take his eyes from her as she allowed the robe to fall down to her feet and willingly accept his hand, lowering herself into the pulsating rhythms of the aromatic bath. All he could manage was to watch her movements for the first few seconds. In his mind he'd imagined what she'd look like in all her delicate nakedness, but it paled in comparison to what stood before him. She was beautiful. But somehow that often used description seemed to fall woefully short. As she made her way into his waiting arms, his heart speed surged. Looking into his blue eyes, and pressing her breasts against the silver brush of his hairy chest, she whispered, "I'm yours tonight."

Darias reached for and opened the small bottle of warmed, fragrant oil left alongside the Jacuzzi, pouring the contents over and down the slant of her back and between her fully round breasts. Using both hands in a circular motion, he gently smoothed the elixir around her perfectly proportioned upper body. She in turn used the dripping oil from her body to smoothly massage his extended manhood.

"Ary, let me protect you forever," he whispered in her ear.

"Be my shield of armor and keep me safe in your arms," she answered.

He held her tighter, mindful of her delicate frame, but eager to demonstrate his prowess.

Her thoughts interrupted her emotions when she briefly imagined Dwayne. She could almost hear his deep voice professing his true feelings, holding her, loving her, forgiving her.

But as their lips touched, any further reflections were immediately quelled. The feel of his toned, forty-eight year young body, the gentle strength of his arms, and now metrical beat of his heart was what the 28 year old craved. She needed to be held, to be caressed and made love to—to be assured that everything would turn out right both personally and professionally, even if she didn't quite believe it herself.

CHAPTER 17

"OKAY G, sounds good. I really appreciate your understanding and I'm going to take the next week or so to refocus, and come back better than I was before."

"Well Dwayne," he declared with a hearty laugh." I don't know how you could improve on the contributions you've already made at NPI. But hey man, I can't wait to find out. Enjoy your vacation on my dime and I'll see you in a week's time."

Dwayne had reached out to an old friend and confidant to discuss what returning to his old job might mean for his career moving forward. Eventually, he was convinced to stay for a while longer in hopes of making a quicker move to the position of Vice President before going to another firm. It ultimately made sense to remain at NPI where G would certainly be willing to consider his promotion with Joseph and Marguerite out of the way and then perhaps move to a competing firm with not only the title of VP but a huge salary bump as a lure away from the growing prestige of NPI. But right now, he wanted to get out of town—to an unfamiliar place, where no one knew him. He craved solitude and tranquility. And after the disastrous fling with Deidra, he wanted to reprogram his thoughts and concentrate on himself, not on his next sexual or business conquest. He thought back to the last conversation he'd had with his barber, Ricky, promising to go to the Mediterranean with a special someone. Well, he'd keep his promise, but this time, he would be taking the trip solo.

Yeah, the Mediterranean sounds real nice, he thought. "I can kick back for a few days—all expenses paid and get reenergized. I certainly deserve it after all the shit I've been through," finishing his inner thoughts out loud. Dwayne powered up his tablet, searched for packages to Zakynthos, or Santorini Greece, the Italian coast of Tuscany or Sardinia, Corsica, France or Menorca Spain. He settled on Corsica, a mix of French and Italian culture.

CHAPTER 18

ARY and Darias spent lazy days and romantic evenings on Randheli Island, traveling to Malé along the Majeedhee Magu in the afternoons for unique treasures including a surprise stop at Sifani's, a luxury jeweler, and favorite of Darias' for a beautiful 18kt yellow gold pendant set with pink sapphires and white diamonds for Ary. This time away from home was like nothing she'd expected and everything she'd needed. Ary let her mind drift with no responsibilities of timelines, deadlines, presentations, confrontations or thoughts of thousand dollar commissions. Although she'd tried not to, thoughts of family and visions of Dwayne silently invaded when she'd least expected. As he gifted her with the opulent pendant, she imagined Dwayne taking the jewel from the hands of the proprietor, slowly turning her around and planting an arousing kiss just beneath her hairline, before gently placing the bauble around her slender neck. Her knees felt weak, her body shivered unnoticed, before reality once again reminded her of where she was and who she was with.

"It's gorgeous," she managed, looking down at the pendant which had been paired with a gleaming 24kt yellow gold chain. "Thank you for rescuing me from my difficulties back home. This time with you has been magical, and I'll forever cherish each and every moment."

Looking into her hazel eyes, which seemed to have absorbed the turquoise colors of the lagoons in the surrounding coral atolls, he noticed her exposed shoulders, glistening from the golden tan she'd acquired while lazing on the private beach of the resort. Aided by the rays of the tropical sun, streaks of brilliant yellows kissed her natural sandy colored hair, all of which helped to solidify in his mind that she was indeed a portrait of *natural* beauty.

"Ary, stay with me when we get home," he proposed, unexpectedly. "You don't have to answer me now, but think about it. I know we could be great together. Our combined ambitions are limitless and our connection as friends and lovers would only add to future successes."

She was speechless. This was not supposed to happen. He was her confidant, not her soul mate. He was supposed to rescue her from professional and personal conflicts, not impose them on her. What could she say without feeling a sense of guilt for all that he'd done to help when her world at NPI came crumbling down and her personal life unhinged. He was beginning to sound like Joseph Larsen. She was beholden to no man. She was grateful, yes, but obliged, *hell no.*

"Let me think about it Darias. I'm still not sure about my job at the firm or if I'm ready to get right back in the game. Also, I have so much work to do in reconciling with my family, which in and of itself is a full-time endeavor," she added, trying to inject a bit of humor into an awkward conversation.

"As I said Ary, don't answer me right now. I don't want to spoil the time we've shared here. I want to remember us lying together on the beach, making love under the stars. I want to remember you in your exquisite nudity as you stepped into my arms in the Jacuzzi in Dubai. I want to remember you clumsily, but oh so sexily ordering your meal and wine in your broken Arabic. No, I don't need an answer now. We only have one day left in this tropical paradise and I'd like to continue the fantasy we've enjoyed." His eyes were intoxicating, his voice, mesmerizing, and his commanding physical stature made it almost impossible to resist. But she knew she'd have to, sooner rather than later. Her friendship with him was extraordinarily special, and she'd hoped that it would remain that way. But as she'd learned over time and past relationships—remaining friends with a lover was at best, problematic and at worst, an awkward dance.

CHAPTER 19

DWAYNE enjoyed every moment of his time away from home. Ordering room service for breakfast in bed, sampling the richness of local delicacies for lunch at cafes carved into mountainsides overlooking the Golo river, pausing at ancient sights as he wandered through and around tiny villages on a one-man walking tour, all the while listening to locals chat and greet him in their native tongues, moving over slightly to share narrow walkways and jagged passages. Yes, this was what he'd needed—crystal blue waters, skies filled with thin blankets of clouds providing just the right amount of cover from the intense rays of the Mediterranean sun and evenings spent at lavishly appointed hidden local restaurants, recommended by hotel staff hoping to garner an extra tip from the handsome American at the end of his stay. But still, no matter how hard he tried to not think of her, his mind painted her picture, walking beside him, holding tight to his arm before stopping suddenly, underneath a satiny night sky, as he turned to face her while simultaneously pulling her closely into his longing body. They would kiss, long, hard and heated, indifferent to any onlookers who may have curiously watched and undaunted by what they may have whispered, said out loud or thought of the young American couple. They were lovers, in every imaginable sense of the word. She made him feel whole, alive, and manly and he vowed to do whatever it took to make her realize they were meant for each other.

"Mi li putissitu essiri Mad sulu tonight, vassia?" (*Will you be dining alone tonight, sir?*) a heavily accented host asked, welcoming him into the eatery. With his thoughts of her now interrupted, Dwayne awkwardly placed both hands in his pockets, pulled in his lips and answered a quick and unexpectedly disappointing, '*yes*,' following the man to a small ornate table near an open window, filtering in a balmy Corsican breeze.

CHAPTER 20

"I'M telling you Caroline, it's okay now. Mama is finally alright with our relationship and your connection to Matthew. I don't really know how it all happened, but everything seems to have been sorted out." Marcus held her close in his arms as they sat on a bench in Central Park. He'd invited her to meet him after work and surprised her with a bouquet of yellow and white roses. The sun was setting in the western sky creating a memorable backdrop to his explanation and declaration. "I don't know how else to say it, except to just blurt it out. I love you Caroline Grant, with all my heart. You are the first person I want to see when I open my eyes in the morning and the one I want to feel in my arms when I fall asleep at night. I know I've taken you through hell and back and I apologize and hope you can find a way to forgive me. But what I've come to realize is, like my family, you've stood by me through my confusion and foolishness and your love for me never wavered." Marcus turned to face her as he knelt to the ground on one knee, taking her hands into his. "I'm asking you again, this time with the proper hardware, to be my wife." The ring was a 3.5 carat, round cut solitaire white diamond with a 14 carat yellow gold band to match the flowers that lay in her lap. He slid the jewel onto her freshly polished ring finger, waiting for her formal response.

"Marcus, I love you," she insisted, staring at the sparkling jewel then looking deeply into his probing eyes. "You know there is no one I'd rather spend the rest of my life with. But I have to be certain that *you're* sure, not only about us, but mostly about you. I can't enter into a marriage like you yourself once said, not knowing who my husband really is. I believe that you *are* the man you've shown me to be. My question to you is—do *you* truly believe it?"

Marcus was stunned and shaken. That was not the response he'd expected from the woman he'd just declared his love and intentions to. What had changed? Had he waited too long? Did she see something in him that he wasn't yet willing to admit to himself? Was it the antics of his family that caused her to question his devotion or even his masculinity?

Caroline waited for his answer. She needed an explanation. *Why now?* she wondered. *How could everything just miraculously turn itself around in such a positive way, providing him with the clarity he'd been searching for over the past few months?* There was no doubt in her mind that she loved him, but she'd come from a family of divorce—parents, aunts and uncles, and it was something she'd never envisioned for herself.

"Marcus," she asserted, realizing that his profound disappointment prevented an immediate response. "It's beautiful and it's perfect, but now I'm afraid that *we* may not be. I'm terrified that the time is not right, for reasons that might well be beyond our control."

Letting go of her hands he rose slowly from his bended knee, trying to steady himself from the shock of her revelation. His heart pounded as though it would leap from his chest at the slightest movement. He sat down next to her, searching her face, her expression, her azure eyes for an even deeper truth. With his confidence shattered, his emotions took charge and rose from the depths of his soul, even allowing tears to flow from his saddened eyes.

"I'm not gay Caroline, I'm not," he tried convincing her, his voice trembling, "Or bi-sexual. I'm a heterosexual man who's deeply in love with you," this time summoning the deepest, most masculine tone he could muster. "I've tried to be as honest as I could with all that I've gone through with my family and in my childhood, and if, right now, you're questioning *your* trust, love and belief in me, well, there's nothing I can do to change that. It's something *you'll* have to decide for yourself. I can tell you that I'm willing to wait, but please don't make me wait only to find that you've moved on to someone whose sexuality you never had to consider," he finished.

Abruptly shifting away, Caroline stood up and blurted, "I wasn't the one who questioned your sexuality, Marcus—it was you, not me! All I'm saying is I don't want to end up in the same situation your mother found herself in, or my uncle Matthew for that matter. I want children, a family, a husband who will be my confidant and partner for what I hope will be our lifetime. I know I may sound somewhat naïve, maybe even old fashioned and just the opposite of what it means to be a feminist these days, but I don't care. It's what I want and know I deserve. So Marcus, this time, I'm asking *you* to wait and trust that if we're meant for each other, the time will come for me to accept your beautiful gesture." And with that, she leaned down, kissed the top of his head, returned the ring and headed towards Sheep Meadow.

CHAPTER 21

THE sudden rainstorm was the perfect ending to what had been a perfect getaway for Dwayne. He didn't mind the large, fragrant drops dancing against the windows of his hotel room while enjoying his last night tucked comfortably underneath the incredibly soft cotton sheets, or even having to make a mad dash into a spirited bar to prevent his sheer island fashion from becoming drenched and revealingly tempting to the local women or sparking masculine jealousy among the men. He watched as the curtains of rain fell from the night sky, and then closed his eyes to concentrate on the natural rhythms of nature. His time in Corsica had been magical. What would have made it even more memorable would have been spending it with the woman who continued to occupy the empty place in his heart.

CHAPTER 22

ALTHOUGH she'd preferred to have flown directly home, Darias explained that they would be stopping over in Athens, Greece not only to refuel but also to check on one of the two villas he'd rented out to vacationers. She settled into the comfortably large leather seat and closed her eyes, conceding that the beauty of Greece would provide one last bastion of solace before tackling the grind of work and any Alexander family issues that awaited her. She'd also hoped that by doing so, he wouldn't press her, at least for now, for an answer to his unforeseen and unsettling question of living together.

CHAPTER 23

"THANKS for arranging this on such short notice," he gushed, acknowledging that he'd always wanted to visit Athens. "Hey, this is all on my boss's dime, so why the hell not, right?" The concierge had worked hard to find a flight and hotel, knowing that the already generous American would not disappoint in the form of gratuities.

CHAPTER 24

DARIAS worked feverishly on his laptop as they flew over countries and villages along massive oceans and winding rivers. At times, he looked at her as she pretended to sleep. *Was this the right time for them to live together?* he second guessed himself. *What if her answer is 'no,'* how would that reflect on their working relationship if and once she returns to NPI and has business with BP? At times it became hard to concentrate on business. Everything that had taken place prior to their get-away was mind boggling. He'd helped to bring down one of the most successful oil men in New York at a firm whose reputation was rapidly growing not only in the states but abroad as well. He'd spoken to G in the days following the firing of Joseph and his breakup with Marguerite and had suggested that he get away for a few days just to put it all in perspective and come back fresh. G reassured him that his mind was clear and that working hard and smart was in fact his therapy. The decision to award the BP contract would be announced soon and he wondered if the resulting award would have any effect on her decision to stay at NPI or whether or not to move in with him.

Ary could feel his eyes on her, making her even more determined to keep them closed. She squirmed left and right in her spacious seat and turned even further toward the window, adjusting the down-filled pillow and pulling the silk covered blanket around her shoulders. Her thoughts were focused once again on family and sitting down with Sonya to understand her newfound relationship with Matthew. *What would it all mean for she and Marcus and holiday celebrations?* The mere thought of her father and his partner sitting down to dinner at Sonya's was too much for her to even conceptualize. *Wasn't that how it all began? How could she possibly move forward and accept them all as one big happy family again?*

Suddenly, a fierce turbulence caused her eyes to flicker. "Oh my God!" she screamed, turning to face him. "Are we ok? What the hell is going on?"

"What's wrong? It's just a few bumps," he stressed, reassuringly. "We're on a smaller plane this time so you're going to feel them a bit more than when we came over."

Totally dismissing his explanation, she warned, "If this keeps up I'm gonna need something strong to drink. What do you have that can take my mind off of the fact that we're trapped in this flying seesaw?"

"Were you having a bad dream? Maybe that's why the strong winds startled you even more."

"Maybe, could've, I don't know," she answered, still shaken. "I think I also panicked knowing that the reality of life will be staring me in the face soon and I'm not so sure I'm ready to face it."

He signaled for the on-board assistant, "Two scotch on the rocks and make hers a double," he ordered, unbuttoning her seatbelt and raising the arm rest to hold her in his arms. "Everything's going to be alright Ary, I promise. You won't have to face anything you're not prepared to handle."

The plane continued on to its destination, maneuvering up and around to avoid any further disturbances.

CHAPTER 25

WHEW. *I didn't realize just how relaxed I'd gotten,* Dwayne thought as he found himself lagging behind other travelers, making his way through Athens International airport. Remembering the plane had landed early, and that his driver wouldn't be at the pickup location for another forty-five minutes, he decided to visit some of the exquisite shops lining the renovated spaces on the upper level of the airport to while away the time. *Ah, Boggi Milano, just the temptation I need to spend some of my* own *money,* he laughed, walking into the softly lit, fashionably exclusive men's store.

As Dwayne described the sports jacket he'd seen on their website, showing a picture on his iPhone and hoping they'd have it in store or at least something similar, Darias and Ary walked past on their way to Ermenegildo Zegna, another fine men's shop, and a favorite of Darias'. Ary swore she'd heard a familiar voice. *It couldn't possibly be,* she thought, shaking her head as though it would clear her suspicion.

But just as she'd turned around to make certain that who she thought she'd heard was not that person, Dwayne walked out from the shop and met her stare.

"Dwayne?" she screamed, taken aback by the surprise. "What the hell? I mean, how? When? What are you doing in Greece?"

Just as shocked, and taking a step backwards across the threshold of the store, he shook his head before stumbling out an explanation. "Oh my God, Ary, this is, this is, unbelievable! I'm here on the last leg of my vacation from another vacation in Corsica and out of all the people I could have run into in a foreign country, I run into you," he finished, without noticing Darias, who'd walked a few steps ahead. As he walked closer to hug her, he was suddenly unnerved.

"Whoa! Oh! Hey man," he managed, forcing the words out from his lips. "What a coincidence. Never in my wildest dreams did I expect to see…the *two* of you here. Are you guys here on business or…?" he lingered awkwardly.

"Hello Dwayne. This *is* a surprise. You came all the way to Athens to go to Boggi Milano's?" he questioned, without offering any answers. "You do know they have a store in New York, right?" he asked, trying to lessen the uncomfortable encounter. They all let out a collective, uneasy laugh. "But hey, who could blame you for wanting a change in scenery from what I guess can best be described as, 'difficult times'? Even if it does involve traveling 5,000 miles for a pair of Italian leather shoes you could have just as easily had shipped to your house."

Ary turned to face him, catching his smirk and sarcastic bite before turning back to Dwayne, who by now had figured out that they were there on vacation while simultaneously trying to reconcile his own emotions.

"Yeah, you're right man. It has been one wild ride. And as far as the shoes, I was actually looking for a sports jacket. But you're right, I could've just relied on familiarity and done the boring thing—taxiing cross town to pick it up or even had it delivered to my doorstep. But this seemed *soooo* much more tempting. And by the look on your face, you probably felt the same way when it came to satisfying the lure of temptation, five-thousand miles from home," he shot back with equal sarcasm.

Ary knew it was time to quell the '*mano a mano*' hostility brewing between them before it escalated into something more. "Dwayne, did you say you were in Corsica? Where'd you stay? For how long?" she asked, rattling off the questions while trying to diffuse the tension. "Why did you go to Corsica first and *then* come to Greece? It seems a little backwards."

"It was a last minute decision to come to Athens," he explained, staring deep into her eyes. "I figured I'd extend the time away before immersing myself back into the grind of business with all of my favorite, *old*, *white*, oil barons," he nudged, turning to Darias. "So no, I wouldn't so much as call it backwards, as I'd describe it as adventurous, spontaneous, and well played."

"Well played?" she asked, puzzled.

"Hey, I'm here, you're here, thousands of miles away from home, neither one of us consulting the other before venturing abroad, but both ending up in Athens—on the second level of a busy airport mall—in front of an expensive men's shop. Yeah, I'd call it well-played," he finished, this time fixing his eyes on his imposed rival.

"Well-played or not," Darias interjected, feeling the friction rising to a boil, "We'd better get going. I'd like to pick up the rental car and head out to the villa before the sun goes down," he urged, meeting Dwayne's gaze with equal hostility. "And hey, if you need a *lavish* place to stay, one of my rentals is opening up tomorrow. But don't worry, I'd be happy to lower the cost to make it more affordable."

Dwayne fumed. He turned to Ary to try and assess whether she was in agreement with Darias' obvious insults. He also didn't want to make a scene in the middle of a foreign airport. She was staring in disbelief. This was a side of him she hadn't seen. *What was going on in* his *head*, she wondered. She hadn't yet agreed to move in with him. *Why was he being so possessive?*

"I'm pretty certain that Dwayne could afford to stay wherever he chooses, and going by the pugnacious stare on his face, I don't think your *'lavish'* villas would be his first choice."

But careful not to align herself with either one, she continued.

"And Dwayne, I don't think you can tell by the look on *anyone's* face, that they've been *lured* by the temptations of a foreign land, five, ten or fifty-thousand miles away. I would also think that by now you'd know that I'm not influenced or *'played'* as you say, by any man or woman. I make my own choices, whenever, however and wherever they take me," she interposed, with all the muster she was able to conjure.

For just a moment, he was speechless. Thousands of miles from home and she was still causing him angst. *She's even beautiful when she's making a fool out of two grown men,* he thought. *I can't ever seem to escape this fucking grip she has on me. But right now I'd better have a quasi-intelligent comeback or else I'm gonna end up with the same dumbass look as that jerk she's here with.*

"You know what? You're right, Ms. Alexander. I apologize for suggesting otherwise and I'm *more* than aware that you make your own choices, whenever, however and wherever the *fuck*..." he started, before catching his belligerent tone. "I'm sorry, what I meant was, wherever those select *choices* may take you," he corrected himself, flaunting a Cheshire cat grin. "It was a pleasure seeing you here and I wish you both a safe journey on your final destination. Αντίο, Avvedeci, and goodbye," he sang in impressive Greek and Corsu.

Not impressed, Darias waited until Dwayne walked away before countering with, "What American speaks Corsican? Just stick with French or even Italian, you'll be fine, I'm sure."

Ary stood there, watching as Dwayne made his way through the horde of travelers. Darias watched her watching Dwayne and grew increasingly annoyed.

"C'mon Ary, We really need to get going."

"Okay, I know. But what was all that about? I'm beginning to feel like a pawn in a chess game. I feel like all of what just happened was entirely uncalled for."

"I'm sorry Ary. I don't ordinarily behave that way, and I actually like Dwayne. So I have no rational explanation or plausible excuse," he offered, biting his bottom lip. "Let's just say that it was a clash of the alpha males. Good old dominant, masculine conflict when in the presence of a desirably stunning female. Call it instinct, I guess. How else do you expect a man to react when he feels as if another man is encroaching on his territory?" he explained, kissing her gently on the lips and forehead.

She bristled at his last statement. *This man did* not *just refer to me as his 'territory'.* "Darias, we have to talk," she swore, as he grabbed her hand, leading her through the teeming concourse.

CHAPTER 26

DWAYNE regained the strength that had escaped him prior to the startling encounter with Ary and Darias and nearly sprinted past other travelers, maneuvering fluidly through the throngs of people. Remembering he'd left the men's store without buying the jacket, and noticing he'd still have at least twenty minutes to waste before his driver would be downstairs outside baggage claim, he thought, *I'd rather wait out the rest of my time in a bar sooner than chance another awkward run-in with those two.* He darted into the first pub he came upon and ordered a Johnnie Walker, Double Black Label scotch. *It's like a fucking curse,* he reflected, downing his drink in one hard swallow, and gesturing for a refill. *What the hell does a brother have to do to prove how he feels about a sister? Is she clueless? Has she been so far removed from her own people that her 'black-man-game' is off?* But before he could reconcile his own thoughts and finish his second round, he heard his name being called over the paging system, first in Greek; *Dwayne Hargis, parakaloúme na antapokritheí o odigós sas stin piátsa ton taxi.* Then repeated twice in English; *Dwayne Hargis, please meet your driver at the taxi stand. Mr. Hargis, your driver is waiting for you downstairs at the taxi stand.*

Checking the clock above the massive wall of liquors, he reached into his breast pocket, pulled out his credit card, motioned to the bartender that he was anxious to settle the tab and just as quickly signed the bill without scrutinizing the charges, totally out of character for the financially savvy executive. He then raced toward the escalators where the overhead signs pointed to '*baggage claim*' and hoped that his luggage was waiting on the carousel. He was more than anxious to begin the second relaxing leg of his trip, or so he'd hoped.

CHAPTER 27

A week had passed since Marcus had seen or even heard from Caroline. He'd gone back to the bench where he'd declared his love for her and proposed with a ring of engagement. His thoughts were unrestrained and his confidence fading with each passing hour. Would she really wait for him again or had he blown his chance at happiness for good? What else could he possibly do to convince her of his love or that he was indeed the man she'd met almost a year ago. He wasn't ready to let her go or accept that it was time to move on. "I need to call Ary. Maybe *she* can talk to Caroline, make her understand that I am who I say I am," he declared with a newfound assurance. Feeling as though he'd made the right decision, he buried his hands in his pants pockets and walked in the direction of the setting sun.

CHAPTER 28

DARIAS and Ary barely spoke during the drive to the villa. She was still seething from his *'territory'* remark but wanted to wait for the right moment to remind him that she belonged to no one. After stopping at the property, she was taken aback by its size and architectural splendor. She'd concluded long ago that he had money, not only based on his New York penthouse, but from unsubstantiated rumors around NPI that he'd come from a long line of Scottish coal wealth.

"So, here we are, finally. I just want to check on the vacationers staying in the ground floor suite. They're a young, recently married couple I'd met in Spain last summer who didn't want to stay in traditional hotels as they island hopped their way on an extended honeymoon, and I wanted to personally make sure everything was what they'd expected—and of course that they'd tell their friends and family about the place," he explained to his uninterested passenger. Ary smiled, then turned to open the door.

"It's beautiful. I think I'll walk around the grounds before meeting you inside, if that's okay?"

"Sure, that's fine," he agreed, feeling a little uneasy. "Is everything okay Ary? You were awfully quiet during the ride and I really want you to see the place..."

"I'm fine. Go, conduct your business. I promise, I'll be inside in just a little while. I really want to take in the sights and sounds of the sea."

In actuality, she needed to get away from him. Although she was equally upset with Dwayne's presumptions, somehow she understood his jealousy. He had, after all declared his love for her back home and risked his career to make sure hers remained intact. She visualized him driving out to her mother's house, only to be turned away without explanation. She wondered how many times she could keep disappointing him before he wrote her off completely. Looking back toward the villa, she noticed Darias and the stylish couple walking toward the perfectly landscaped gardens. She could hear him speaking in broken Spanish, laughing at himself as the couple encouraged his attempts before they all opted for English. Ary watched as the handsome Spaniard curved his arm around the petite waist of his bride. Her heart raced as Darias turned slowly towards her, motioning to come and join them. Part of her wanted to, if only not to be rude, but she turned instead to face the Cyclades Islands in the distance, home to Santorini and Mykonos, secretly wishing to be anywhere but here.

CHAPTER 29

DWAYNE'S driver had taken the scenic route to the private hotel, pointing out the history of the islands and the fierce pride of the Greek people. Although he was exhausted, it gave him time to sort out the confusion waging between his heart and mind. As the driver spoke in broken, heavily accented English, Dwayne's thoughts were consumed with finally reconciling his on-again, off-again, so-called relationship with Ary.

"Greece has given the world many wonderful things, Mr. Hargis," the self-appointed tour guide announced suddenly. "Socrates, Plato, Aristotle and the Olympic Games. And of course, I'm sure you know that Athens was the cradle of democracy in western civilization," he maintained most assuredly. "But with all that knowledge, to me personally, Mr. Hargis, nothing is as meaningful as the Greek goddesses of love and beauty—Aphrodite, Venus, Iris," he finished, looking through the rearview mirror at his obviously lost in thought traveler. "And from what I know and have seen in all my 66 years, you look like a man who's either running *from* or running *to* his goddess," he laughed.

Dwayne, instantly shaken from his private musings, was forced into an unrehearsed answer. "*From*, running *from* someone I guess you could say. And I agree—what better place to do it in, than Greece." As they made their way on the winding, rugged roads leading up to the hotel entrance, Dwayne's iPhone buzzed, alerting him to a text message: *I've made my choice and I'd like to spend the rest of my time here with you. Text back if you agree. Ary*

"What the fuck?!" he blurted out as they crossed over a rough patch of roadway.

"I'm sorry sir, but the streets are not all as smooth as you might have in America."

"Oh no, it wasn't the bump. It's my phone. It was a message on my phone," he explained, still staring at the screen. "I can't believe this shit," he griped, this time in a more hushed tone. *She really does live in an alternate universe. One where* she *makes all the rules and everyone else is expected to live by them. But not this time, uh uh, oh hell no, not again,* he swore, finishing his thoughts in private.

Startled by the car's sudden stop, he noticed colorfully costumed hotel staff racing towards the rear as the trunk slowly opened, waiting to retrieve his luggage. The driver hurried out and made his way around to Dwayne's door, holding it open. But he sat there, unable to move, staring at the ancient, pristine white stoned structure shimmering against the golden colors of a fading sun. He couldn't help himself. He thought of her—that moment in his apartment, watching as the glow of a moonlit sky cast a perfect silhouette around her naked body—their hearts beating in chorus to the soulful jazz saxophone of Coltrane in the background.

"Mr. Hargis, we've arrived at your hotel. Is everything okay?"

"Yep, yes. Everything's fine. I was just, just," he stammered, "just lost for a quick second. Enamored by the, the beauty of the architecture," he asserted, only telling a half truth, trying to save himself from further questioning. "Hey, here's a little extra for the guided tour and conversation," he offered, reaching into his pocket for the loose bills he'd gotten at the currency exchange at the airport. And thank you, efharisto, efharisto," he said, practicing his limited Greek phrases.

"Parakalo, Mr. Hargis and efharisto. It was my pleasure to spend a little time with you and introduce you to my great country. And I hope, with all sincerity, you find your true goddess here or at home. But don't wait too long because living might not last a lifetime."

Dwayne watched as the driver sped off circling the driveway and down the hill. *'Living might not last a lifetime?' That's all I need right now is a modern day, limo driving, Socrates filling my head with some philosophical bullshit,* he thought, as he turned toward the looming wooden lobby doors, making his way to the check-in counter.

"Kalispéra kai kalosorísate, Mr. Hargis. Good evening and welcome to the Palace Acropolis. Welcome to your home for the next several days. I am Kostas, the hotel manager. If there is anything that you require during your stay, *anything*, please, just ask and it will be done," he stated effortlessly after being informed of his newest guest by the baggage handlers.

Dwayne breathed a sigh of relief. All he wanted and needed was a soft bed and a stiff drink. "Efharisto, Kostas. Please send up a bottle of Blue Label and a bucket of ice. That'll do for now." Before heading to the elevator, he swept a quick look around the lobby, noticing the imposing, nude Greek sculptures and striking artwork and was glad he'd decided to stop over as one last respite before heading back to the realities awaiting him at work and at home.

CHAPTER 30

AS she walked around the spacious property, praying that she'd done right by texting Dwayne, although knowing deep down that he was still reeling from their encounter at the airport, she'd hoped that he would forgive her one last time. *Come on Dwayne, answer me, text me back, let me know that you still really care. I'll admit that I can be a handful at times, which I'm sure you'd agree, but I need you to forgive me. I really want to spend the rest of my time here with you. It's so beautiful…*

But before she could complete her thoughts, her phone rang.

"Oh thank God!" she beamed, before looking at the caller's name. "Wait, Marcus?" she asked disappointedly.

"What's wrong? Is everything okay?"

"Hello? Hey Ary, can you hear me?"

"Yes Marcus. What is it? Are you okay? Is Mama…"

"Mama's fine. Me? Not so much. I need your advice Ary and it can't wait until you get home…*whenever* that might be."

"I don't know what *that's* supposed to mean, but what is it that can't wait?"

"It's Caroline. She wouldn't accept the ring."

"Whaaaat? What ring? What are you talking about? I thought you two were already engaged. I'm confused."

"Stop talking for a minute and let me explain," he chastened, interrupting her successive questioning. "Caroline doesn't believe that I'm not really a younger version of dad. She's not 100 percent convinced that I'm not gonna up and fuckin' leave her like he left us and I need you to tell her that that's not the case, Ary. I need you to explain it to her—tell her that I'm a straight man who's had many women in the past, but that I'm ready to settle down with one woman—her! The woman of my dreams, the one I've been searching for all my life. I need you to tell her that, Ary," he finished, completely out of breath.

She was stunned to hear him pleading with *her* to confess *his* love to *his* fiancée.

"Soooo, there you are," he whispered, sneaking up behind her, playfully wrapping his arms around her waist.

"Not now please!" she chided, pulling away and pushing the mute button "Can't you see I'm on the phone in the middle of a serious conversation?"

"Sorry, no I didn't," he apologized, only half meaning it. He looked at her, trying to comprehend the cold stare in her eyes. "I *thought* you were trying to get away from all the *serious* shit back home, not pack it up and bring it with you. Unless of course you just happen to have found it *unexpectedly*, right here in Athens," he ended with intentional irony.

"I don't know *what* you're talking about, but right now I need to get back to this call. We can discuss your concerns later." She watched as he looked almost through her, stunned and confused, then turned her attention back to her brother who was still talking as she unmuted the phone.

"Ary, are you there? Can you still hear me?"

"Yes, I'm here. Now slow down and tell me what the hell you're talking about."

Darias walked back toward the villa, turning to catch a glimpse of the woman he could barely recognize from just minutes before. He pondered his next move. *How could she do this?* he wondered, after having poured his heart out, even suggesting they move in together. When his relationship with Marguerite ended years ago, he'd vowed to be a confirmed bachelor, just play the field of smart, beautiful women who were themselves looking for handsome, wealthy, and equally brilliant men. And although there had been plenty of possibilities, the right one had yet to find her way into his heart. None, until Ary Alexander came along. In a lot of ways she'd reminded him of Marguerite, before, he felt, the oil industry had corrupted her and her personal demons had gotten the best of her. But Ary was young, beautiful, personable and exceptionally bright. He even thought she could be the one to sway his mind from bachelorhood.

Now, he felt offended and betrayed—emotions he'd restricted to business dealings with powerful and sometimes underhanded competitors from less-than-honorable moneyed oil men. He'd promised himself after his breakup with Marguerite never to be vulnerable to the diversions of attractive women ever again. In the end it had been a heartbreaking experience and one in which he was in no hurry to relive. *I don't know for sure who was on the other end of that line, but I'm willing to bet it wasn't work related.*

With his thoughts distracted, and his ego bruised, he walked around the driveway of the villa, jumped in the rental car and sped off.

Still listening to her brother go on about his engagement dilemma, Ary heard the car engine roar and made her way to the front of the house where she noticed rising dust and tire tracks against the rugged pavement. "Oh shit, what am I supposed to do now?"

"Are you talking to me Ary?" Marcus inquired.

"No Marcus, I'm not talking to you! He just drove off and left me here, by myself, in Greece!" she yelled. "And I don't speak the language!" she continued, pacing back and forth. "I don't know the people in this house and I don't have any transportation. I don't even know if he's coming back or if there are empty rooms here!" she explained desperately. "Marcus, I'm sorry but I'll have to talk to you later. I'll call you back once I've figured out what the hell is going on here, okay? I love you. I'll talk to you later."

She hung up without waiting to hear his response, looking frantically around the property, trying to orient herself. *Dwayne, if ever I needed you, it's never been more than right now. Please, please call or text me back.*

CHAPTER 31

MARCUS gripped the phone long after Ary had disconnected. Now *he* worried about his sister who sounded anxious and alone. He wondered who she might be with in Greece. All she'd told him before leaving was that she'd be in the Maldives with someone other than Dwayne. Now she was stranded in Greece. Marcus scrolled through his contacts and call list, hoping that he hadn't deleted Dwayne's number from weeks ago. Maybe he'd know who she was with and could shed some light on the vagueness of her conversation.

Dwayne lie in bed watching what seemed to be a Greek reality show while savoring the smooth scotch sent up to his suite by the concierge. "I see they watch mindless shit just like folks back home," he laughed. But his laughter was short lived, interrupted by the sudden ringing of his phone.

"What the…! Hello?" he answered, not recognizing the incoming number.

"Hello Dwayne, it's Marcus Alexander, Ary's brother. Sorry to bother you."

Dwayne's emotions went from shock, to disbelief, to concern.

"Hey Marcus, what's up?" he asked, cautiously.

"I hate to trouble you man, but I'm a little concerned about my sister and I didn't know who else to call."

At first he was stunned to think that the first person to come to mind, *and* call in an emergency would be him. *What is this really about?* he wondered. Did Marcus somehow know that he'd seen her at the airport in Athens? Did he even know that he was *in* the country?

"Marcus, what's going on? What's your concern?"

"Well, this probably sounds somewhat *'out there'* but I was just talking to her on the phone, knowing she was vacationing in the Maldives, then come to find out she's in Greece, stranded. It's seems that whoever she was with has left her and she's alone. That's what I know. And the reason I called you was because I figured you, being her boss might have some idea of who she was traveling with," he finished.

"Huh?! Why would I know that?"

"Well, I didn't know if Greece was a business trip or what after having gone off to the middle of nowhere and…"

"Whoa, Marcus, wait," he cautioned, stopping him mid-sentence. "First of all, back up. What did you mean by *'stranded'*? Look, I'm in Greece as well and I just saw her a few hours ago with her uh, friend, boyfriend, colleague or whatever and she didn't look like there was anything wrong. So, I'm not sure why she'd be by herself right now."

"I'm not sure either Dwayne. All I *do* know is what she said before abruptly hanging up on me, clearly upset and…wait a minute, did you say you're in Greece too?"

"Yeah, I am," he answered, swallowing hard. "Look Marcus, I can try calling her cell and hope she answers, see what the hell is going on and have her reach out to you to let you know she's okay. That's all I can do. I really don't want to get involved in whatever is going on between two adults, okay?"

"Appreciate it, man. And again, I'm sorry to get you mixed up in this, but she's family. And as strong-willed as she can be sometimes—she means more to me than anything."

"Family…," he whispered, trailing off. "Yeah, I know."

CHAPTER 32

"HEY mama, yeah, I spoke to her boss, he's there too and he'll call once he finds her. Don't worry, I know she'll be okay and knowing her, in the end, she'll say it was nothing, that I overreacted and worry too much."

"Thank you for letting me know what was going on, Marcus. I wasn't informed about her trip and neither have I seen or heard from Ary since she ran off like a chastised child that day after seeing Matthew and Bruce here at home."

"Speaking of them mama, are things still good? Still copa-setic?" he asked, injecting humor into a conversation that could have easily evolved into more than he wanted to handle at that moment.

"I think so, baby. I think we've all come to the understanding that it just takes too much energy to keep up the disappointments we've all shared over the years."

'Disappointments'? he thought to himself. *Hatred* would have been a more fitting description. But he chose not to rehash a dialogue that would have surely conjured up hurt feelings, and instead, ended the conversation with a simple, "I agree, mama. So, I'll let you know how she is after I hear from her or her boss."

"Thank you, Marcus. I love you and keep me updated."

He considered for a moment bringing up his own situation with Caroline, but quickly decided against it, remembering what Sonya had just gone through because of him. He certainly didn't want to be the cause of a medical relapse. Although he marveled at her strength, he reasoned that she could only take one Alexander crises at a time. "Love you too, mama."

CHAPTER 33

AFTER hanging up from his call with Marcus, Dwayne thumped the phone against his impressive six-pack, then scrolled through his contacts, stopping at her name. He hesitated before choosing her number, secretly hoping she wouldn't pick up.

"Oh Dwayne," she answered, crying. "He left me here, alone. I don't know what to do."

His emotions immediately took control of his common sense after hearing her distraught voice. "Ary listen, try and calm down, tell me where you are and I'll come and get you." Before he even realized what he was doing, he'd reached for his shirt, slipped on his shoes and grabbed his room key and wallet. His mind raced a hundred miles an hour, trying to keep up with the pounding of his head and heart as he made his way down to the lobby.

CHAPTER 34

ARY sat on a bench in the gardens, awestruck by the majestic beauty of golden hues and purple shadows cast by the setting sun over the distant mountain range. An approaching car engine was all that interrupted her passing captivity. *Oh my God. I hope it's him*, she thought, jumping to her feet, racing towards the driveway.

Dwayne parked near the front door entrance, noticing her right away, standing off to the side of the villa. She nervously watched as he came closer, putting both hands in the pockets of her flowing white maxi dress, unsure if he'd curse her out, or symbolically ring her neck. He did neither. Instead he stood in front of her, face to face, so close she could feel his breath and see his heart throbbing against his chest.

"I'm really sorry. I didn't..."

Before she could finish her explanation, he pulled her into his arms and kissed her quivering lips. Feeling the sanctuary of his embrace, her tears flowed freely. She wrapped her arms around his ample neck and finally exhaled. All of his anger seemed to diminish with the softness of each kiss. Instead of prosecuting her for the hell he'd decided she deserved, he was now protecting her from a scene that might have been.

"You're safe now. Let's go."

CHAPTER 35

DARIAS walked along the beach, hoping the sound of crashing waves would help ease his pain. *How could she do this?* he wondered, still wrongly convinced that she'd been on the phone with Dwayne. *To me, me, out of all the men who've broken her heart. She must have known that he'd be there and contacted him while we were still at the resort, arranging their 'surprise' meeting at the airport. It's hard to believe that that was a coincidence. I truly believe they planned their little rendezvous, and that's just fucked up.*

He rolled up his pant legs, removed his shoes, socks and shirt, leaving them visible in the sand and ran as hard as he could. It would take more than a casual stroll to work off his anger.

CHAPTER 36

DWAYNE tried reversing the directions he'd gotten from the concierge as he drove on roads that seemed to meet a steeper curve at each turn.

After having explained his emergency to Kostas, he was given access to a rental car at the hotel that had been reserved for a guest checking in tomorrow afternoon.

"I need to find my way back to the hotel before tomorrow cause this rental is not really mine. I kinda borrowed it by saying I had to rescue a damsel in distress." he confessed, chuckling.

"Is that all it took," she replied, wiping away the leftover tears.

"Well, that and a hundred dollar bribe." They both laughed.

"But seriously Ary, we're gonna have to talk once we get to the hotel. I can't keep doing this. I promised your brother I'd do what I could to find you and make sure you were okay and…"

"What are you saying?" she interrupted. "What do you mean, my brother? I texted you. I thought you were responding to *my* text."

Trying to keep his eyes on the darkened, unfamiliar roads, he silently repeated the prayer of St. Christopher for safe travel: *Each time I drive Lord, may I feel Your hands on mine upon the wheel.* He then turned his attention to her as her tone seemed to rise with each query. "Really, Ary? Does it matter whose text I replied to? I came when you needed me, even after your little airport theatrics. I came when I thought you were in trouble. Give me credit for something," he implored, his irritation growing. "I'm not the one who left you at some house on a hill. I'm the man who would never think of leaving *any* lady stranded at home or in a foreign country, whether it was because of a fight or whatever it was that took place between the two of you. It's as if everything has changed because you think I only came because your brother asked me to, who, by the way, you should probably call to let him know you're okay. But before you do, stop the drama Ary, grow up. *I'm* here, *he's* not," he said, briefly turning to address her. "Look, I don't know how many times a man has to prove to you that he cares, but that shit's gettin' old. I feel like I've been there for you at every turn, since the first time we met at NPI," he explained, his disposition calming after recognizing a familiar street leading up to the hotel.

"I apologize. I don't mean to upset you Dwayne, but I'd texted you earlier because after seeing you at the airport, I knew for sure that it was *you* I wanted to be with. I wanted to explain it all to you back home. I'd even prepared a romantic dinner to make up for the misunderstanding of coming out to my mother's house on the Island. Dwayne, I agree, we *do* need to talk, but please keep an open mind and give me a chance to try and clarify everything before completely writing me off."

"We're here, finally," he announced, exhaling and wiping his brow. "That was some pretty harrowing shit! I don't think I've ever driven in a foreign country not having the slightest idea where the hell I was going—at night—on winding roads—near frightening cliffs, and made it back alive in one piece to tell about it!"

She watched as he got out of the car, walked around to her side, opened the door and gestured for her hand.

"Thank you," she said, demurely, allowing him to lead her through the lobby doors and up to the guest check-in counter.

"Hello Kostas, and again, efharisto for the use of the car," he pronounced, feeling relieved to have made it back to his temporary home. "You're a good man, eísai kalós ánthropos, a good man, right?"

"Naí, málista kýrie, yes, yes sir! You are picking up the language quite well, Mr. Hargis."

"So, Kostas, I do have one other request before I retire up to my suite."

"Otidípote, anything sir."

"I'll need another room for the lady. Can you help me with that?"

Ary looked up from her handbag, astonished. Her eyes went from Dwayne to Kostas, not knowing how to respond.

"Of course sir. Of course. Now, would this be added to your bill or…"

"Yes, naí, Kostas, yes. And please, see to it that she has everything she needs tonight."

"Naí, sir, naí."

Turning to his red-faced companion, and taking both her hands into his, he said, "Ary, I'm exhausted, so I'll see you tomorrow morning around nine o'clock for breakfast. Have a good night." He spun around and walked toward the elevator, sensing that she was still confused, dumbfounded, and oddly staring at him, but he refused to look back in her direction.

"Signomi, excuse me ma'am, ma'am," Kostas repeated, trying to gain her wavering attention. "Would you prefer an ocean view?"

"What?! Are you kidding me?" she blurted, reflecting utter bewilderment.

"I'd like to know your preference for your room please. We only have a few left and I want your stay with us to be a pleasant one. So, Ms…" he began, hoping she'd volunteer her name.

She turned to fully face him and with all the mettle she could summon, answered, "Ms. Ariel Marie Alexander. Would you like to see my passport as I.D.?"

CHAPTER 37

DARIAS returned to where he thought he'd left his belongings, only to find them drifting slowly towards the ocean by the ebbing tide. "Shit! My shoes!" he yelled, grabbing them and shaking off the sand and surf. "This is turning into a fucking nightmare." Gathering his soggy socks and shirt, anxiously checking his pants pockets to make certain his keys hadn't fallen out during his run, he thought, *Thank God. At least I can drive back to the villa, dry my clothes and rest in the empty suite.* His thoughts suddenly turned to Ary as he walked to the car. *Why I feel terrible for leaving her is even puzzling for me,* his more compassionate side once again resurfacing. *But I'm sure by now she would have had the good sense to go inside and chose one of the available suites, and hopefully think about this ridiculously childish situation.*

Remembering he hadn't been in contact with the pilot of the private jet who had been trying to reach him for the last several hours, he awkwardly retrieved his cell from the glove compartment and called. Without going into detail, he offered to be responsible for any additional cost because of the extra day in Greece. The pilot, who'd been waiting in the airport pilot's lounge, was relieved to know that his passengers were okay, but annoyed that he hadn't been notified earlier.

"We should be ready to take off no later than two o'clock tomorrow afternoon, so try and get some rest," Darias urged. "I know there are hotels right near the airport, and again, don't worry about anything, I'll cover the cost of your stay, meals and transportation. I appreciate your patience."

Now with his head firmly planted against the headrest, he sighed, taking a deep breath before checking to see if he'd missed a call from Ary. "Hmmm, so this is how she wants to play? Well, she'll find out sooner rather than later that I don't play foolish games, personally or professionally. I'd have thought you'd known that already, especially after having enlisted my help with all that bullshit you just went through with Joseph at NPI. I *really* thought we had something special here and I hope you have a good explanation for all of this nonsense," he finished, as if he were speaking to her directly.

Looking down at his bare feet, cool against the accelerator, he shook his head, pursed his lips and inserted the key into the ignition and headed towards his villa.

CHAPTER 38

AS the sun rose, Ary stretched out her arms and turned to look across the massive bed. *Was I dreaming?* Sitting up, she leaned forward, looking around towards the small living room area and then out towards the balcony. She lowered her head, deep in thought, trying to remember if it were him who lifted her hair, kissing her lightly on her neck. Was it him who climbed in bed, startling her at first, but then reassuring her that she was in safe hands? Was it him who took her in his arms and held her gently? But before she could answer her own thoughts or conclude if it was indeed a dream, a sudden knock on the door announcing "*Room service*" halted any further determination.

"What?! Room service? I didn't order any…Just a minute please," she yelled. Rising out of bed, she noticed the only clothing she was wearing were her bra and panties. "Oh God! Hold on, hold on."

"Don't worry," he assured her, coming out from the bathroom. "I've got this."

Displaying a boyish grin after opening the door, he said to the hotel staff, "Wait here while I find out if she's decent."

He walked into the bedroom and found her holding the bed sheets up to her chest, shocked and astonished.

"Come in," he called out to the server, "and leave the table in the middle of the room. Thank you, efharisto,"

Ary's eyes grew wide with confusion as she searched his face for answers.

Once the food trays, juice glasses and flatware were properly arranged around the white linen draped table, Dwayne signed the bill and watched the server leave the room, listening for the closing door.

"You overslept," he scolded. "I did say breakfast at nine."

"Then, it *was* really you? she asked, still unsure. It *wasn't* a dream?"

"No, it wasn't a dream. It's really me," he answered, standing at the foot of the bed trying to relieve her troubled stare.

"When? How? Did we…?"

"Let's see," he bragged, teasingly touching the tip of her nose. "When and how? Right after you were checked in I went back downstairs to get an extra card key to your room. And at about three o'clock this morning I knocked on your door. When you didn't answer, I used the key to come in and found you sleeping like Cinderella," he ended, smiling. "Let me stop lying. You were snoring like a drunken sailor," he laughed. "But still as beautiful as I've ever seen you."

She smiled, throwing several pillows at him.

"Listen Ary, I really came down here to talk to you 'cause as tired as I was from all the craziness of yesterday, I couldn't sleep. My thoughts were all over the place, from literally wanting to strangle the life out of you again, to wanting to protect you at all cost. But after seeing you lying there underneath the sheets, I decided the best thing to do at that moment, was to climb in bed next to you, inhale your scent and kiss you. I wanted to try and forget every bad thing that had happened."

"But did we…I dreamt that we…"

"We what?" he asked, playfully. "Did we talk? No we didn't."

"You know what I mean Dwayne. Right now I can't distinguish between a sweet dream, a stimulating fantasy or plain reality."

"No we didn't. I didn't need to. I only wanted to be near you while you slept, listen to you breathe, and watch the cadence of your heartbeat. I wanted to know that you felt protected. So if you dreamed or fantasized that we did, that's fine, I hope it was memorable. But like I mentioned to you before Ary, we have to figure this shit out. I really can't keep this up. I need to know once and for all what the hell is going on with this, this, I don't even know what to call it. This quasi-relationship—friendship—understanding *thing*."

"I know, Dwayne, I know. Sometimes I feel as though my world is spinning out of control and I honestly don't know how to stop it or at least slow it down. There are so many things I want and need to accomplish before I'm 30 years old, which is something I'm *sure* you can identify with," she interjected, putting on a sober face. "But then something always seems to get in the way."

"Wait, are you suggesting that *I'm* standing in the way of you reaching your goals? I'm not sure I follow you."

"No, no, not at all. Please don't feel that way. I must sound silly for even saying that when I have a salary most people would envy, a beautiful condo with amazing views of the GWB and the river, and a job that up until recently, fed my ego and my desire for the *ginormous* challenges that I *deliberately* sought out for myself!"

"Not to mention an incredibly handsome and brilliant boss who taught you everything you needed to know to get up and running at lightning speed in this exciting industry," he finished with a wink.

"Well, that last part could easily be debated. But I cannot deny, for one second, the veracity of an incredibly handsome and oh so extraordinarily gifted boss," she beamed, rising up on her knees to meet him with a slow, moist kiss on his lips.

Ignoring the tempting aroma of breakfast, they embraced, falling slowly onto the bed where at first he'd appeared as her fantasy, but now he was all too real.

CHAPTER 39

HE'D tried calling her throughout the night, only to be greeted by her voicemail message. Growing even more worried after noticing it was already 10:30 in the morning, he'd calculated that they'd need to be back at the airport no later than 1:00pm for their 2:00pm takeoff. *Where the hell is she? It's time for the games to end. We have to get on that plane and head home. I refuse to spend another dime on flight and pilot time, not to mention fuel cost. And I don't care if we speak to one another the entire trip home, we have to leave today. All of this crap can be settled once we get back to the states.*

Ary couldn't have answered his calls—she'd muted her phone after Dwayne rescued her from the villa. Darias had been replaced by the man whose love she so desperately wanted to accept.

He paced around the suite, scratching his head, trying to figure out his next move. *Jesus, I can't just leave her here. How far could she have gone last night? And her luggage is still on the jet. Okay Woolfolk, pull yourself together and think.*

But before he could continue his thoughts, his phone beeped a text message: *In case you were worried, I'm fine and I forgive you for abandoning me yesterday. Please leave my luggage at the airport in the storage area, because as you might have guessed, I will not be traveling back to the states with you. Thx, Ary.*

"Ahhhh, shit," he yelled. "I knew it. I knew it was him on the phone," he concluded. "The question is why? Why did I let myself fall into the trap of another woman? Didn't I learn anything from my relationship with Marguerite? I have *got* to stop being pulled into these bullshit situations with women. It's too fucking distracting. All they want to do is use you." Turning around to face the olive wood-framed mirror hanging in the foyer, he continued his one man tirade. "You know what Woolfolk, it's not *them* using you, it's *you* letting your guard down! You really need to start treating women like business transactions. Get in, close the deal, get the fuck out and move on to the next one. No more trying to establish a '*relationship*,'" he gestured, using air quotes. "You're a rich, white, handsome, middle-aged man who has the pick of the litter when it comes to beautiful women. Stop it with these man devourers! Maybe you should take a page out of the Joseph Larsen playbook. Just get back to what you do best…bringing in multi-million dollar deals and increasing your financial portfolio."

He thought about tearing the mirror from the wall, but quickly remembered it was an expensive, one of a kind piece and he'd only be destroying his own property.

"I need a hot shower and a cold drink," he determined, walking over to the mini bar, only to find that in his current state of mind, he couldn't recall the combination to the locked case. "Goddamit!" he yelled, punching the wall, watching helplessly as he turned to see the traditionally handmade mirror come crashing down, splintering into shards of worthless glass.

CHAPTER 40

"HEY, we're gonna have to try and find you a ticket back home young lady. I think your ride may have flown the coop without you," he hinted, slightly laughing.

"No kidding! I just hope he left my luggage at the airport. I have two weeks of clothes packed in those bags and they're not easily replaceable."

"Well, look, you're welcomed to stay here. I'll be around for another two days and I fully intend to take advantage of my visit because when I do return home, there're some serious things I'll have to consider."

"Like what?" she asked, offering him her full attention.

"Like, do I go back to NPI, especially after G has offered me my job back and footed the bill for this little excursion? Or, look for something else within the industry. And just keepin' it 100, how responsible is it to work in the same office with someone you're involved with…meaning you, if I wasn't being clear."

"I know what you meant, silly. But Dwayne…"

"Wait, I'm not finished. Let me think this through while it's on my mind."

"Yes sir!" she saluted.

"If I'm being perfectly honest with myself, I absolutely thrive in this business, if nothing else but to prove to them that I'm better than how I'm perceived. At the same time, I make a shit load of money, as well as all the invaluable contacts I've cultivated over the years. And Ary, if I wanted to," he concluded, taking an even more serious tone, "I could just pick up the phone and call any number of folks who would either hire me on the spot or tell me who to talk to for a new opportunity. How many of *us* can do that? It used to be, '*Last one hired, first one fired and your golden egg is fried.*' Now it's just, 'Don't freakin' hire them if you can manage to stay under the government's discrimination radar.'"

"Wow, Dwayne, do you really feel that way? In this day and age? Look at us."

"Yeah, *look* at us. There's only a handful of *us* working in the oil industry, in this country anyway. And at NPI, which I truly respect, there's me, you and six other people of color, well, five now that the infamous Marguerite has been exposed and dethroned," he laughed. "And that's out of seventy-five employees!" he yelled for emphasis. "So as I said, yeah, I feel that way and you're being naïve if you don't recognize it too."

"Dwayne, I'm *not* naïve and I wish you'd stop saying that. I know the struggles we confront on a daily basis at work *and* in life. And no matter what you think, I *don't* live in a bubble. I mean damn, look at what I've...actually, *we've* just gone through with Joseph! All I'm saying is that we can't let those barriers stop us. This is America, and as much as we're told that it's *not* our country, it's gonna take more than a few loud mouthed, ignorant, woefully uninformed, hangin' on to a lost war assholes, to convince me otherwise. So yeah, I understand all that it means to be a minority in this *and* in other countries, but I hold onto what my parents always taught me and my brother, which was, '*armed with pride, education, knowledge and intelligence, if you allow them to win, even on an uneven playing field, then ultimately, you've only yourself to blame.*'"

"Hmmm, okay, I like that. Your parents are very wise people. But the question still remains, should I go or should I stay? Should I remain loyal to G, and we all know that loyalty means little to nothing these days. Or should I just move on to bigger and brighter things outside of the industry? Or maybe find *you* something else in another department within NPI, or another firm where I have contacts and I know you'll be taken care of. Hmmm, I'm thinking, I'm thinking…"

She could feel her temperature rising and her frenetic thoughts spinning out of control.

Why Lord, she wondered. *Why would this man even suggest something like that for me? Didn't we already cross that bridge? And no matter how much we've accomplished as women, they still want to insist that we need their help or that we have to be 'taken care of' when it comes to business. That is pure B.S. And I'm not trying to school the entire male species on the do's and don'ts of talking to a professional woman. But I would have hoped that* this *man, who I'm involved with, especially with everything that we've been through, would know all this by now, or at least realize it about me!*

"So, once again I find myself with so much to reflect on," he mused, this time tapping his own nose. "But, right now, let's enjoy our *cold* breakfast, take a relaxing warm shower afterwards, together of course, head out to the airport to retrieve your luggage and then discover the amazing and historic sights of Greece!"

She stared into his eyes, wondering, *what made this man tick*? She felt mixed emotions—desire, disappointment, apprehension, curiosity and a sudden need to escape. She weighed for a moment if it were *worth* the fight to correct most of everything he'd decided would be best for her. Ultimately, conceding to a deeper consciousness, she simply answered, "Yes, lets."

CHAPTER 41

DARIAS walked out to the car, took one last look around the property and noticed the white sand glistening like sparkling jewels against the morning sky. He briefly thought about the necklace he'd bought for Ary, how satisfied he was with his choice after placing it around her flawless neck, watching her reaction and thinking how lovely she looked wearing it. He'd felt she'd deserved it after all she'd gone through at work and at home with her family. Now all he could feel was frustration, doubt and anger. As he drove slowly through the mountainous terrain, his emotions pushed him to speed. *The faster I can get there, the quicker this'll all be over and I can get back to what's important,* he reflected. But better judgment prevailed and kept him within the legal limit. No matter how hard he tried to think of other things, anything, even listening to a deafening, Greek rock band on the radio, flashes of their time together crept into his memory. A single tear rolled down his cheek and his chest seemed to tighten at every mile. Gripping the steering wheel, he eased his foot off the accelerator, took a deep, slow breath and steadied his position in the narrow lane of the winding road, lowering both visors to block the intense rays of the Athenian sun. He reminded himself that this was not the time for panic or self-pity. He had to get to the airport and begin the journey back to the states without her.

CHAPTER 42

DWAYNE was able to secure a short-term rental car through the hotel manager in whose confidence he also relied on to find a flight back to the states for Ary.

"Do you think he'll be able to help in getting me home in the next day or so, or should I pursue it on my own? I really need to get back soon and like you said, make some important decisions about work and…"

"Did you see that?!" he interrupted, with utter excitement.

"What?!"

"Over there, in the distance, I think that's the Acropolis!"

"Yessss," she dragged. "I see it. But Dwayne, did you hear what I was saying about…?"

"Of course I did babe. I'm sorry. I just wasn't expecting to be driving and then right before my very eyes, up creeps the Acropolis, home to the Parthenon, the Temple of Athena Nike and the Theater of Dionysus…in all its historical wonder!" he recited with the excitement of a child entering the Magic Kingdom for the very first time. "So, no, I don't think you need to worry about the flight, Kostas will take care of it. He hasn't let me down yet. And I agree, we both have serious decisions to make. But Ary, right now, let's just enjoy these last couple of days, together, 'cause reality kicks in once we touch down on American soil and there's no turning back. Agreed?"

With a reluctant sigh, she pulled her sunshades down from the top of her head to shield her eyes and mask her irritation, saying, "Dwayne, somehow you manage to always be my voice of reason. And you're right, we're here, together, in Athens! Home to Aphrodite, Athena, Apollo and Zeus!" she shouted.

"Hail Zeus!" he roared exuberantly, fist pumping with his free hand. "Zeus, the King of Gods, which, from now on is how you should address me while we're here and when we're making love," he announced, along with an exaggerated grin. "And you are my Queen Hera—Queen of the Gods!"

"I am *not* calling you Zeus," she laughed. "But you are my only prince."

"I'll take that."

They both chuckled boisterously as he leaned over, turning slightly towards her for a quick kiss, still careful to keep his eyes on unfamiliar roads.

CHAPTER 43

THE Hertz rental car return sign provided a faint sense of relief, a feeling that his journey home would soon be underway. *Alright now, let's get this done quickly so I can get back to business*, he thought, racing inside.

The drop-off was hassle-free with a courtesy car waiting to take him to the private hanger housing the Gulfstream jet. Approaching the aircraft, he noticed Ary's luggage being taken away by a small, flatbed vehicle. He'd called ahead to the pilot instructing him to have a crew member arrange for her bags to be taken to the main terminal storage area. Although she had finally invested in a set of TUMI luggage, he was careful to point out not to confuse her cayenne colored hardsides, with his red and gold, limited edition Globe-Trotter pieces.

The last few days had been difficult, and as hard as he'd tried to ditch the sweet memories of the past week, seeing her bags made it all too real again. He waited and watched as the vehicle turned away from the hanger and head in the direction of the terminal before getting out of the car. And with renewed energy, rushed up the stairs, greeting the pilot in the cockpit and the crewman standing in the luxurious cabin before making his way down the narrow aisle, leaning back against the soft, cream colored leather crested seat, fastening his seatbelt, and saying with authority, "Let's put this beauty in the air."

CHAPTER 44

DWAYNE and Ary were exhausted after touring the sites of the Acropolis. The traffic getting there had been horrific and the crowds made it feel even hotter than the actual 85 degrees. "I think we should try and get to the airport Dwayne. I'm soaking wet and I don't have a change of clothes, remember?"

"Yeah, I know what you mean," he answered, lifting his arms to expose the saturated underarms of his shirtsleeves. "Listen, before we do anything else though, I meant to ask if you'd called your brother to let him know you were okay."

"Oh God! With everything that's happened, I forgot to call him back. I'm sure he's probably worried."

"Well now's as good a time as any….almost a half-day later," he smirked.

Dwayne kissed her on the cheek and walked off to view the Erechtheum temple, giving her the privacy he assumed she'd want and the time she'd most likely need.

Finding a spot where a tour group had just dispersed, she quickly rushed over to claim the empty bench before anyone else had a similar thought. But she hesitated before dialing Marcus' number, imagining that he would have called Sonya after their earlier conversation while she was still in the throes of what she felt may have been misconstrued as a mini-meltdown. She didn't want to hear a second-handed lecture from her mother about how the men in her life were leading her down a path of total devastation or contributing to her ostensibly perilous lifestyle. *I'm not in the mood for a sermon from anyone right now so I'll tell him that it was all just a huge misunderstanding and that I've got it under control.* And seeing *as though I still have to face mama about that little family feel-good session I walked away from back home, I'm gonna need more energy than I care to expend right now.*

She moved to the edge of the bench and instructed Siri to dial his number.

"Hi Marcus, it's me."

"What the hell? Are you okay? Where've you been? You hung up on me and I ended up calling your boss…ummm…what's his name…"

"Dwayne."

"Yeah, Dwayne and he…"

"I know, I know. I apologize," she interrupted. "Look, things got a little mixed up and feelings got hurt, but I'm okay, really. Please tell mama not to worry, and you shouldn't either. I'll be home in a couple of days."

"Well to be honest, it wasn't really mama who was worried about you, it was more, me. She guessed you were with one of your, let's see, how did she put it? Oh yeah, '*wealthy, white lovers*' and the two of you probably got into a heated argument which lead to him leaving your ass marooned somewhere. She said you never even told her you were leaving town and that she hadn't heard a word from you since you'd left the house the day daddy and Matthew were there, so…"

"Listen Marcus," she broke through, her irritation clearly evident. "I'm fine, and I'll *try* and explain it all to mama once I get home."

"Hey, don't go all nuts on me. I just did what any caring sibling would have done to find his *ungrateful* sister, who, by the way, sounded like she was losing her friggin' mind and 'bout to be in all kinds of trouble," he rattled on sarcastically. "I'll be sure to let mama know that you'll be in touch. And one last thing," he continued, not giving her a chance to respond. "Thank your boss for me because I guess we, rather I, wouldn't have ever gotten a return call from you without his persuasion." He disconnected before she could answer, but it didn't stop her from yelling into the phone.

"You called me, remember? You called me to talk about *your* problems with *your* 'fiancé'. I didn't call your ass or mama for that matter because I can handle shit on my own," she screamed.

Hearing the commotion, Dwayne turned and started walking in her direction. Others looked too, but just as quickly decided there was nothing to see.

"Hey, hey, hey, what's the matter?" he asked, nearing her. "What happened?"

"Nothing," she answered, wiping away falling tears. "It's okay. I'm fine."

Cocking his head sideways and leaning down to look up into her eyes, he reached in his pants pocket and offered his handkerchief. "You don't *look* fine. What did Marcus say?"

"No, it's nothing, really," she answered, accepting his monogrammed kerchief and dabbing the corners of her eyes. "I just don't understand why nothing seems to go smoothly when it comes to my family."

"Ary, it's not just *your* family, believe me. There's not a week that goes by that one of my knuckleheaded brothers isn't calling me about some petty nonsense, whether it's trouble over a *new* woman, anxiety over an *old* one, stress on the job or at school or another request for some desperately needed, *'borrowed'* cash to tide somebody over 'til the next paycheck. But I'm the oldest, and I have a responsibility, especially with my folks getting up in age and dealing with so many health issues. And the last thing I want is for them to be in the middle of sibling craziness. I guess it's just how we were raised—to look out for each other when my parents are gone. But it always seems like they want to get a jump on things and drive my 'ole ass insane," he laughed. "But hey, I love 'em, no matter what and I'll always be there. So, don't be too hard on Marcus, he's family and I really think they come into the world hardwired to make life *in-ner--est-in'* for us first-borns," he said, smiling, conjuring up his West Virginia twang for emphasis.

"Thank you, Dwayne. Thank you for always understanding. I love you for that," she revealed, feeling humiliated that it was *always* him coming to her rescue whenever she found herself in trouble.

"Whoa, wait…wait...did I hear you *admit* that you *love* me or just that you love me for *that*?"

"C'mon silly, we really need to get going."

"So you're *not* gonna admit it, right here, right now, when we're not making love?" he shouted.

"You're embarrassing me, Dwayne, she whispered, looking around for anyone staring back at them. "You know how I feel about you."

"No, no I don't. Not really. I only know how you feel when we're being intimate, Ary. But when it comes to that everyday love, the get-down dirty, funky, I got'cha back no matter who, what or where kinda love, no, I'm not certain that I do know."

"What?!" she asked, a puzzled look splashing across her face.

"Look, I know how *I* feel about you and I think I've proven it more times than I care to recall. But I'd like to know, once and for all, right here in Athens, for all the Greek gods to witness, how you *really* feel about me. Is that too much to ask, Ary Alexander from *somewhere* on Long Island, New York?"

"Dwayne," she whispered, pulling him along. I *do* love you, but my life is so chaotic right now, both personally and professionally, that it just wouldn't be fair to you or anyone else to say that I could be exclusively committed, knowing how much that means to you. I just don't see myself in the next year or two settling down, or having children and having to put my career on hold."

"No one is asking you to settle down right now, Ary," he asserted, stepping in front of her, abruptly freezing her steps. "And believe me, I'm a witness to your chaos, and most of the time, an *unwilling* participant," he laughed. "But I'm here, and all of what you said is *precisely* why I love you. I've seen your strengths as well as your vulnerabilities and I admire how you always confront them, head on, right or wrong. I know all of your imperfections, well, I hope that's all of them," he joked, "And I accept them because I know none of us is perfect, especially me. But I want to be imperfect with someone I admire, and who's ambitious to a fault, like me," he rationalized with a slanted grin. "And most of all, I want someone who keeps the excitement of life alive at every turn—if any of this makes sense."

For that moment, all she could think about were his words. Her soggy clothes were no longer at the forefront of her thoughts. She repeated them over and over in her mind, '*But I'm here, and all of that is precisely why I love you.*' He *was* there. He'd driven on treacherous roadsides in an unfamiliar country to rescue her from another man. He'd put up with more than most men would ever consider—past, present or possibly in the future. But the question that nagged her was *why* she couldn't fully love him or totally commit herself to *this* man, who had, on more than one occasion, professed his love for her and was willing to put up with all her flaws.

"We really should go," she pressed, tears once again streaming down her cheeks, hoping to deflect any further conversation. "There'll be tons of traffic."

CHAPTER 45

G arrived to the office even earlier than his usual 6:00a.m. and relished in the quietness. He thought about everything that had happened and changed during the last several weeks and wondered how it had all escaped him—Joseph's deception, Marguerite's true identity, Dwayne's vulnerability and Ary's discovery of it all. He was grateful that everything had finally come to light but wondered if she hadn't come to work for NPI, how would it have played out in the end? He walked around to Joseph's office, staring at the closed oak door before grabbing the brass handle, then hesitating; ultimately deciding it was too soon to go inside. He still needed time to process how Joseph, a man he'd considered a brother, could have betrayed him in such an implausible manner. Lowering his head, he turned around and headed down to Marguerite's former office. Her door was wide open and visibly displayed on her desk were the expensive trinkets he'd brought back from his business travels around the world. Understandably, his heart sank. He'd asked himself *'why?'* countless times over the past weeks, *why she wouldn't have shared who she really was?* Did she honestly feel as though it would make her less desirable if he knew she had African-American blood flowing through her veins? What could have given her the impression that he would have cared? Did she see *him* as racist or intolerant? Had he said something derogatory about minorities in her presence or in an environment where there were no other persons of color? G didn't think of himself as bigoted. He'd gone to school with people of all races and mingled with them after classes and on weekends. *But,* he'd asked himself, *as an adult, who are* my *friends*? Who were his business partners, aside from his Saudi connections? His colleagues? When he and Marguerite dined out, gone to the theater, or on more than one occasion, vacationed with other couples, were there ever any non-whites included? G knew the answer, but it wasn't because he'd held a racist bone in his body. It was simply because he never had to think about or even consider it. The world in which he operated stateside was a white world, and he was at the top of the privilege chain. G never had to consider whether something was fair or unfair based on the color of his skin or his religious beliefs. All of his successes or failures were, he felt, because he'd either bid too high, too low, undervalued the scope of the project, or he'd ultimately determined that his firm wasn't the right fit for a large, multi-pronged undertaking. Nothing ever had to do with his outward appearance or whether he'd possessed the aptitude to accomplish something.

"I'm a fool," he shouted, after returning to his office and hammering his fist against his desk. *How could I have* not *ever* considered *what a minority in this country encounters in the oil business or any business for that matter that's owned or run by men who look like me? I'm Italian for God's sake. We were treated like trash not too long ago ourselves, but as time went by we could blend in to the larger, white society. Maybe you conveniently forget once you're accepted and turn a blind eye to others who could use the same help on the way up,* he thought. *The fact is, you should really turn around and reach back—offer your hand because you know where they're coming from.* He paced around his office, contemplating his thoughts. *How many people of color do I even have working for me? I've never even thought about it. I left the hiring up to Senior Management, except on a few rare occasions or when it came to actually* hiring *Senior Management, and at that level, I didn't hire any, without giving it as much as a second thought. Shame on me. My parents would be disappointed, knowing that I grew up in the crowded melting pot of Little Italy and made it out, never looking back with derision because of my own hardships, but always paying it forward with scholarships and charitable donations once I was financially able. I have to change this and I will. I'll start by talking to Dwayne once he returns from vacation to get his opinion and advice on what I can do to rectify this.*

CHAPTER 46

ARY and Dwayne arrived at the airport and headed straight for the storage department. After talking with an employee, they asked to speak with someone who had more than a working knowledge of English so Ary could describe her luggage and situation in detail. Finally, a woman came out of the back office and inquired whether Ary had a claim ticket.

"Look, you don't understand. I tried explaining as best I could to the first guy but I'll try again. I came here on a private jet and now I'm going home on a commercial airliner. The person I was with was *supposed* to leave my bags here because, well, because he said he would, and I have no reason to doubt that he didn't," she persisted, trying to also convince herself. Dwayne looked at her and could see her growing frustration.

"Ary, what color are your bags and who's the designer?"

"They're red, well, cayenne actually with a silver metal lining along the sides. And they're not designer they're TUMI hardsides."

"Okay, *now* we're making progress."

She gave him a confusing stare. *Is he inferring that I* wasn't *making myself clear?*

'So," he continued. "Her cayenne colored luggage was dropped off, probably sometime this morning or afternoon because she would no longer be traveling on a private jet. And her companion, being the gentleman that he is known to be, wanted her to have her personal belongings. Now, *I* was hoping that a person of your position over this department would be able to help us in locating them."

"I can try to help you sir, but we have hundreds of pieces in the back and they've all been tagged with a ticket, mostly from the commercial flights they came here on..."

"But I *just* said I didn't fly commercial, so how could they possibly have been ticketed?" she explained, her exasperation at the tipping point. "I don't understand. I'm sure there are other private jets that have at one time or another required use of your storage facilities?" her pitch increasingly rising.

The woman looked away from Ary and directed her explanation to Dwayne. "Sir, there *is* a smaller department that handles most of the luggage we receive from private aircraft needing storage. Some have tickets, some don't. So they may possibly be over there. What I was trying to explain to *her* before she enírgise san énas gáidaros, *(acted like an ass)*, was that I'll have someone look here in the back, but I also suggest you walk just around the corner and ask as well because it may take us a while since they were not tagged and I'd hate for *you* to just wait here unnecessarily. It's how you say in English, killing a bird with a stone."

"Oh! Killing *two* birds with *one* stone! Yep, of course, that makes perfect sense," he agreed, trying to diffuse what he saw as an avoidable escalation brewing between two obstinate women—one who was physically and emotionally drained—the other who felt her authority was being demeaned by who she'd determined to be an obnoxious, wealthy American. "Many thanks, polá efcharistó, Ms. Christopoulos," he said, looking closely at the plastic nametag pinned on her blouse.

"You speak a little Greek I see," she smiled.

"No, he doesn't," Ary answered, annoyed by her flirtation. "Let's go."

Dwayne smirked, feeling a little pleasure from her jealousy. He followed her out the door, but not before turning to the woman and whispering, "She's had a few unfortunate mishaps while here, so don't take it personally."

The woman winked and said, "Tha káno ó, ti boró gia na voithíso kýri *(I'll do what I can to help sir)*."

Ary stopped and turned to look at him. "You really felt the need to make an excuse for me?"

"You heard that? I was trying to be discreet," he laughed. "And I wasn't making an excuse, I was just trying to make sure she wasn't gonna destroy or toss your bags if she found them first."

"I don't think there was a need to explain *anything* to her because she was the one acting so egregious. And not, might I add, being very helpful because I don't speak '*a little Greek*,'" she repeated sarcastically. "I was merely trying as best as I could to explain and reclaim my belongings. Oh, and one other thing Mr. Hargis."

"What's that, Ms. Alexander?"

"She was obviously flirting with you and you were relishing in it! How dare she! I think it was disrespectful, especially not knowing our situation."

"Situation?! Hell *I* don't even know our '*situation*'" he said, using air quotes and laughing.

"Oh my God, Dwayne. Can we just go and find my bags without getting into a cogent discussion?!"

He grabbed her hand.

"I'm feeling frazzled right now because what if he decided *not* to drop them off out of spite! Then I'd have to go and buy new outfits for the next few days and I'm not really in a shopping mood."

He could only summon a blank stare. His first thought was, *I don't think I've ever heard a woman turn down the opportunity to shop while on vacation.* Then, in all seriousness, he wondered if she were really so naïve as to think that Darias was above being spiteful after having been dumped. *I might have done it,* he thought, *just to see the look on her face,* he laughed to himself. *In business, she'd projected a woman who could take on the world with unceasing confidence,* b*ut in her personal life, she appears to unravel at the drop of a pin.*

"Don't worry, we'll either find your luggage or I'll personally splurge for a shopping spree in Greece."

"That's very sweet of you Dwayne, and I appreciate it. But I'm perfectly capable of purchasing my own clothes."

"Not the ones I had in mind," he cooed with a devilish grin. "I happened to pass a Victoria's Secret while I was browsing yesterday and right next door was a shop called, '*Mile High Stilettos*,'" he laughed.

"You are truly *out* of your mind," she said, pinching his arm.

"Ouch! That hurt," he pretended.

"Now, where'd you say that shoe store was again?" she questioned, displaying the proverbial side eye.

They both laughed and walked around the corner to find the smaller storage area.

CHAPTER 47

DARIAS relaxed on the plane with a glass of his favorite Bordeaux, trying *not* to think of what exactly went wrong. But after reaching cruising altitude, and right as he was drifting off into a deep sleep, he recalled how satisfied he'd felt after placing the jewel around her slender neck. *No matter what happens,* he thought, *she should keep it.*

CHAPTER 48

ARY waited in the claustrophobic waiting room while a customer service rep searched the back room for her bags. Dwayne excused himself, telling her he needed to find a men's room. He returned 20 minutes later to find her excitedly greeting him. "They found them Dwayne, they found my bags!" she beamed. "Now I can relax and enjoy the rest of my time here with you."

"Whew," he breathed, wiping his brow, "I guess that lets me off the hook for an *entire* vacation wardrobe," he laughed. "But I did happen to buy one little outfit, just in case. I hope you like it."

Ary looked at the packages in his hands and shook her head. "Really, Dwayne? Seriously? After everything I've just gone through? All you can think of, right now, is Victoria's Secret and stilettos?"

"What? Too soon?"

Pursing her lips and placing both hands on her hips, she said, "Size 8s and a small I'm hoping?"

"Girl give me that luggage so we can get up outta here," he said, playfully grabbing them from behind her. "Let's get this two-day, mini-vacation love-fest started."

Ary laughed hard, letting go of the stress from the past day and night, quickly following him out the door.

CHAPTER 49

G spent the day calling friends and colleagues inquiring about potential candidates for the Marketing and Customer Relations VP positions left vacant by Joseph and Marguerite's unceremonious exits before reaching out to the Executive Recruiting Firm he'd utilized in the past. A few names had been suggested, but in the end, he declined to meet with any of them. Betrayal was still fresh in his mind although he knew he'd have to fill the slots sooner rather than later. His mind wandered over and over as to why he hadn't been able to detect Joseph's plans. *He had to have been planning this for some time. Was it because he was more like a brother than just my VP? Is that how he thought he could get away with it? And now, how will it all work out, knowing we'll be competing for some of the same projects and dealing with the same executives here in the states? I don't ever want to see him again if I can help it,* he thought, his anger resurfacing.

His cell phone rang preventing any further musings about staffing up the C-suite. The number displayed was *'unknown caller.'* Reluctant to answer at first, knowing that only a handful of people had his personal number, he pressed the answer symbol just prior to the final ring.

"G, please don't hang up, please. Let me explain. You at least owe me that don't you?"

"I don't *owe* you a damn thing," he yelled, unaware and not caring whether others were nearby in the office. "You have some fucking nerve calling me, Marguerite. I put my trust in you, shared my plans, my goals, my intentions and you threw it all away!" he yelled. "And for what? For what? Because you thought I held the same bigoted, racist, ignorant feelings as you? You disgust me, you and your scheming partner Joseph Larson. Maybe the two of you should go into business together and call it, '*Racists R' Us*' or maybe you could launch your own lingerie line and call it, 'Marguerite's Secret,' for those wanting to hide their race and ethnicity. How about that? There you go. I just gave you two perfectly fitting ideas for your next filthy business ventures. And you thought I was upset? Listen to me woman, I don't know why you thought it would be okay to call my number. Did you think all would be forgiven if you just waited a little while before getting in touch—let the steam blow over? That you could just come running back into my life…"

"G," she interrupted. "Please let me explain. There's more to it than you know."

"Go to hell Marguerite Armstead and take your fucking explanations with you."

Throwing the phone as forcefully as he could against the wall, he watched as the screen separated from its case and scatter bits of broken glass over the floor.

"Is she fucking crazy?" he asked, rhetorically. "Who in their right mind would call someone they've deceived? What kind of narcissistic personality would even think it was ok to dial the number of a lover whose company they were conniving to destroy? Joseph I could see, but you?" he asked, pacing around his suite, posing the questions as if she were still on the line. "No, hell no. I'm *not* ready to talk to you and I'm sure as hell not willing to *forgive* you. And to be clear, I will *not* change my phone number, so you'd better delete it from your illusive fucking memory."

Connie had walked into the office thinking that her boss was engaged in an unscheduled and apparently heated meeting and discussion, certainly one she knew nothing about. It wasn't until she peeked into his partially opened door that she noticed he was there alone. Looking down near the threshold, she saw his phone in scattered pieces.

G turned around, smiled and said, "Oh, good morning Connie, what's on my calendar for today?"

CHAPTER 50

AFTER arriving home, Darias decided to take an extra few days away from the office. He knew the BP contract would be announced on Friday and he was privy to the fact that NPI was number two on the list of the last four contenders. He'd placed a call to the Chief of Staff on Monday requesting a Wednesday meeting with his CEO and other VPs whose input in the award decision was crucial. He weighed the options of G's company handling such a huge, five-year contract against the turmoil NPI was facing without their two top executives. Although he loathed Joseph Larsen for more reasons than he cared to remember, and his relationship with Marguerite had definitely seen better times, he couldn't deny their skills as talented, savvy business professionals. Could he forgive Joseph for what he'd done to G and the fact that he was now a supposed competitor in their tight-knit industry? Or was this just something to be expected from an oilman's ego? He was, after all, instrumental in helping to expose the plot. And how would G fair without the cunning prowess of his former partner and lover. She did have an enviable relationship with most of the top local oilmen. So what now? Did G owe him for saving his firm or would he be complicit in rewarding NPI a multi-million dollar contract for essentially nothing in return. His thoughts even shocked him. Why was he questioning such obvious choices? Was it really all about business or was he still reeling from the scene in Greece with Ary and Dwayne who essentially had made a fool of him. They were still both G's employees, and he had referred to them on numerous occasions as his '*superstars*'. They would both benefit handsomely from a BP contract, catapulting their already skyrocketing careers further into orbit. *You do need a day or two to get your act together man,* he thought. *Never have you let business and pleasure influence any professional decisions and now is* not *the time to start.* But as hard as he tried, he couldn't shake the negative feelings. *Just when I thought no other woman could be as ruthless, smart and ambitious as Marguerite Armstead, in walks Ary Alexander, all tied up in a shiny red ribbon of beauty—a younger more stunning version of the same, digging her persuasive nails and shapely shrewd ass into every vulnerable, impetuous, moneyed oilman who has to have the latest trophy to boast about and flaunt to his fellow titans.* He brushed his brow and walked from his bedroom through the living and dining rooms and into the porcelain white designer kitchen, pouring himself a cup of freshly brewed coffee. *And here I am, never thinking this could happen to me after my breakup with Marguerite, contemplating how to influence a major contract because another woman took my heart and played chess with it, only to be crowned a fool. Am I just feeling sorry for myself?*" he questioned, setting down the coffee and opting instead for a shot of vodka. *What am I, a twelve year old boy trying to exact revenge on the schoolyard bully? This is ludicrous Woolfolk, this isn't like you at all. Pull yourself together man and do the right thing.* Feeling the need to drive, he called down to the concierge requesting his red, Maserati Gran Turismo convertible from the garage. What he actually needed was an escape from his lingering thoughts of her.

CHAPTER 51

HIS heart and mind felt empty and numb. He felt alone, even while surrounded by his colleagues. *What do I have to do to have a sustained period of happiness in my life? What can I do to convince her, better yet, convince myself that I'm worthy of love and the joy that seems to elude me but seems to shower down on everybody I see? I know I love her. I can feel it in my bones. I don't want to go on without her in my life. And now that mama has found peace and the power of forgiveness, somehow I've lost it or maybe never really had it.* Marcus stared out the window of his tiny office, going over every conversation he'd had with Caroline, every argument, every agreement, and every intimate moment. Why was she having doubts when he was ready to settle down? They'd discussed their wedding plans—a small ceremony with family and a few friends—the memorable honeymoon vacation they'd take on Italy's Amalfi Coast—whose apartment they'd live in afterwards until a larger one fit their combined budgets—when they'd start a family and what names they'd give to a son or daughter. He wanted to be the father he'd never had and he'd hoped she'd be the mother he'd always loved. Marcus sat back in his pre-ergonomic-era office chair and reminisced about early childhood memories. He remembered Sonya rushing to drop Ary off at her competitive swimming classes, then racing to deposit him at a private violin lesson. As he grew older, he became envious of his sister's athletic prowess and his father's reaction whenever he was able to make it to one of her field hockey or swim competitions. He'd never seen Bruce smile so wide or cheer so loud. He remembered looking out into the audience before a holiday orchestra or choral concert, hoping to see his entire family. But more often than not, his father was there in absentia, according to his mother who'd always made excuses for the man she adored. He was always either traveling, working late or stuck in a meeting, *He wasn't even responsible for an apology*, Marcus thought. *What will life be like if and when Caroline does come around to saying 'yes' to his second, more formal proposal? What about holidays, children's birthdays, christenings, and graduations? What kind of memories will he have to relive about his own childhood if Bruce chooses to become part of his life once he marries and produces grandchildren?* Marcus' mind wondered random thoughts for more than half an hour before a knock on his door brought him back to his present certainty.

A colleague pushing it open asked, "Hey man, we're all going out for drinks tonight. Can you come or do you have classes?"

"Oh. Ahhh, yeah, well, I do have classes, but I think a night off will do me good. Count me in, dude," he finally decided, grateful for the distraction. "I'll meet you downstairs in a few minutes."

As Marcus gathered his sports coat, checking to make sure his apartment keys were securely inside his breast pocket, he looked around his office and thought, *I really need to finish law school and prove to her that I'm serious about making some* real *money. Maybe that's why she's hesitant too, and just didn't want to say it to spare my feelings. I need to make the kind of money that we're both accustomed to having. Maybe she thinks I won't be able to provide her with the type of lifestyle she grew up in and what she wants for any kids we have together. And since the market is flooded with out of work or underpaid attorneys, she's worried I'd be one of 'em, which leaves me no other choice but to call dad once I'm done with school and pass the bar, and ask him to reach out to his hot-shot lawyer friends to help a brotha out at a prestigious firm,* he ended, laughing. *And as much as I'd hate doing it, I don't have the luxury of time or the patience to send out hundreds of resumes begging for a well-paying position. Yeah, this is something I definitely need to think about doing if I want to get her back.*

As he closed the door to his office, he heard the phone ringing and paused. "Hey, sorry, I'm off to drink away my problems."

CHAPTER 52

ARY kissed him goodbye at the airport. She'd arranged from Greece to have a car service drive her back home to Fort Lee. Dwayne jumped in a taxi for the forty-five minute drive from JFK airport in Queens to his apartment in Manhattan, which he knew would take longer because of rush hour traffic. But today he didn't mind. He could relish in the memory of their time together before any serious career decisions would have to be made.

CHAPTER 53

"OH please be careful with my luggage," she implored the driver. "They've been through so much already."

He stared at her with a look only a New Yorker could comprehend and she responded in kind, verbally.

"I mean it. I'm watching how you handle my bags. Your tip is *literally* riding on it."

Satisfied that her instructions and warning had been heeded, she settled back into the comfort of the spacious, soft black leather interior and kicked off her shoes. As the driver pulled into the heavy traffic along the rough and tumble road of the Van Wyck Expressway, she noticed a gigantic glowing sun, radiant orange and gold, as it began setting in the western sky. The colors were breathtaking she thought, as it slowly disappeared beneath large, cottony clouds, bidding farewell and moving swiftly beneath the backdrop of the darkening expanse. Childhood recollections invaded her mind, evoking warm feelings of running into the family room and finding her mother painting her next '*masterpiece*.' Closing her eyes and taking in an extended breath, she pondered whether or not she would call Sonya to let her know that she'd arrived home safely and that she would try and see her over the coming weekend.

No, she thought before drifting off to sleep. *Not tonight. I want this vacation to end just as it began.*

CHAPTER 54

DWAYNE requested the driver make a quick stop at NPI before continuing home. He'd felt an urgent need to talk to G and wanted the conversation to happen before he officially returned to work. Walking into the glistening atrium he immediately became startled by the enormous crowds gathered around what looked like a well-dressed, male body lying near one of the many marble pillars. He began walking towards the commotion but his curiosity was briefly interrupted by another man hurrying away from the crowd of onlookers and into one of the many elevators, stopping only to poke his head out for one last suspicious look before quickly disappearing behind the closing doors, but not before Dwayne made eye contact.

Joseph? Was that you? Why would you *be here?* he wondered, still unsure of what was happening. He nudged closer to the figure on the floor, this time noticing the man's blood soaked clothes, lying face up, eyes wide opened. He let out a deafening scream after making the discovery. *Oh my God! G? What the fuck? Who did this?* As he stood there, the crowd began to oddly disperse, backing away from the body in a coordinated circular formation.

One person stepped forward, releasing an icy laugh, touching him lightly on his shoulder. He shuddered, unable to move. Standing directly behind him was a woman, unrecognizable at first, her clothes bloodied, and a 12-inch blade dangling dangerously from her hands while a frozen smile held tightly on her face. She spoke slowly while the crowd looked on in silence. "Someone had to pay, Dwayne. And you or Ary weren't around."

He spun around as she raised her arms toward the high,

domed ceilings, her eyes lit with flashes of fiery rage as her body whirled furiously until her presence was nothing more than a thin grey haze of smoke.

"No!!!! Marguerite!!!! No!!!!," he shouted, causing the taxi driver to erratically swerve from his lane into the path of adjacent cars. A flurry of furious horns blowing, lurid cussing, and angry gesticulations came steadily before he was able to gain control and corrected his course.

"Hey man, what the hell? You alright back there?"

Dwayne's eyes opened quickly as he looked around, orientating his whereabouts. Exhaustion had been instantaneous. He'd fallen asleep the moment his head hit the headrest with his gruesome dream coming fast and furious.

"Whoa! Damn! Sorry 'bout that! I guess I was having a nightmare."

"Well your '*nightmare*' almost got us killed man," the driver countered, visibly shaken, gripping his unsteady hands around the steering wheel. "How 'bout you stay awake for the rest of the ride so we can both get to our destinations in one solid piece tonight."

"Duly noted, man, duly noted," he agreed, ignominiously, using his shirt sleeve to wipe away the beads of sweat pouring from his forehead while mumbling slightly under his breath. *Jesus, that was rough. Maybe that was my sign,* he thought. *Whatever it was, that was some fucked up shit.* He closed his eyes briefly before determining that it wasn't a good idea to chance another nightmare.

"How much longer?" he asked, eager for the safety of home.

"About fifteen more minutes," the driver answered annoyingly, just as eager to drop off his unnerving passenger.

CHAPTER 55

ALMOST two hours later they'd reached Fort Lee. It was a struggle to even open her eyes. Jet lag had officially kicked in and she secretly wished she could tip him into carrying both she *and* her luggage all the way upstairs.

"Oh wow, already. I guess I was more tired than I'd even imagined."

"Yes ma'am," he responded indifferently before getting out to carefully retrieve her bags from the trunk of the car, remembering what she'd threatened about his tip before placing them in front of the glass lobby door. He returned to open the passenger door.

"Would you mind helping me take them inside, near the elevator? I don't think I have the strength to even *pull* them in."

Without answering, he waited as she burrowed through her handbag, searching for her keys. "I guess it would have made more sense to look for them before I'd fallen asleep, right?" He only stared, anxious to get on his way. "Let's see. Okay, got 'em," she announced, relieved.

Taking one piece at a time, he followed her into the lobby and placed it in front of the elevator door. After bringing in the last bag he took off his baseball cap and thanked her, obviously waiting to see if he'd passed her obnoxious test. Giving her luggage a quick, once over, she pulled a fifty dollar bill from her wallet, and said, "We thank you for treating them with respect."

Perplexed at her speaking for her luggage, all he could muster was a simple, "Thank you," tipping his hat before disappearing through the lobby door.

Ary pushed the button and waited for what seemed like

minutes for it to descend from the fifteenth floor. "Come on, come on, I'm exhausted. I just want to see my bed and fall into it, all-by-myself." Finally, the doors opened and she pulled the luggage in with all the diminishing strength she had left. Confident that no one else was getting on, she pushed the number 24 on the panel, leaned back against the back wall and closed her eyes. After a few moments, the soft bell rang, indicating she'd reached her destination. Grabbing each bag's handle, she exited slowly, walking around the quiet corridor to her apartment. "Home, I'm home!" she said, putting the key in and unlocking the door to her sanctuary. The sweet scent of roses she'd bought to add to the ambience she'd wanted to create for Dwayne's surprise dinner still permeated throughout the space. "Emmmm, that's nice. What a lovely way to be welcomed home." Leaving the luggage near the front door, she kicked off her shoes, walked into the bedroom and took off all but her underwear. She crawled underneath the inviting, 600-thread count soft cotton sheets, and within minutes, had fallen asleep, never checking her cell phone to see that her mother had left a lengthy voicemail message expressing her concern.

CHAPTER 56

"WELL, I tried. That's all a mother can do," Sonya sighed, placing a small load of dishes in the dishwasher. She couldn't help but think of, *and* worry about her daughter. 'N*o matter how old you get'* she always told them, *'you'll always be my babies.'* Though this time she wished it were different. Ary was twenty-eight years old and no matter how brilliant she'd been in school, in sports and early on in her career, able to navigate the changing lanes of the corporate highway, somehow, this seemed different. Now she was dealing with the crude, enormously wealthy world of white, powerful oil executives who appeared to enjoy playing a more sinister game of racing to the top. She worried that her daughter's involvement in this industry, filled with false relationships, risky fortunes and misplaced principles might lead to her professional destruction.

Like most mothers, Sonya still wanted to be viewed as relevant in her adult children's lives. Not in any intrusive or invasive way, just as a matter of wanting to feel needed for her wisdom and advice. She felt that she and Marcus were in a good place now that she'd given her blessing for his impending marriage to Caroline, and all that that would mean for the family. Her relationship with Bruce and Matthew was on the mend after years of guilt, anger, blame, mistrust and depression. Her hospitalization, she often felt, was a wakeup call for how she wanted to live out the rest of her days. *Maybe I'll start looking for someone,* she considered—a *companion maybe. The kids have been trying to get me to do it for years and it would be nice to have someone to confide in besides a few friends and family. I so want to trust again. And hopefully this time, I can be sure he won't leave me for a younger, male model,* she thought, forcing a '*humpf,*' and a muted laugh.

With her energy level slipping away after a half day of painting and a full day absorbed in thought, she said, finally, "I'd better call it a night and get to bed. I do have that meeting in the morning to discuss my showing at the Dorothy Kaye Gallery in the West Village." She'd spent the last few weeks painting landscapes, some of which were beautiful scenes she'd experienced traveling to exotic locales with her family over the years, others, places in her vibrant imagination. Although '*landscape*' painting was not necessarily seen as 'exciting' in the 21st century art world, certainly as compared to abstract and discursive art, her skillful use of mixing mediums within the same picture—pastels and ink, tempera and water-color were stirring and causing a buzz among those young and old, experienced and novice, all of whom were inspired by her novel expressions. As she walked out of the den, which had only recently been converted to an art studio, her way of subliminally erasing the memories of Bruce's infidelity and years of personal despair, she angled between easels that held unfinished works and three sculptor's pedestals; one made of wood from African pine in the shape of the great pyramids of Giza; a Hulien Jade marble stand imported from China; and her prized possession—a mid-century stand and stool she'd bought years ago at an estate sale while visiting a friend in the Hampton's, which ironically, was just two houses away from the beach house Matthew would eventually purchase and where he and Bruce would go on to share memorable evenings on the generous deck facing Ditch Plains Beach in Montauk, watching massive waves and discussing their combined futures after shedding their former lives.

Although she was able to convert the space into a new

beginning, the forces of its past had not fully transformed each member of the Alexander family.

CHAPTER 57

OKAY, *I can do this,* he thought, trying hard to convince himself. *I'll just walk in, greet the staff, make my way to G's office and start the negotiations. But I'll also be prepared to walk out the door if things start to go left.* Dwayne had spent the last few days going over his career plans and his future with NPI. With Joseph and Marguerite out of the way, he felt he was more than deserving of a hefty raise and well positioned for a possible promotion to VP. *I don't want to come across as ungrateful, especially after the man just spent a king's ransom on a wonderful vacation, but why should I wait? My life was turned upside down after his 'best-boy' and 'babe-in-denial' tried to destroy me, and sometimes we black folks are just too damned forgiving and willing to accept crumbs and a disingenuous apology. Not me. My mama and daddy ain't raised no fools now,* he recalled affectionately, conjuring up his southern dialect, something he'd practiced on retiring when he moved to New York and entered the corporate world. *I'm one of those Negroes who knows what his value and worth are to a company and will make damn sure I get what I deserve and a whole lot more.*

The elevator reached its destination on the eleventh floor. But as he prepared to walk out through the opening doors, he was stopped by the sight of Ary and G waiting in the hallway.

"Oh hey! Morning guys," he greeted, surprised to see Ary so early. He'd spoken to her a few days before and she'd told him that because of some medical issues and appointments, she wouldn't be in the office until ten o'clock the first few days of this week. It was seven-thirty.

"Dwayne!" G said, holding out his hand. "Welcome back man! I, we, hell, NPI missed you. It is *definitely* not the same here without you leading the marketing charge. I take it that you had an exciting as well as a restful time away from our demanding world?" he inquired with an enthusiastic laugh.

Dwayne, still confused at seeing Ary, and even more at seeing them together, obviously on their way to a meeting, reciprocated a cautious handshake. His mind raced with thoughts of deception before he could utter a decipherable word.

"Uh, yeah. I uh, I had an exciting time. Thank you G. It was... definitely exciting *and* restful. Thank you again for your generosity," he stuttered.

Ary hadn't spoken a word. She'd stood there, next to G, wearing a professional smile on her face as Dwayne swept his glances from left to right.

"Well, I'd like to hear all about it and see the pictures—the decent ones of course," G laughed. "But right now, we're off to an unscheduled BP meeting. I'll catch up with you this afternoon and fill you in."

"Yeah, yeah, sure. I'll check with Connie and get on your calendar."

"Good man. We'll talk later."

As the elevator doors reopened, G gestured with a sweep of his hand saying, "After you, Ms. Alexander."

Dwayne stood there, staring at the closing doors, finally asking himself, "What the fuck just happened and why wasn't I made aware of it?"

CHAPTER 58

G and Ary retrieved their visitor's passes and headed up to the boardroom on the 30th floor of BP's Headquarter building on Park and 59th. He'd instructed her as they were driven over in his private Town car that he would take the lead when asked about the impending contract, explaining that because of the uncertainty of the discussion, she should wait for a visible cue from him before commenting on or answering any questions specifically directed at her. The emergency meeting, which had been requested by members of the Board, had taken him by surprise.

As they were escorted into the room, G was taken aback at the number of people present, but was adept at never revealing his hand. Filled with mostly white men in their fifties and sixties and a couple of American and Middle Eastern forty-something year old women dressed in designer suits, all stopped their conversations to look up as the NPI couple entered. Sitting at the far end of the enormous mahogany table were a sprinkling of male early-thirty something's, totally engaged in their electronic devices, never bothering to look up or acknowledge G or Ary.

Ary swept the room to see if Darias was there or anyone else she may have met in the past. There weren't. Although outwardly she appeared the picture of business perfection, dressed in an Elie Tahari fitted navy blue sheath dress and matching jacket, black leather Altuzarra three-inch Mary Jane pumps and a Phillip Lim black and navy color-block leather handbag, inwardly, her nerves were anything but confident. Like G, she wondered why BP had called this hasty meeting. *Was it because NPI was a finalist in the upcoming selection process and there were a few outstanding issues needing clarification? Was it because they were being eliminated and the Board wanted to personally assure G that his proposal offering would be considered at a future date? Or, she thought, could it have anything to do with her disastrous last few days with Darias, and he wanted some type of personal and public revenge that would not only be professionally damaging, but detrimental to her overall career.* No, she thought, *not even* I *think I'm that important.*

She second guessed her wardrobe choice, wishing she'd gone with her first selection of a black peplum jacket, classic white cotton blouse and pleated trousers, an outfit that would have easily absorbed the perspiration she felt trickling down her back and underarms and the probable knocking of her knees. But before she could ponder any further digressions about her fashion choice, a slow walking, silver haired man entered the room.

"Good morning everyone and thank you for rearranging your schedules on such short notice to be here," he said, still walking to take his seat, left of the head of the table. "I know some of you came from as far away as Connecticut and New Jersey," he joked. "But we felt it was important that we meet before the official award announcement for the, shall we say, *coveted*, BP contract that not only we in the industry are excited about, but also the national and international press."

With still no sign of Darias, she watched G for any positive or negative indication and covertly looked around the table and room for any competitors who, she assumed, would have been summoned to hear any supposed outcomes. She recognized no one. After a few more remarks and praises from BPs Board Chairman, Charles Floyd, known simply as the '*Chairman*' by internal and external executives, regarding the stability and growth of the company, the glass double doors swung open and Julian Dorchak, BPs CEO walked in along with Darias, the CFO and a young man trailing closely behind the trio. Ary's heart skipped several beats and she felt as though any minute, it would nosedive right onto the conference room table.

What the hell? she wondered, keenly aware of the sweat now beading between her breasts.

Julian walked swiftly to the head of the table, taking a seat. The CFO sat to the right of the Chairman while Darias turned and headed towards the opposite end. The young man sat near the wall, adjacent to the boardroom table with his tablet on his lap.

"I hope you all weren't too terribly inconvenienced this morning," Julian started.

"We already covered that portion of the meeting Julian," the Chairman interjected, laughing and placing a hand on the shoulder of the gregarious CEO.

"Okay good," he acknowledged. "So we convened this meeting for the sole purpose of awarding the latest contract that was put out to bid to the many capable firms who applied and that eventually, were winnowed down to the most capable two out of four corporations. I'm sure that most, if not all of you know John G. Gicardi, President and CEO of National Petroleum Incorporated. G, please stand up."

G stood up and waved his hand to the attendees, taking a moment to scan the room for any of his competitors, thinking they may have slipped in without him noticing. There weren't. He sat down and returned his attention to Julian who turned to the assistant in the corner and asked, "Is he in the building yet?"

"He's running ten minutes late, sir."

"Ok, fine. We can start the initial conversation without him."

Now G was confused. He felt totally in the dark as to what was happening and what was to come. Had he missed something during all the confusion that had taken place at the firm during the disruption with Joseph and Marguerite? Was there an email, a letter, a phone call, an announcement he'd overlooked or maybe had gone unnoticed by Connie. *No,* he thought. *That could never have happened. Not on my watch, even in the midst of chaos. But then again Joseph did pull a pretty spectacular feat right under my trusting nose,* he surmised. *What is this? Why am I being summoned to hear about an award with the CEO, CFO, SVPs* and *the Board of Directors and Chairman? I know this contract is huge, but why all the pomp and circumstance?*

Darias, standing far away from the rest of the executives did not once acknowledge Ary. She glanced his way in the middle of the CEO's statements, but he kept his head high and his eyes focused on his boss.

After a few more minutes of profitability stats and market positioning from the CFO, the doors opened and a stylishly dressed, dark haired man in his forties was ushered in by the receptionist.

"Please forgive me, ladies, gentlemen. My flight from L.A. was delayed."

G quickly glanced at Ary to gauge whether or not she knew who the man was. She returned an even more curious look. Julian motioned for him to join him near the head of the table. G's curiosity was quickly turning into consternation. He watched as the stranger worked the room, stopping to shake hands, pat backs and offer good wishes to the many attendees, before sitting in the seat that was obviously left vacant for him. *Okay, this better be good,* he thought. *I'm all for surprises, but not when it comes to multi-million dollar contracts involving* my *company.*

"G," Julian finally said, interrupting his frenzied thoughts. "I'd like to introduce you to the man who'll be working with you on this extraordinarily important contract."

Astounded, G all but skyrocketed out of his chair. *Working with me? What the hell is going on here?*

"This is Dave Winters, CEO of The Oil Trust, or T.O.T, out of Los Angeles. Both NPI and Dave's company tied in your bids for the contract and because I know both your reputations and I trust the Board in their recommendation, we've decided to split the award to cover both coasts. The Oil Trust will cover the second year drilling project out in the Pacific and assist you with the upfront project covering two of the four northeastern states."

G was speechless. *How could this be happening? Whose decision was this?* he wondered. *Why didn't my sources warn me that this was a possibility? At least give me a fucking heads up?* He turned to where Darias had stood and noticed he was gone.

Dave got up, walked towards G with a wide grin, placing one hand on Ary's back and extending the other to G saying, "This is gonna be fun."

The room erupted with applause and congratulations. The men and women all rose from their seats as the CEO, Chairman and CFO got up to leave.

"G, the Board and I have other business so of course our finance department will contact yours with the details of the contract and the memorandum of understanding for the new partnership between NPI and T.O.T. We'll talk soon. Plan on a big celebration! And congratulations again to the two of you. I fought hard for this one," he whispered in G's ear before rushing out of the busy room.

T.O.T? I'm working with a company whose acronym is T-O-T? I have never, since I started this company worked on a contract with anyone *and now I find out in a fucking meeting that we've won with a stipulation of forming a partnership? Are they serious? Is it worth it? What's the catch? I've never heard of this guy or his fucking company. Could this be a favor to some asshole on the Board and just to make it look legit, they had to bring in my reputable firm to keep it under the FERC and SEC radar? But then again, how often does a quarter-billion dollars over a five-year period fall in your lap?* G's thoughts were flashing as fast as the lights on a patrol car in hot pursuit, but he didn't want to appear as though he wasn't pleased or didn't want to accept the deal. This was of course, a game changer for NPI and upped his already well established status in the industry, ten-fold. Although he'd been known and respected as a brilliant entrepreneur, stellar businessman, and stupendous negotiator, this deal, if successful, stood to propel him up there with larger international oil firms. On the one hand he was proud of the work from his firm putting together a winning bid. But on the other, he wondered, at what cost?

CHAPTER 59

"YEAH, it's done. You should have seen his fucking face, it was priceless. I only wish you could have been here for it man. We're on our way to *infamy* and it's all because of, how should I put it, let's see, my very *favorable* relationship with the Chairman. We can think of ourselves as his *beneficiaries*!" he crooned, laughing. "Listen Joseph, I'll bet that never in your wildest dreams did you think you'd be able to get revenge this quickly, never in your freakin' wildest dreams man, and for so much money. Lawrence is a genius for bringing us all together! And hey, I'm really sorry that your relationship with G had to go south, but our fortunes are definitely heading north. What? Yeah, yeah, he's arranging for the first payment to come through as soon as that former boss of yours signs the partnership agreement and then the second part of this epic saga will be put in play and NPI's days will be numbered."

"This is all sweet music to my ears, Dave. And he thought I would just lie down and die, tuck my tail between my ass and go away, disappear completely from the industry? Hell, did he forget I learned from the best, John G. Gicardi himself?!" Both men laughed for a solid minute.

"Look, I'll call Lawrence to let him know that it's a go and to kick everything into high gear," Joseph advised, recovering from his euphoria. This is gonna be one *wild ass ride* and I can't wait to get behind the wheel."

"Good deal, man. I'll be back in L.A. in a couple of days. But listen, we still have to be extremely careful. No one, and I mean no one can know that you're involved with this company."

"Yeah, yeah, yeah," Joseph snapped, "We all know the arrangement. No need to remind me, okay? There's too much money at stake to fuck anything up and taking G down in the process is just caviar on the blinis."

"Listen, the Chairman has someone in New York that I think is slated to get a small chunk of this too, one of his female '*conquests*' who's providing information we might be able to utilize."

"Are you kidding me, man?" Joseph asked, uneasy. "What does he consider a '*small chunk?*' We're already dividing this thing up four different ways."

"I don't know. But I'll tell you this, with the amount of money we stand to profit from this deal I don't think his '*lust fund*' will make a dent. So I wouldn't make a big deal out of it, okay?"

"All I'm saying is that the more people that get pulled into this, the messier it becomes, believe me, I know from my time at NPI."

"Well, my friend, not this time. This is the 'real deal' the 'big leagues.' G thought NPI was going to be the next savior in the oil industry. I'm here to say that T.O.T will be like nothing anyone has ever witnessed before. Even the old timers will have to wait their turn in line if they want to do business with us in the next year or two. They'll all be talking about *us*, Joseph! Nobody will remember NPI or its little CEO anymore. He'll fade away just like the ones that came before him who tried to shake up the industry and had to learn the hard way. He'll have to start all over again when I'm done with him. And I can assure you, he'll be too demoralized to even have the *energy* to do it, pardon the pun," Dave laughed, loud and hard.

Joseph took the phone away from his ear and put it on speaker, increasing the volume and placing it on his desk. He was suddenly taken aback at the extreme vindictiveness in Dave's voice. Although he wanted revenge and he'd planned on presenting a challenge to G in the industry, he'd never planned on actually destroying him, something his newfound partner seemed hell bent on achieving.

Lawrence Finney, Joseph's friend and partner on the west coast had introduced him to Dave at the Oil, Gas and Energy conference two years earlier, when they'd begun planning the launch of their own venture. After later learning of Dave's family connection, being the cousin of the Chairman's son-in-law, Joseph felt they would be solidly positioned for the anticipated BP contract. And the fact that the Chairman was looking to retire next year and replace his seat with his son-in-law, notwithstanding any impervious objections from the already bought and sold voting body, made it even more palatable that the two of them should collaborate with Dave's firm.

Lawrence, reluctant at first because of what he'd heard from others in the industry out West that Dave, although smart, sometimes acted on impulse rather than thinking things through and with a long range vision, tried talking Joseph out of it. But he was resolute in his decision. Joseph had reasoned that Dave was the next best thing considering he could no longer count on his New York contacts or his past relationship with Ary, urging her to pass along any classified information she may have gotten from Darias. And the fact that Dave lacked the combined experience of he and Lawrence, and was willing to split the initial wealth in order to gain some much needed recognition, would all work to their ultimate advantage. So he went about convincing Lawrence to follow his lead, explaining how his plan would eventually work in *their* best interest.

"Hey man, like you said, you'll provide the caviar and blinis and I'll bring the Magnum Grey Goose. This is gonna be a celebration like no other any of us has ever experienced."

Joseph pinched his bottom lip between his thumb and index finger, picked up the phone and said, "Yeah, like no other."

CHAPTER 60

STILL in shock from the meeting, Ary wasn't sure whether to congratulate G as they rode back to the office or keep quiet. They'd ridden down BPs elevator without saying a word. She'd never seen G speechless and she could neither read his face nor his thoughts. The fact that NPI had won the contract was in and of itself amazing, she thought, especially since it was up against larger, more prominent firms. But to win with the stipulation of forming a partnership was almost unfathomable. G had always said that NPI was *his* baby, and *his* alone. He'd taken pride in his storied professional accomplishments, but none as prideful as the creation and success of what he'd often referred to as, '*my own private oil conglomerate*.' She nervously checked her iPhone for messages and emails. The silence was deafening. Finally, G said, "I'm not sure what to think about what just took place, I'm still processing it. I'll have to make some calls, so don't mention this to anyone just yet. I don't know if we should be celebrating or strategizing our next move, understand?"

"Yes, of course G. Can I say that I'm still in a bit of a fog about what happened and how it transpired? I thought we were just going there to maybe clarify some things in the proposal, or negotiate on some of the deliverables. But to come out of that meeting with an award announcement, in our favor, was like being handed a bucket of gold."

"I'm not so sure it *is* a bucket of gold, Ary. I've never heard of this Dave Winters person or The Oil Trust and I'm not certain of a partnership of *any* kind whether it be with a known, or in this case, an unknown entity. This is all a little strange to say the least," he continued, pursing his lips and looking out through the tinted windows. As they neared the entrance to the Philips building, G warned, "Ary, remember, not a word to anyone just yet. I have another stop to make, so I'll catch up with you later this afternoon."

With a look of concern, she concurred. "Of course G, not a word."

She got out of the car and headed towards the secure entrance. "Hi Bob, it's so nice to see you at your station again. It just wasn't the same without you," she said, displaying her badge.

"Good to see you too, Ms. Ary. It feels *alllll right* to be back on duty, he said, emphatically."

She thought how unusual it was to see him smile and realized how important this job was to him. She wanted to ask him about Marguerite and wondered if he'd been in contact with her or had any plans to do so, especially after she'd had him fired. *I don't think it would be a good idea to bring her up right now, especially in light of what I'm about to do,* she mused. *Besides, I'm not sure I could be that forgiving so soon,* she thought, conjuring up her father's image. *But everyone has their own demons I suppose, and only they can determine how they'll deal with them.*

Walking past him through the security gate, as she'd done countless times before, a moment of déjà vu from the first day they'd met came over her. Bob had become an almost surrogate father figure to her, and because of that, she held a soft spot in her heart for his wellbeing.

CHAPTER 61

DWAYNE sat in his office, his mind drifting from curiosity to irritation to full-on frustration. He wasn't willing to return to NPI the same way he'd left, feeling as if there was no one he could trust—not his CEO, or any of his direct reports, and right now, not even the one he wished he could call '*his girl*.' He looked out of his tiny office window, down at the people walking along 5th Avenue, wondering how many of them were satisfied with life, work, relationships or a combination of all three. He also felt a tinge of guilt for feeling this way after just having returned from an enviable vacation. But he couldn't help but wonder what G and Ary were up to. Why wasn't he invited or even told about the meeting with BP? G could've reached him by calling or emailing, even while he was on vacation. It had never stopped him before in the three and a half years he'd worked for NPI—or was Ary up to her *questionable*, ladder-climbing-take-no-prisoners, work-related schemes again? Who was there that he could confide in? He pressed his head hard against the windowpane, his hands spread eagle onto opposite sides. He felt the energy slowly escaping his body and his mood descending into an irritating funk.

A soft knock and cautious opening of his office door by his subordinate startled him.

"Whoa, hey Mike, I didn't hear you knock."

"Hey Dwayne welcome back," he offered, walking into the tiny space.

"Thanks a lot. I was just, just reminiscing about my vacation," he lied.

"Already?! Didn't you just get back?" he laughed. "Or did

you take some additional time off before returning to this insane, always interesting and endlessly challenging world?"

"No, yeah," he answered, awkwardly. "I ahhh…, I came back a few days ago but needed to rest up from my relaxing time away. I figured I'd need it before getting back into the grind."

"Well, it's been crazy here with all the changes you know, with Joseph and Marguerite suddenly gone. And I'm not sure that we, meaning the '*minions*,' were fully briefed on what all went down. Soooo…"

"Oh, okay." Dwayne interrupted. "Well, as soon as I'm able to sit down with G and get a sense of where everything stands, I'll brief the team on what effect, if any, those changes will have on everybody," he explained, not fully aware of how the changes will affect him and what his position, current or future will be at the firm. Dwayne was even more convinced that he had to have a conversation with G before the day ended, and the more he thought about it, the more it troubled him. He thought of questioning Mike about what he *did* know, but he didn't want to appear uninformed.

"Listen, I'd better return some calls. I'll have Ann send out a calendar invite for our marketing meeting which should be in the next day or so, as soon as I'm clear on the direction G wants to go."

"Sounds good. It's been…how should I put this diplomatically, a little *tense* in the office with G feeling as though he should be spearheading *everything*. And let me just say that, even though Joseph was always thought of as G's ace, there were a lot of us who always knew that he couldn't have succeeded in accomplishing all that he did without you having to clean up after his, let's call them, *lapses in business judgment*."

Dwayne was shocked to hear how candid and frank his staff felt confiding in him. Was he just trying to remain on his good side because employee evaluations were coming due, or was it because of something he'd heard? His trust factor had already taken a nosedive because of the '*undisclosed*' BP meeting. And the mention of G being '*tense*' was so out of character, it was hard to imagine.

"Hey, that's all water under the bridge now and we're moving forward with the sole purpose of growing this business and expanding our market share while increasing our personal portfolios in the process," he ended, with a slight laugh. "So, watch out for that invite. I'm sure we'll have a lot to cover."

"Will do Dwayne. And again, welcome back."

Dwayne smiled, giving a salute of confidence to his subordinate. He followed him to the door, peering outside of it, making sure he'd walked a good distance down the corridor. He needed time to plan for his afternoon meeting with G and he didn't *want* or *need* anymore uninvited guests.

CHAPTER 62

ARY walked in the office and quietly greeted Ann before heading around the hallway to her cubical. She looked over the movable wall to see if anyone else was within earshot of the conversation she was preparing to have. The office was empty except for a few interns gathering research documents and placing them neatly into gold colored folders with the bold, black, *NPI* logo blazoned across the front cover. She wondered whether or not she should even make the call from her desk or taxi across town to a restaurant not frequented by the oil establishment. *There's always that possibility of someone who just happens to walk by and hears something they shouldn't*, she thought before checking her wallet. *I should probably do it from outside these walls and use cash instead of a credit card*, she concluded. *I don't want to leave a trail.*

After grabbing her navy blue jacket and handbag, she quickly circled back towards the reception area and stopped for a quick explanation. "Ann I have a few, ah, personal appointments to go to. They shouldn't take long and I should be back in a couple of hours. If anyone needs me, they can reach me by cell."

"Okay sweetie. Everything alright?" she asked, always displaying her maternal nature.

"Oh yes, I'm fine. Everything's good. See you soon."

Ann's gaze followed Ary as she paced nervously around the outer hallway waiting for the elevator to arrive—turning back to her station only after the young protégé sprinted through the opening doors.

"There is *never* a dull moment around here," she whispered under her breath.

CHAPTER 63

RELIEVED to be alone, Ary took a deep breath and leaned back against the side wall of the elevator. As she descended eleven floors down to the lobby she noticed G, laughing in conversation with Bob. She mingled in with a crowd exiting other elevators, hoping to avoid being noticed by either man. She was able to make her way inconspicuously through the atrium and onto 5th Avenue to hail a taxi. *Lord please let me get there and get this over with. You know I don't need this stress or anxiety in my life right now.* A yellow cab pulled up to the curb and she hopped inside, immediately directing the driver.

"The Smyth Hotel in TriBeCa. West Broadway between Chambers and Warren, please," deciding at the last minute to head downtown instead of cross-town. She'd eaten at the *'Little Park'* restaurant in the hotel's lobby with a few girlfriends when it first opened and reasoned that she would be relatively safe from running into any oil colleagues, especially during the 11 o'clock late breakfast hour.

"I think it's better to take the FDR and get off near Chambers rather than the West Side Highway to Broadway at this hour," she said, checking her smartphone map app, assuring him that she was not a tourist to be taken for an expensive ride.

"The FDR it is," he answered, looking at her through the rear-view mirror.

Ary settled into the faux leather seats of the car and checked her phone for any missed texts. There was one from Dwayne: *Where are you? We need to talk.*

"Oh boy!"

"Excuse me?"

"No no, not you. I was thinking out loud."

He turned his attention back to the mounting traffic.

Not now, Dwayne, she thought. *I'll talk to you once I get this over and done with.*

CHAPTER 64

"THANKS for coming to the City, mama. I wasn't sure if you still enjoyed the '*exhilaration*' of being at the center of the universe," Marcus laughed.

"Well, I don't know if I'd call it '*exhilarating*,'" she countered, returning a smile. "But there's always a certain energy here that you can't find anywhere else."

Marcus had invited his mother to breakfast to discuss his marriage issues with Caroline. It all seemed surreal to him that the very woman who was to be the topic of conversation, was the same one whose name and family had caused the sudden collapse of his mother over a month ago. And now, he was seeking her advice.

"When was the last time you were here, mama?"

"A couple of weeks ago. I had a meeting with the studio to talk about placement, capacity, and lighting," she offered.

"Oh yeah, the showing!" he hollered, causing a few heads to turn. "Oh, sorry y'all, It's just that my mom is a famous artist and if I were you, I'd get her autograph now before you have to pay through the *you-know-what* for her signature art work that's being shown at the…what's the name of the gallery, mama?"

"Marcus Alexander, you're too much!" she said, as one of the curious customers inquired about the exhibit.

"It's the Dorothy Kaye Gallery in the West Village, Saturday night at 7:30pm…" Sonya tried explaining before Marcus interrupted.

"Check out her website, '*smaartworks.com.*' It's easy to remember because it's *smart, art* and *works*. Notice how she incorporated all the right words in there?" he winked. Do you have business cards with you, mama?"

"Maybe I should fire my publicist and hire my own son from now on," she said to laughter, while handing out a few cards.

"I'm telling you mama, like I've been saying for umpteen years—you could be raking in even more guap than you already are if you let me handle the publicity."

"If by '*guap*,' you're referring to money, Marcus, I think I scratch out a pretty decent living with the pace of my showings and the sales generated both online and through my agent," she laughed, returning to browse the breakfast menu. "And besides, Mr. Publicist, I've just been commissioned to do some artwork for a friend's client. She recently sold a beautiful mansion in Greenwich, Connecticut to a lovely couple and they want me to provide pieces for their living and dining rooms and the master suite. I'm also working on a sculptured piece for the grand entrance in the center hall."

"Wow, that sounds great, mama. Have I told you lately how proud I am of you?" he asked, switching from jollity to sincerity. "I don't think I say it enough, but I am. How you forgave daddy and Matthew and finally put the past away to be able to live in the present and work towards a more contented future. I've always learned so much from you, mama, and you still amaze me with your strength and resilience, your knowledge, wisdom and bravery. I'm blessed to be able to call you my mom."

"Marcus, that was beautiful! I really appreciate knowing how you feel. Sometimes a mother needs to hear the spoken words from her kids to know that they care and understand."

"We do mama. We really do, even though we may have strange and sometimes stupid ways of showing it. And I think you know how much we love you. There's nothing we wouldn't do for you, nothing."

"I know baby, and that's good to hear, because I need you and your sister to be available to accompany me to a very special occasion," she appealed, watching his widening eyes.

"O-kaaayy. That was fast. Am I to assume you're putting us to the test on this?"

"Don't be silly, Marcus. I'm not '*testing*' you. I'm merely *asking* if you'd be willing to go out West with me for your father's surprise, sixtieth birthday party. Matthew invited me and I'd like to go. But I don't think I'm ready to go it alone. I'm sure you and Ary will be receiving invitations, but I wanted to ask first."

Marcus was stunned and his face couldn't hide it. His resting elbows gave way to his weakened muscles, causing both arms to fall from the table down by his sides, as if they were bearing fifty pound weights. He leaned further back in his chair and said, "I can't believe what I'm hearing. What's next? Are *you* gonna end up engaged to one of Matthew's relatives too?"

Sonya was puzzled. She'd thought he was fine with the direction the family had taken when it came to accepting Bruce and Matthew. Based on his reaction at the house after seeing both men and sharing food and drinks, she felt the healing process for the Alexander's, all except for Ary, had begun. Maybe it was in fact, too soon. *Maybe*, she thought, *it would have been best to have kept her invitation private and waited to see if Marcus and Ary were indeed invited.*

"I really don't appreciate your sarcasm Marcus, so let's keep it in check."

"But mom…"

"There's nothing to '*but*' about Marcus Bruce. I'm sorry if I offended or shocked you. I just figured that we were all moving ahead with our lives, especially you with your imminent marriage to Caroline. Last I heard, she was still Matthew's niece, right?"

"I know mama, I know and I'm sorry. I really am. But you have to admit that we've been through hell and back and hell again with your hospitalization, not knowing if and how you would come though that and knowing that it was all because of me and…"

"Stop it Marcus!" she interrupted. "Let's not rehash painful memories. I think we're all pushing forward and trying to be better people. If there's one thing I've learned from all of this and my unfortunate time in the hospital and subsequent recovery, is that life is short, and so is the time to be with the one's we love. So make the most of what God has blessed you with and be thankful for the things you've worked hard to acquire. And lastly, ignore the noise that persistently surrounds us."

Marcus lowered his head before regaining his posture and pulled his chair closer to the table. "Truth be told, ma, I did receive the invitation a few weeks ago and put it aside. I wasn't thinking of it as a family affair, especially after neither you nor Ary mentioned it. So I never brought it up. And I really hadn't planned on going. I guess I still have some issues of my own to work through and that's one of the reasons I invited you here today."

Sonya smiled at her son, placed her hand on his nervous knee and said, "I don't think there's any rush to work through any lingering issues Marcus, and I'll understand completely if you don't want to go. I didn't mean to sound selfish in asking you. Maybe I'm not as ready as I think I am either. Marcus, we're all on the mend and it's perfectly fine to take as much time as we need to work through our collective concerns. So in the meantime," she said, sliding her finger down the menu, "I'm starving! Let's get some sustenance in us before tackling anymore serious conversations."

CHAPTER 65

ARY walked into the restaurant giving the space a quick scan before approaching the host's desk.

"Good morning. Table for one please and I'd prefer to be seated towards the back."

"Hello and welcome to Little Park. Right this way."

Ary followed him through the stylishly modern space. There were obvious tourists sitting with young children and business men and women working from tablets, laptops and oversized smartphones, oblivious to anyone or anything except for the coffee, tea or food sitting in front of them. *Yes,* she thought, *this was a good choice.* No one would recognize her or have any interest in her conversation.

"Is this fine ma'am?"

"Yes, it's perfect," she confirmed, placing her handbag in the opposite chair. "I'll just have tea for now, and if you have any raw sugar, please."

"I'll let your waiter know to bring it right out."

"Thank you."

Settling down she reached across the table to retrieve her phone from her purse. She could hear laughter off to the other side of the restaurant. *I wish I could find something to laugh about right now,* she thought. *Why is my life always so complicated? I never had this kind of stress at my old job. But then again, I didn't make this kind of money there either or come in contact with the multi-million dollar egos I have to deal with on a daily basis. Is it all worth it to be living in an enviable condo, traveling the world and not having to dish out my own money, expanding my serious designer shoe collection and chic wardrobe? Yep!* she laughed. *It is. But now I have to make this…"*

"I thought that was you hiding in the corner!"

"Marcus! What the hell are you doing here? How did you…?"

"We noticed you when you came in, but thought you might have been with some colleagues or clients and didn't want to bombard or embarrass you. So we waited a minute."

"Wait. '*We'?* We who?"

"Me and mama. I invited her to breakfast in the City and I'd heard great things about this spot, and obviously, you did too!" he ended, laughing. "She just ordered coffee."

This is a freaking nightmare, she thought. *There are thousands of f-ing restaurants in this city and I chose the one my mother and brother decide to have their morning meal! Jesus Christ!*

"Wow Marcus! How lucky am I?"

"Right?! And sis, maybe this was fate."

"Huh? What do you mean?"

"The talk I wanted to have with mama is the same one I was trying to have with you about Caroline when you disrespectfully ended the conversation while you were over in…wherever the hell you were."

"Oh, ok. Is she still upset with me? Should I go over?"

"No, just wait here. I'll see if she wants you to change seats or if we should come over to your table—it's a little more secluded. I'll be right back," he said, maneuvering around tables and chairs.

How can I make the call now? I don't know what to do. Shit!

Ary noticed Sonya and Marcus making their way towards her. She grabbed an empty chair from a nearby table, pulling it up to hers. She knew the window of opportunity for making the call was all but lost, so she put her cell phone back in her purse, set it down beside her and heaved a long sigh.

"What a wonderful surprise mama," she greeted, standing up to kiss her on the cheek. "You look beautiful."

CHAPTER 66

DWAYNE'S personal cell phone rang, startling him, causing him to answer without noticing the caller ID.

"Hey big brotha, hope I didn't catch you in the middle of somethin'. I just wanted to call and give you an update on what's going on at home."

"Hey Dion," he answered wearily, closing his eyes and blowing out a long breath. "Naw, I can talk for a minute or two. What's up? How's mom and pops? I meant to call when I got back from vacation, but there's so much shit going on already that it just slipped my mind."

"Well, let's see," he started. "Pop's condition is, ya' know, 'bout the same as the last time we spoke, and Darrell is still workin' his butt off, you know, back in school for his master's and holdin' down a full time *j-o-b* while tryna' pay rent in that small apartment he got on the other side of town. I guess he's tryna' walk in his big bro's footsteps, man," he chimed with a nervous laugh. "And me, I feel like I'm holdin' down the fort here all by my lonesome most times without the proper…"

"Whoa, wait a minute. Can you be a little bit more precise man, about the parents?" Dwayne interrupted. "I already know Darrell is back in school 'cause I'm making up the difference with the tuition bill," he snarled, growing increasingly frustrated. "And I do occasionally help you '*hold down the fort*' so you're not doing it all *by yo' lonesome*," he said, sarcastically. "Look, I'm gettin' ready to go to a meeting and I'd like to know if there's something I need to do or send before I get off the phone, Dion. So tell me what needs to get done, or who needs what?" he asked, his voice rising with each question.

"Hey man, why you gettin' all irritated? I'm just the brotha who's tryna' keep it together down here all by my fuckin' self, ya' know? I don't *really* have to call your black ass and tell you nothin'—cause if you cared like you always professin' you do, tellin' mom and pops how successful you are—sendin' that big city change instead of showing your damn face once in a while, it might just make some kinda difference."

"What the hell are you talking about man? Look, I'm sorry if I sounded annoyed. I'm just going through some shit that I'm not really sure is *shit* at all. Dion, I apologize, really. I know I haven't been in touch and you're right, sending money is definitely no substitute for being there. So I'll try and come down in a couple of weeks, right after I straighten some things out here."

"I think a couple of weeks might be too late, big brotha."

"Too late? Too late for what? For who?" he asked, nervously.

"Mom's in the hospital and…"

"What?!" he yelled. "In the hospital? For what, man? I spoke to her and pops before I went on vacation a few weeks back and she said they were both feeling okay and that she'd received the money I deposited into her account—all six-thousand of it to help cover the cost of some outstanding medical bills, her and pop's medicine and I included a little extra for whatever they wanted or needed it for. Wasn't she taking her medication? And why are you just now tellin' me this? When was she taken to the hospital? How serious is it?"

Dion tried his best to hide the anger he felt mounting towards his older brother before answering. "They took her to the emergency room two days ago and admitted her."

Dwayne felt the hairs on the back of his neck rising with his body temperature.

"Cause of her Parkinson's disease, walking was gettin' worse and worse and when I left her sittin' on the front porch with pops the other day, for just a minute, while I went to the bathroom, I came back and found her lying there on her face. Pops was tryna' pick her up but…"

"What the hell?!" he yelled.

"She wasn't responsive, so I called 9-1-1 and they came and got her. Then 'bout three or four hours later, I find out they want to keep her and run some additional tests…"

"Whoa, whoa, whoa, wait one effin' minute. They took her to the emergency room *two* fuckin' days ago and *nobody* thought to call or tell me anything!!! Not you, not Darrell, not even pops? What kind of bullshit is that?" he screamed. "Anytime you two need some extra '*change*' nobody forgets to call me. I'm so freakin' tired of being the responsible one! Just because I'm the oldest doesn't mean I should have to do every goddamned thing. I mean, Lord…"

"You wait one effin' minute, big brotha. I *just* called you! You haven't called me, mom *or* pops in weeks and *you* yellin' at me?! I don't think so! If you cared as much as you say you do, you'd show up in Greenbrier County more than two or three times a year instead of thinkin' that your fuckin' fancy-job money was enough to keep us country hicks quiet. Did you also forget you have a *son* down here, man? A son whose mama drops him off unannounced—leavin' him for mom and pops to look after when she needs a so-called '*break*' from workin' at that coal miners bar downtown. You know the one, where men go when they want more than just a drink," he jeered, landing a virtual sucker punch. "Oh, but wait, I forgot, you do send for him a couple times a year to go up north to get that culture he can't get down here in the boonies, right? Get the hell up outta here with all that screamin' and yellin' shit—tryna' be all big-city important. We might be lil' country ass folks to you since you left home, but you still gotta responsibility to your folks and your son. And pops don't owe you no phone call, you should be checkin' up on him! And now that mom has been diagnosed with colorectal cancer, maybe you'll think about showin' up more often."

Dwayne had reached a fever pitch, prompting him to hurl his phone against the wall, shattering it into pieces. He picked up his chair, throwing it across his desk where it crashed against his office door, causing his college degrees to fall off their hinges, while those nearby wondered if he was becoming unhinged.

"What the hell did I do to deserve all this? What-did-I-fuckin'-do?!"

CHAPTER 67

DARIAS paced around his office, walking from the wall of windows overlooking the majestic greens of Central Park, to the view of the Hudson River glistening against the morning sun underneath the George Washington Bridge to the west. He waited for his electronic assistant to summon him to the meeting with Julian and a few other VPs. *What's next?* he wondered. *I'm all for business bombshells, but even I didn't see this coming. Who's behind it? All I wanted was to have her name taken out of consideration as the possible lead from the account, teach her a lesson, and bring her ungrateful ass down a notch. I didn't know about this partnership shit.* He felt blindsided. *Hopefully this meeting will shed some light on this new situation. Maybe it was a mistake on my part thinking I had more critical input than I actually had in this award. There's only a few folks on the board capable of pulling this kind of coup, but for what reason and for how much?*

But before any prolonged thoughts or suppositions could continue, his electronic assistant reminded him: *'Mr. Woolfolk, your meeting with Mr. Dorchak begins in two minutes.'*

"Damn, here we go." He grabbed his suit jacket from the back of his leather-mesh office chair and headed down the corridor.

CHAPTER 68

"HELLO Ariel. This is a wonderful surprise."

"Oh oh mama, am I in trouble? Whenever you call me by my birth name I know *something's* coming," she laughed. "What'd I do this time?"

"Nothin' lil' girl," Sonya laughed. "Can't a mother call her child by the name she was gifted?"

"Yes of course, mama. But seeing as though I did leave home in a rush the last time I saw you, which to some, could have been misinterpreted as childish behavior and..."

"*Misinterpreted*?! Ha!" Marcus laughed, cutting her off from any further explanation. "It was more like, '*hey baby brother, I can't handle this family dynamic right now, so I'ma check y'all later. Bye.*'"

"Okay funnyman, it wasn't like that at all. I was just exercising my right to own my own feelings…as they always taught us, right, mama?" she asked, looking to Sonya for a sliver of maternal support. Sonya lifted her cup of coffee and winked her acquiescence.

"And, family, I've thought about it and I'd like to offer my sincerest apologies for that unceremonious exit."

"Forgiven, baby."

"Wait! That's it mama? Uh uh, not so fast," Marcus chimed. "How come she always gets off so easy? Nothing ever changes in this family when it comes to the *chosen* one."

"Oh! Now *I'm* the chosen one, Marcus? Don't even get me started on how many times I took the fall for your scrawny butt so you could come off looking all innocent. And what about those homework assignments you supposedly aced, *all-by-yourself?* Uh huh, okay, don't even get me started."

They broke out in simultaneous laughter. Ary could feel the stress and tension easing around her neck and shoulders. She almost felt relieved having to put off the call until later in the day.

"Alright, you two," Sonya interrupted, delighted to be in the company of her children, "the waiter's coming over. I think we should take another look at our menus."

Marcus punched Ary lightly on her shoulder. "I love you anyways, big sis, and thanks for always havin' my back. But can I *please* talk about why we're here? Sheesh!"

CHAPTER 69

"GOOD morning gentlemen," he said, walking into Julian's office suite where he found the CFO, and three VPs already seated around the octagonal, cherry wood table. He was shocked to see the Chairman and two members of the board also in attendance.

"So, that went well," he started, trying to gauge whether anyone was willing to offer any further insight. "I have to confess, I didn't think number two was going to be The Oil Trust. I thought it was agreed that the contracts were to be divided between NPI and SKG, with a possible third split to be decided by a quorum to include ChemCo in the last year for any drilling cleanup.

"Well Woolfolk," the Chairman interrupted, flaunting a wrinkled scowl on his forehead. "There *was* a quorum. But unfortunately, it took place while you were away. And not one of us in this room has the time or the proclivity to wait around to make important decisions such as this because you found it necessary to go half way around the world with one of Larsen's former, or current—I can't keep up with his shenanigans anymore, sexual conquests," he ended, with a hearty laugh.

Darias was shocked. "I beg your pardon? What business is it of yours or anyone else's for that matter, who I spend my time with? It has no bearing on how I perform or conduct my professional responsibilities." He looked to his CEO for agreement or at the very least, backup. All he got was a head shake and a taut pursing of his lips, indicating his hands were tied.

"You see, Woolfolk. I've known Mr. Dave Winters for a very long time. You could say he's like a son to me," he continued. "So,

I'll admit that I'm flexing a little muscle and cashing in some well-deserved chips so my 'son' can finally realize his dream and make a dent in the industry with his very capable firm, just like our friend, John Gicardi did not too long ago. And I think we can all agree that he isn't the only bright, handsome, oilman that could use a helping hand during these hostile government, regulatory times. These guys could all benefit from a little influence, knowledge and mentoring. And G, as some of you still *affectionately* refer to him," he said, winking and looking around the table for agreement, "is still very useful in that regard. Dave stands to learn a lot from him. But don't be too disappointed Woolfolk, BP stands to make a small fortune with these new drilling contracts out West, as will all of these hardworking, talented folks sitting around this beautiful table. That includes you too," he scoffed, fixing his eyes directly on Darias. "Yes gentlemen, I think we'll all benefit quite handsomely from this transaction. So get on board Woolfolk, and keep earning that very significant paycheck you find in your bank account every week or month, however often you get paid. And in case you've forgotten, it's the board that so graciously consents to that continuous financial flow. So fall in line. And oh, one last thing Woolfolk, next time try and find another pretty young thing to spend your valuable time with and stop picking up Larsen's leftovers. It really does nothing for that solid reputation you've worked so hard to cultivate." The Chairman, CFO and VPs all rose. Darias remained seated. He was seething. His face was flush and his fingers had automatically tightened into fists. He could only stare at the wall of art behind Julian's enormous desk to keep from punching the Chairman.

"Good day gentlemen. I think we're all on the same page and I expect everything will proceed as discussed and the plans can be thrust into high gear with absolutely *no* mishaps." The men and women all agreed with small whispers and affirmative head shaking. They followed the Chairman out of the office, leaving Darias and Julian behind.

"Hey man, I'm sorry if you were blindsided by this…"

"*If?*" he asked, emphatically. "*If* I was blindsided? I'm still waiting for the second Mac truck to finish me off! Listen, no disrespect Julian, but what the hell was that? I know he can be a dick *most* times and there've been many days and nights when I've prayed that he would have a heart attack while he was in the arms of some other man's wife, which is where he prefers to be. But this? This is beyond the pale, Julian. This is Joseph Larsen type shit. Please tell me you had nothing to do with this. You and I had talked about replacing G's protégé with your choice for team lead. So what gives? Will Sarah still be involved? Ary Alexander doesn't deserve this. It seems that wherever she goes lately, trouble follows and we don't need that with such a high profile contract. Every federal and state regulatory body will be looking at this, making sure we comply with all of their OSHA rules, environmental impact assessments, pipeline transportation, waste regulations and…"

"Darias," he interrupted. "We both know that Ary Alexander is really the female version of Gicardi, which means that she's more than capable of leading the first phase of this project and ensuring that the mandates are followed to completion. And let's be honest here, the only reason you want her kicked off and replaced with Sarah is because she chose to spend the rest of her vacation with Hargis."

"I told you that in confidence," he said, gritting his teeth.

"And it'll remain that way if you don't push the issue."

He was baffled. He'd always been able to trust and confide in Julian. But now, everything seemed to be coming unglued. He wondered what could have changed over such a short period of time.

"Look Darias, I agree, this smells to high heaven. But it's above me, man. Let's wait and see what direction the wind blows. While you were gone, the Chairman and a few other board members contacted me and requested an emergency meeting at his estate in Southampton. This wasn't a *'get here by train or by car conference.'* This was a *'get on a friggin' helicopter or private jet and get your asses out here in an hour,'* type meeting. I tried calling you, but it went straight to voicemail, so I made the trip alone."

"So what happened? What couldn't wait?"

"When I arrived, Winters was already there, sitting in the library with the Chairman. That's the first time I'd ever seen or met him or heard of his company. I knew right away something was off."

"What do you mean? How?"

"I don't know, a gut feeling I guess. You and I have been in this business a long time. And because I've spent most of my time at BP, I know exactly how the board works. They're different from most other boards because they, unlike the CEO, hold the majority of power, stock and influence. It's just the way the charter was written a bazillion years ago and no one is willing to change it, challenge it or even bring it up because of the founders' two sons who, as you very well know, rule with an iron fist. And I, like so many other executives have been wishing for them to retire or just fade away into golden dust and get blown away to that section of heaven set aside for the oligarchy."

"Yeah, I think the entire industry's been waiting for that day to come."

"So the Chairman made it quite clear that Winters was getting the contract with no questions asked. He laid out how it was all going down, with all the players in agreement, including the sons, a few more board members and now us. I couldn't object, because like you, I rather enjoy my lifestyle with all its perks, power and financial rewards. Plus, I figured everything would get back to normal once this contract was awarded and…"

"And nothing, Julian!" he interrupted. "This is bullshit! If we let him get away with this now, who knows what's coming next. What if he wants to replace you as CEO or me as a Senior Executive VP for no other reason than a vindictive whim? And what if there's another Dave Winters waiting in the wings for another favor? How did this all happen? I *never* trusted that asshole," he professed, pounding his fist on his boss' desk. "I always knew he was waiting for just the right moment for the ultimate power grab, but what I didn't know was who he was willing to destroy and what he'd have to do to get it."

"Now hold on. I think you're getting a little ahead of yourself here. This is just a contract that's been awarded to a friend or a '*son*' as he calls him. It's not like it hasn't been done before. C'mon now, let's not be naïve. Other board members have made requests and flexed their muscles for contract awards in the past."

"This is different Julian. Somehow this feels different," he said, staring into his CEO's penetrating grey eyes for answers that weren't readily forthcoming.

CHAPTER 70

"SO mama, tell me, what's your initial feeling about it? As a woman, a wife, well, a former wife," he said, correcting himself. "For what possible reason would she be stalling after all we've gone through together?"

"Marcus," Ary interrupted, before her mother even had the chance to respond. "Have you thought about just straight up *asking* her, challenging her to be open and honest?"

"I was asking mama for *her* opinion, Ary," he said, clearly annoyed. "And, I'm not stupid or the *little* brother who needs you to guide him in the artful discourse of a simple Q&A."

"I was just…"

"If *I* might have a chance at offering some motherly wisdom," Sonya intervened, averting what could have been a lengthy tit-for-tat between siblings. "Marcus, you're a grown man who says he's professed his love to the woman he wants to spend the rest of his life with, start a family and experience all that that means, including the highs and lows of a marriage. Yet now you're suggesting your fiancé is having doubts, no matter how hard you try and convince her otherwise? I would only say that either *both* of you are 100 percent certain that this is a contract you're both willing to sign or it's not. I know that might sound harsh honey, but I don't want you to go into something where you're wondering and waiting for the other shoe to drop. I'm sure you understand what it's like to be caught in the middle of someone else's mistake. And honestly, if I had to do it all over again, believe me baby, I would have widened my eyes and been more willing to accept the consequences that followed long before it got to the point of him feeling as though he had no other choice but to walk out."

Briefly looking away from her children, thoughts of that Thanksgiving toast crept into her memory.

Marcus grew concerned, wondering if his mother could mentally offer sound advice at that moment, watching as she easily faded back to thirteen years ago. What he didn't want was to cause her anymore emotional distress.

Sonya looked down at the white cloth napkin lying across her lap. She took a deep breath and said, "So Marcus, give her time. What's the rush? Let her be certain that you're the one before she trades her single life and livelihood for one where she might well have to put the needs of others before her very own for more times than she can ever imagine. Let her come to grips, if she hasn't already, with the fact that her whiteness and all the privileges she enjoys in this society because of it, will be clouded just a bit because of the ignorance, intolerance, bigotry and hatred of others. You'll also be giving up some of your blackness to exist in facets of her world Marcus, whether we want to admit it or not," she suggested. "And sweetheart, it's more than likely, if she has a solid foundation, you'll be thrust into her family circle and her friendships, not only because of your marriage to each other, but because of your father and Matthew's relationship as well. And that means sharing in their traditions during holidays, which might be different than your own. And once you bring children into the family fold, it'll only deepen the connection."

"That doesn't mean I'm giving up spending holidays with my *own* family, mama. Uh uh, no way. We have our own traditions, right Ary?"

Ary smiled. "That's not what mama's saying, knucklehead. Of course we'll always be there for each other—holidays and non-holidays. But really, Marcus, I've seen it time and time again that once the kiddos come, they spend more time with the wife's family."

"Is that true, mama? Is that how it was with us?"

"I wouldn't necessarily make that blanket statement, but it does happen more often than not. You guys did spend more time with my family, but it wasn't because I planned it that way. I loved Bruce's family, even his combative, '*king of his castle*' father, and felt it equally important that they were part of your lives. So we talked about it as we were planning our family—what holidays we'd spend with my family and which one's we'd share with his. And believe me, someone always feels slighted. So there is no easy answer, but I think you'll be okay as long as you both put forth an honest effort and discuss these things before the children come."

"Wow mama. You just spit some gems of wisdom right there. I'm already feeling the energy!"

Ary laughed, "Silly child."

"And you're right, if we *are* meant to be together, she'll say '*yes.*' And if not, as difficult as it would be for me to move on, I'd have no other choice. I certainly don't want to replay that infamous day in my head again, this time watching *her* walk out the door right after a memorable toast and a holiday spread on the dining room table."

Ary and Sonya winced. The mere fact that he would bring up such horrific and painful memories, Ary thought, was naive at best and insensitive at worst.

Her cell phone rang before she could switch it to vibrate. She glanced to see if it was the person she'd promised to call. It was.

"Should you have taken that sweetheart?" Sonya asked.

"No, no. It's fine, I can call them back after breakfast. They can wait. They'll wait," she continued explaining, arousing her mother's suspicion.

"Ary, if you need to return the call, please excuse yourself and do so," Sonya admonished. "It never pays to delay what could be accomplished right now," she continued, reminding Ary of the pressure she'd felt from her mother and father as a teenager.

"Mama, I can call them back or they'll call later. I'm telling you, it's fine," she responded, with an air of nervous irritation.

"Okay sis, but don't blame us when the crap hits the fan because you weren't available 24 and 7 to your handlers," Marcus quipped.

"Marcus, please," she said, throwing him a sustained stern look. "Can we continue our conversation before breakfast arrives?"

Sonya stared at her daughter, sensing there was something wrong, but decided not to inquire any further. She had yet to have the conversation about attending Bruce's surprise party and wasn't sure this would be the time to bring it up to her.

At just the right moment, the waiter brought over a tray of breakfast staples—scrambled eggs, smoked Canadian bacon, waffles and hash browns for Marcus—a spinach and feta cheese omelet for Sonya, mixed fruit with a bowl of oatmeal for Ary, and a basket of artisan muffins for the table.

"Oooh, that looks good. I'm gonna need this food to help me digest all that *advisability* mama just laid on me," Marcus joked.

Ary laughed hard before turning to the waiter. "It does look appetizing, thank you. Oh, and please refill my mother's coffee and I'll have another cup of tea."

"Yes, ma'am, I'll be back in a moment."

Sonya smiled, pleased that her daughter's tone had become less stressful.

"Mama," she said, looking directly into Sonya's eyes, "without you even knowing it, you've lightened what could have been an onerous morning, and I love you for it." She leaned over and kissed her mother's cheek."

"It was my pleasure, Ariel Marie," Sonya answered, affectionately brushing her daughter's tresses.

CHAPTER 71

DWAYNE'S hands went from rubbing his hair, determining it was time for a cut, to pounding his fists on his desk. He turned again to look out the window, but this time instead of wondering about the lives of the passersby on 5th Avenue, he decided to join them, reasoning that the air and an escape from anyone else who might unexpectedly walk in or call his office would provide at least a moment of solace. Connie hadn't been able to schedule a meeting with G until 4:00pm and he wanted to use this time to figure out what he would say once he came face to face with his CEO.

This was one of those times he thought, having a significant other would be appreciated. He wished he'd had a special someone to call, solicit advice from, or relay his true feelings to. But the one he had in mind wasn't fully his, no matter how much he wanted her to be.

Walking around his desk towards the door, he uprighted his office chair, reminded of the results of his mini-rage. His shattered cell phone lay near the wall with fragments of plastic and glass crunching underneath his shoes. Stopping to pick up what was left of it, he sighed. "Damn, something's always broke. If it's not family, it's this fucking job or my on-again, off-again relationship with her," he said, sweeping scores of tiny pieces under his desk. "Well, at least I have insurance to replace the damn phone. Too bad you can't replace your heart when it breaks."

Dwayne took a deep breath and reached for his suit jacket dangling on the back of the door hook. "Whoever said '*you have to first* learn *the* rules *of the game and then play better than anyone else,*' should have been given a medal for making the *understatement* of all time, cause around here, you have to become a fuckin' all-star without even knowing the game you're playing." He walked out of his office, pulling the door hard until he heard it lock.

CHAPTER 72

"HELLO?" she answered, leaning into the phone, trying to sound as upbeat as she could, especially in light of her circumstances. "Yes, he called me last night. Congratulations. I'm sure there'll be plenty of celebrations to come."

"Hey babe, you gotta give me a little more than that! Some enthusiasm maybe? At least a pretend laugh. Don't you want revenge? He tossed you to the curb like a piece of non-recyclable trash and *I*, of all people, know you didn't deserve it," he said, pausing, believing he'd given her something warranting a response. "Look, Marguerite, we've know each other for over twenty years and dated for what, four or five?"

"*One*. We dated for *one* year," she interjected.

"Well, one. But the way you made me feel babe, was like we'd been together for a lifetime," he said, closing his eyes, trying to summon the memories.

"Yeah, I know, me too," she answered, raising her eyes in disgust toward the ceiling.

"Nonetheless, like I said, you didn't deserve to lose your job *and* your man all in one fell swoop, and in such an undignified manner! Ooh, that was simply going too far. He could have at least fired you and then waited a week or so later to break it off or vice versa. That's what I would have done," he finished, callously. "And all because he found out you were a half-breed?"

"A what?! What did you just call me?"

"I'm sorry babe, I'm sorry. Was I not being politically correct? What's the term for it these days? I simply *cannot* keep up! And you know Marguerite, there were *always* suspicions among some of the barons. They always whispered about the exotic tint of your skin tone, wondering about your background, you know, your racial makeup."

She could feel flashes of steam rising in her body.

"But it was me babe, me, who took the plunge and dove into that lovely pool of fusion and never wanted to come out."

"Is that your idea of flattery?!" she yelled. "Look Chairman, I only agreed to this because I was devastated and felt that his little hussy protégé was the cause of my life unraveling with him. She came in and immediately began dismantling everything I'd worked so hard for," she laid bare through falling tears. "I put my own hopes and dreams aside to help him reach his vision, and not because I was some dreamy-eyed neophyte who'd do anything for the man she loved just so he wouldn't leave her. I wanted to play a significant role in his success, prove to him that I could take NPI on a course not even he could imagine. And since I'd done it for other small firms, I…"

"Let me stop you right there Marguerite," he interjected. "G is an oilman through and through and no matter how much you thought or wanted to be his equal partner on his way to success in the industry, it was never going to happen, never," he ended, emphatically. "I know it might be hard to hear babe, but it's true—we're oilmen, it's in our blood—it's the air we breathe, what gets us up in the morning, well one of the things that gets us up," he laughed.

Yuck, she thought.

"And it's what causes us to make the decisions we make, no matter the consequences. So don't waste time wallowing in your sorrow, rehashing old wounds, or wondering why somebody wronged you in the past or didn't love you the way you wanted to be loved in the present. Take hold of your reins, get the damn job done. And in this case, the job is to take down that son-of-a-bitch, John G. Gicardi and his precious NPI."

The Chairman laughed so hard, he began coughing uncontrollably.

"You okay?" she asked, mustering a faint concern.

"I'm, I'm fa..fa…fine," he stuttered, trying to control his asthmatic breathing.

"Well, it's like you said, we have a job to do and I hope the people you've put in place are up to the task."

"Don't worry about my *pa…peee…people* babe," he struggled, "I've recruited the smartest in the business, and when all of this is said and done, maybe I'll reinstate you as VP at NPI, or what's left of it," he smirked. "Of course, that's only if you're willing to be nice to me again. You know you've always been my favorite Marguerite.

Ugh, she thought, finding his comments revolting and her frustration deepening.

"I really have to go. But thanks for the update, the pep talk and the charitable compliments. And one last thing Chairman, when is this mystery man who calls me going to finally reveal himself? My curiosity is boiling over."

"Soon enough babe, soon enough. But listen, I meant what I said about you owing me. You of all people know that no good deed goes un…un..." he said, trying to remember the idiom.

"It's *'no good deed goes unpunished.'*"

"What?"

"The saying! The saying is…, oh, never mind," she said, bewildered. "And by the way, that is *not* an expression of flattery." She disconnected the call before he could respond.

How the hell did he ever become Chairman of any company? And what the hell have I gotten myself into? Is this all worth destroying someone I claimed to have loved? And still do. Is this the revenge I was looking for?

She sat up on the edge of her French provincial tapestry-covered accent chair, further reflecting on the conversation she'd tried having with G.

I called to warn you, but you wouldn't listen. I gave you one last chance to make things right again, and you threw it all away. How can I turn back now G? They want to ruin you. What can I possibly do to save NPI? She stood up and paced around the living room, stopping at the chair where she'd fallen into, begging G's forgiveness, and began to cry.

CHAPTER 73

"CONNIE, let Mr. Hargis know I can see him now," G said, rushing into his suite. "And tell him there's something we need to discuss right away."

Connie's eyes followed her boss as he walked past her without the usual '*good afternoon young lady*' or '*now there's the real brains of this organization*,' greeting he'd always offered, making her feel much younger than her fifty plus years, and smarter than she'd ever believed.

"Uh, sir," she said, getting up to follow him. "Mr. Hargis stepped out. He told Ann that he'd return for your scheduled four o'clock meeting. Should I try and reach him?"

Visibly annoyed, he turned around and said, "Yes Connie, reach him please. I need him back here within the hour. Do you think you can handle that?" He stood near his circular conference table looking at her as if he were dismissing an uninvited guest. His brow furled and his enviable tanned face reddened.

"Yes sir. I *think* I can."

"Thank you and close the door behind you," he demanded, not catching the sarcasm she'd thrown back at him. "I don't want to see anyone until he returns."

She was stunned. In all the years she'd worked for G, he'd never once been rude to her, even when she'd mistakenly double booked a meeting or conference call, he'd always comforted her, saying jokingly that there had only been room for one perfect being on this earth and that she'd given birth to him, and by default, NPI. They'd always laugh, no matter how often he'd said it. But today was totally out of character for the man she'd considered the '*nicest and fairest'* CEO she'd ever worked for and someone she'd never grown tired of saying, *'you're the son I never had, but always wished for.'*

Connie was hurt and wanted so badly to slam the door shut. But she knew doing so would only add to his frustration and quite possibly cost her her job.

"Hi Ann, it's me. The boss is raging and he wants to see Mr. Hargis now instead of four. Can you reach out and get him here?"

"Sure, I'll call his cell."

"Thanks. I owe you for this one."

Ann called Dwayne's company issued cell phone repeatedly, only to get his voicemail. *Come on honey, answer your phone. The CEO is on a war footing.*

CHAPTER 74

DWAYNE walked the chic stretch of 5th Avenue to Columbus Circle among tourists, workers and titans. Reaching for his cell phone in his breast pocket caused his waning anxiety to resurface. "Damn!" He looked around for an electronics store and finally resorted to asking a millennial for suggestions. "Thanks man," he said, after getting two referrals. "Appreciate it."

He decided to walk to the furthest recommended store, ten blocks to the '*Mobile Warehouse*,' reasoning that he'd use the time to try and clear his muddled mind. *Will she tell me what's really going on this time or like before, is she at the center of it?*

"All hell just broke out at that freakin' company a month ago and before I can assemble my first fuckin' marketing meeting, there's secrets, surprises and bullshit happening already," his thoughts unexpectedly spilling into spoken words. "Yeah, look at me. I don't care. I could have been talking on my phone for all y'all know. And besides, right now I don't give a shit if anybody thinks I'm nuts. This city is chock full of 'em."

After finally reaching his destination, he walked up to the customer service counter and said with stern authority, "Look, I'm having a shitty day after having busted my phone, so you'll understand if I don't have time for some B.S. sales pitch or half-witted sales person trying to sell me more than I want or will ever need. So here's the deal. I need 256 gigs of storage, a 6 inch screen, front and rear camera and a more than decent lasting battery. I don't care about the brand—I'm no longer loyal to *anyone*. So if you're capable of handling that, tell me what you have that fits my description."

A wide-eyed employee stared with trepidation. "O-kaaay," she answered, looking from side to side, over her shoulder and all around the store. "I can *try* and help you, sir."

Quickly realizing his tone was reflecting his inner feelings, and taking a sweep of the tiny shop, noticing that he was the only African-American customer there, he decided to restate his purpose, this time using a more deferential tenor. "Let me start over," he said, displaying a half-grin. "I could use your expertise in recommending a mobile device, with all the features I mentioned previously and preferably one that won't be obsolete the minute I get back to my office and take it out of the box."

This time she smiled, explaining that she was shaken because of the customer who'd just left in a fiery rage, accusing her of blatantly lying about the extended battery life of the $799 phone she'd sold him a week ago.

Dwayne wondered if that customer was also a well-dressed, dark-hued man of color because by the initial horror-struck expression on her face. It seemed she may have thought he'd come back to further express his dissatisfaction.

"Well, I promise not to bite or yell anymore. By the way, I'm Dwayne Hargis," he said, extending a hand.

"It's nice to meet you Mr. Hargis," she reciprocated, leaning over the glass enclosure. "I'm sure I can help and I promise not to sell you any more than you need."

"Okay then," he said, looking inside the enclosure filled with phones of all sizes, styles and colors. "Now that we're in agreement, shall we begin this conversation again, from the top?"

She smiled an easy relief, handing him a few choices from the case and pointing out the features and functions he'd requested.

CHAPTER 75

JOSEPH spent the rest of the afternoon reading over documents from Dave who had intentionally faxed them from a nearby office store instead of using the fax machines at BP. He was careful not to raise any suspicions from the secretaries or assistants. He also felt there were VPs and board members who might be holding grudges because their first choices were excluded from the list of finalists and awardees.

Joseph couldn't help but smile just thinking about the upheaval happening in the industry. He thought of G, who he felt could have reacted in a more rational manner in his firing. *Yes*, he thought, he would have had the same reaction had he felt one of his most trusted allies had betrayed him, but it was the *way* G tossed him aside that he'd taken issue with. He was humiliated in front of staff, subordinates, other VPs and the fact that word spread overnight throughout the oil elite.

G, you know I couldn't just tag along for much longer, helping to enrich you and your kingdom. I gave you seven good years of my brilliance and I was beginning to feel disrespected and stifled. There was nowhere else for me to go, so I had to create my own empire, one where the riches would be endless, as long as I was willing to work hard and cut the right deals with the people willing to embrace my vision. I really hope we can bury the hatchet one day, man. No matter what you may think, I still look at you as my brother. We just happened to be rivals on our way up the corporate ladder, reaching for that ultimate rung of wealth, power and success, the kind that only a handful have experienced, but all of us desire. And of course, I plan on getting there with all the admiration and accolades that were bestowed on you as you surfed the oil wave. The only difference is that they'll all be surprised to find out that this time it'll be my little company shifting the industry in this sea change. But hey, knowing you G, I have no doubt you'll come back someday. So let's agree that I just needed a head start so we could begin on a somewhat more even keel. "So, here's to an interesting race," he said, holding up the documents in an improvised toast. "May the strongest, savviest, and handsomest bloke be the last man standing," he finished, expelling a hearty laugh.

CHAPTER 76

ARY left Sonya and Marcus at the restaurant, explaining that she had an afternoon meeting with Dwayne. She felt relaxed having spent time with her family and admitted to herself that although everything had not been resolved with her mother since Brookstone, it felt like a good start. Walking through the hotel lobby, she checked her cell phone for any additional missed calls or texts. *I should probably make the call before heading back to the office,* she concluded, looking around for a quiet, discreet corner. After spotting a large, deep seated wingback chair, enough to provide cover, aided by a white Baby Grand piano, adjacent to the bar, she surmised that because it was still early afternoon, no one would be inclined or inebriated enough to try their hand at playing it, allowing her the time she'd need for what she'd hoped would be a quick conversation.

"Hello?"

"It's Ary Alexander."

"I told you to call me before 11 o'clock."

"Look, you're lucky I'm calling you at all. You were the last person I expected to ever speak to again with all that you've…"

"Just hold on before you start castigating me. I have something I know will be useful to G and quite possibly the *only* chance for saving his company."

"I'm listening," she said, reluctantly, scanning the area for anyone who might be eavesdropping. "What is this about?"

Marguerite told Ary about the plan to take down G and NPI, explaining that she'd tried reaching out to him to no avail. She described her devastation at their breakup but stopped short of disavowing her scheme with Joseph to get rid of Dwayne or express any remorse for her role in it. And as much as she hated Ary, she still loved G and felt her nemesis was her only hope of ever getting him back.

Ary's mouth went dry as Marguerite described all that she knew. She spoke about the Chairman and his longtime hatred of G, falsely accusing him of splitting them up. She explained that there was a man who kept her informed of their plans and her proposed part in it, but that he never revealed his name, number or where he was calling from, always using an untraceable phone. She went on to describe her lack of success in trying to unearth *any* information about him.

"Why now Marguerite? And why me?"

"Because right now, you're one of the only people he fully trusts at NPI. I'm guessing it's because of what you were able to uncover with Joseph. So I have no other choice but to confide in you."

"I still don't understand. You did more than betray G. You actively sought to destroy the life and livelihood of your own brother!"

"*Half*-brother. Robert is my half-brother."

"So you *admit* it?! You admit trying to ruin his life?" she screamed, disregarding where she was. "I don't care if he was your *step-brother*, he's family. You would destroy your own blood just to keep an asinine secret? A secret nobody but you gave two shits about?!"

"You wait one goddamned minute, Ary! Just stop it! You have *no* right to lecture me on who I am or my relationship with my, my *brother*. That is *not* the reason I contacted you. I thought you cared about NPI and G. That's why I asked you to call. I'm pretty sure we've established our utter contempt for one another and for no other reason but this, would I'd ever have reached out to you. So are you willing to help or will you just stand by and watch him lose everything? You need to tell me, because now, since I've told you about the Chairman's plans and you do nothing, *you'll* be complicit in its outcome and we'll *all* be responsible for the destruction of a company he loves more than, well, more than anything."

Ary took the phone away from her ear, placing it on her lap. She covered it with both hands and closed her eyes, shaking her head and looking up towards the ceiling before picking it up again. Taking a deep breath, she steadied her voice and asked, "What do you need me to do?"

CHAPTER 77

AFTER his purchase, Dwayne walked out of the electronics store and decided to stop in the park before heading back to the office. He found a bench and pulled out his little black book of names and addresses. *Glad I never tossed you out or threw you against a wall, even though I guess you'd be pretty durable when it came to moments of total, unanticipated fury*, he snickered. *I guess now's as good a time as any to start replacing my contacts since I've destroyed any way of downloading them from the cloud and onto this new phone.* As he began typing names and numbers, a woman walked up to him unnoticed.

"*Never* did I think I'd see you again."

"Oh wow! Same here. How are you Deidra? Didn't think I'd ever hear from or see you again. Married yet?" he asked, sarcastically.

"What?! Oh, well..." she dragged, "That's kind of over. We decided that it was best to go our separate ways. Sometimes it takes something unexpected to walk into your life before you're able to clearly see the truth."

"Huh?" he asked, completely puzzled. "I thought it took us making love that day to open your eyes to the fact that you'd definitely found the right man, and it sure as hell wasn't me."

"I hope I wasn't that unkind, Dwayne."

"Yeah you were," he laughed. "But I was equally as honest in explaining that I was in a, I guess what you'd call an *evolving* relationship."

"Yes. I do recall you saying something to that effect."

"So you'll forgive me if I seem a little clouded that you'd want anything to do with me."

"How about this? How about we start all over—a fresh start if you will," she suggested. "I'd like to get to know you better—the man—the *real* Dwayne Hargis and I'd like to reveal to you who I am."

"I'd like that," he said, smiling.

"Now, may I sit down?"

"Oh yeah, sure. Forgive me. My mind is racing in fifty different directions."

He moved to the center of the bench, so either way she'd be seated near him.

"What brings you to the city?"

"I'm starting a new job here in a few weeks and decided to take some time to get to know *me* again before I take that leap."

"Ooo-kay. Had you *lost* a part of yourself and did I have anything to do with it?"

She smiled. "Haven't we all? And don't flatter yourself *too* much, Mr. Hargis." They both laughed. "But honestly, I think we get so wrapped up in work, love, life and responsibility that we forget what makes *us* happy. That's one of the reasons I decided to leave the trauma unit at the hospital. I hadn't realized how every gunshot victim, drug overdose, cardiac patient, suicide or auto accident that was transported through the door had begun to take its toll on my own well-being and psyche. I had been internalizing all the pain, guilt, and profound sadness of families losing loved ones and not having the chance to say everything that needed to be said before it was too late," she recounted, tearing up. "That's when I took a long, hard look at myself in the mirror and I didn't recognize the person who was staring back at me. I had become this drone, this thing, the nurse who's so accustomed to and rote at her job that that's what it had become for me, just a job, not a career, not a passion, not a calling. So I knew it was time to make a life change and I broke off my engagement, took a one week, solo trip to St. Lucia and got reacquainted with Deidra Scott."

"Wow! That's deep, courageous and some serious food for thought."

He handed her his pocket handkerchief after noticing her tears.

"Why are you staring at me like that?" she asked, half smiling, half curious.

"Just thinking about a recent trip I took to Greece to do just that—clear my mind. Map out what I wanted to do professionally and figure out what was best for me personally. Like you, asking myself should I stay or move on? A reexamination of my life I guess. But I wound up right where I left off. Nothing's changed. I'm back with all the same questions I had before I left."

"Hey," she said, taking his hand in hers. "Since we seem to be in parallel situations, I'd like to suggest getting together for dinner, if you've fully forgiven me. Maybe if we put two confused heads together, who knows, maybe some reasonable advice could come out of it," she laughed.

"At this point, I don't see how it could hurt."

She squinted her tearful eyes and pouted her full lips in disappointment.

"Oh no! I didn't mean it the way it came out. Please, I'm just having trouble putting together a coherent, meaningful sentence these days. I apologize if I sounded insensitive. It's not what I meant at all, look," he said, pulling his hands away and placing them on top of hers, "if you promise not to reunite with your fiancé before this evening, I'd love it if you'd join me for dinner."

Deidra lowered her head, coyishly smiling.

"How about Cloak & Dagger on 67th and Park at seven-thirty tonight? They know me, so it shouldn't be a problem getting a table."

"Cloak & Dagger it is, Mr. '*Man About Town*'," she laughed.

Looking at her watch, she said, "Oh! It's already three o'clock and if I want to be on time for dinner, I'd better get home and change.

"You're going all the way back to Long Island? Just to change clothes? What's wrong with what you're wearing? Don't answer that. It just goes to show that men will *never* understand women," he laughed.

"I disagree Dwayne. It's not that men don't get us. I truly believe that you guys choose *not* to understand us, because if you did, then you'd be held to an even higher standard of comprehension and responsibility.

"Okay, now you're just screwing with my head."

Deidra kissed him on his cheek, wrote her cell phone number on the back of her previous employer's business card, and turned to leave.

"Hey," he called, causing her to stop abruptly. "Thanks for inexplicably walking back into my life, especially now, when I needed it most."

"It's the universe, man," she joked, winking and walking away.

Dwayne watched until he could no longer distinguish her among the crowd. *Alright universe, it'll all be up to you for the rest of the day and night. I'm not so sure I can handle what I might be walking into.*

CHAPTER 78

SONYA hugged Marcus goodbye and told him again how much she enjoyed spending time with the two most important people in her life. She also assured him that having a candid conversation with Caroline about his feelings and their future marriage was something that should be done as soon as possible. *Don't let the giddiness and excitement of an upcoming celebration cloud the sound judgment of two intelligent people,* she'd told him. *If this is meant to be, there'll be plenty of memorable moments in your lives from the time you commit yourselves to one another in front of those you love, to the joys of raising a beautiful family. But the future is just that—the future. You can't get there if you're not presently on the same course.*

Marcus kissed his mother on her forehead, walked out of the restaurant with his arm snuggly around her shoulders and hailed a taxi for her on the corner of West Broadway. His first inclination was to call Caroline and suggest they meet for dinner later that evening. But he quickly decided that a day or two to absorb the acuity from his mother's words might prove more useful in his argument. Checking the time on his Apple watch, it seemed more reasonable to jump on a subway to his office instead catching a cab. He'd at least get back to his office faster, allowing him to work for at least three or four more hours instead of wasting time in traffic.

CHAPTER 79

ARY felt her heart palpitations increasing. She pushed further back in the chair hoping this was all a bad dream. *How could this be happening?* Everything was supposed to have been worked out for her and Dwayne at NPI. G did, after all, call to offer her job back after the recent fiasco. But it felt eerily familiar and disquieting.

Who can I confide in at this point? she wondered, gathering her belongings and rushing through the hotel. *This is too important to handle alone and I'm not so sure if Darias would be willing to help again, especially after our little misunderstanding in Greece.*

As soon as she stepped off the curbside and raised her hand, a taxi swerved over, nearly sideswiping a car to pick up the leggy beauty. "Wow, that was quick. I don't know if it was because of this dress or from all that practice of hailing cabs for the former Queen of Bitches that finally came in handy," she laughed.

"The Philips building", she instructed as she climbed inside. "5th and 53rd and take the FDR."

As they meandered through start-stop traffic, Ary checked the office calendar on her cell phone. *I'm exhausted,* she thought. *I really just want to get home and crawl underneath my covers and dream away this day.*

"Excuse me, driver. Instead of stopping at the front of the building, please drop me off at the side, between 5th and Madison."

"Yes ma'am."

As he pulled towards the middle of the block, Ary instructed him to stop. She pulled out a twenty dollar bill, declined the receipt and rushed towards the garage entrance, racing to the elevator.

Noticing that it was heading up to the lobby, she decided instead to take the stairs to the lower level, not wanting to chance a meeting with anyone from NPI. *I need to get home and figure out if I want to get involved with this or leave it alone. This might well be over my head.*

Ary made it to her car and immediately called Ann to let her know that for the remainder of the day, she would be working off-site, but of course, available to G and Dwayne by phone.

CHAPTER 80

DWAYNE walked into the office waiting area to a frantic Ann.

"Sweetie, I've been trying to reach you. Mr. Gicardi needs to see you immediately."

"Oh. Sorry, Ann. I ended up having to pick up a new personal phone. Mine stopped working suddenly while I was out, so I just replaced it. And I guess I left my work cell in my office."

"Okay," she said, rising up to lean over the countertop. "But heads up, Connie said he's in a foul mood and not being able to reach you didn't help matters. So be forewarned."

"Hmmm, thanks Ann. I thought our meeting was set for four o'clock?"

"Well it was, but it seems that nothing around here is set in stone anymore, if it ever was. I'm so confused sweetie that all I've been wishing for lately is my vacation time, which can't come soon enough."

"Gotcha. I just came back and feel like I need an extra two weeks," he said, laughing.

Ann winked and promptly returned to her duties.

Dwayne walked around the winding corridor, passing Joseph's empty office, briefly stopping and staring at the closed door, remembering the many meetings they'd had, both productive and excruciating. He took a deep breath and continued on to G's suite. Connie looked up and said, "I'll let him know you're *finally* here."

'Finally here,' he thought. *I'm not the one who changed the damn time, and what's with the attitude?*

"Thanks."

Instead of informing him over the wireless intercom system, Connie got up and walked over to G's door, cautiously knocking and edging it open. "Mr. Hargis is here sir."

"Send him in."

Dwayne was already following behind, startling her, and maneuvering around into the lush suite.

"Pardon me Mr. Hargis!" she said, clearly irritated.

He smiled and winked.

"Hey G, my apologies for not being accessible. As I explained to Ann, my phone…"

"Yeah, yeah, ok," he answered before Dwayne could continue his lie. "Listen, I don't know if you've had a chance to speak with Ary or not…"

"Well, no because as I just *trying* to say, I left my phone…"

"Right, your phone. Well, I did instruct her not to breathe a word about the meeting to anyone, so I guess there's no way you would have heard about the bullshit from BP anyway."

"Uh, I'm a little confused? I really have no idea what you're referring to. I wasn't briefed on the BP meeting this morning, remember? You said we'd catch up at 4 o'clock?"

"Well, let me catch you up now," he offered, obviously still cross.

G told Dwayne about the proposed partnership with T.O.T and its CEO, Dave Winters. He questioned Dwayne about his knowledge of the firm or any of its employees. He explained that he was reluctant to sign the agreement until he could uncover the information he'd need to make a sound judgment on the impending partnership and binding contract.

"So I'm relying on you, and a few others to find out anything relevant about this company, which to me, is suspect, until proven otherwise. I don't want this news to spread across the company Dwayne. I don't want staff jumping to conclusions. And oh, we should probably include Ary as well since she's slated to be the Phase 1 Project Manager. So, let's all meet for dinner tonight at Cloak & Dagger to discuss our strategy. I'll have Connie make arrangements for seven o'clock."

Dwayne could feel his ire mounting. *Phase 1 Project Manager? What the hell? What is my role here anyway? Now is as good a time as any to talk to him. It's either keep up the happy façade or move the fuck on.*

"G, I understand the urgency of the matter, but…"

"No, no you don't," he interrupted. "You weren't there Dwayne. Something nefarious is going on and I'll be damned if I just sit by and let them try and take my company down. So either you want to help save NPI and everything we've all worked our asses off to achieve, or you don't. I'm really sorry Dwayne, but right now I don't have time for '*buts*' or hesitation. Do I make myself clear?"

"Very clear sir." He'd never seen G this angry or confrontational. It wasn't his style. He wanted to talk to Ary before tonight's dinner and he knew he'd need to call Deidra to cancel their plans. "I'll see you tonight at seven, sir."

G turned and walked over to his desk, spoke into the intercom system and said, "Connie, make reservations at Cloak & Dagger for six people at seven. I'll need the private dining room upstairs, no exceptions and no excuses from *anyone*." He spilled out the names of those required to attend.

Dwayne turned back to look at the man who at that moment seemed almost unrecognizable, listening as he rattled off tonight's willing and unwilling attendees, totally unaware that he was still standing there.

Dwayne walked past Connie without saying another word and headed to his office. Pacing for a few minutes before pulling out his new phone, he stared at his unfinished contact list and thought, *Damn, this is some real bullshit.*

Looking at the digital clock on his desk, glaring *3:45pm* in bright blue numbers, offered a visual reminder that time was passing quickly. "First things first," he said, pulling out the business card Deidra had given him. "Let's hope this goes better than the conversation I just had," he said, dialing her number.

CHAPTER 81

ARY sat in the middle of her living room floor with her legs loosely crossed in the quarter lotus meditation position—eyes closed—index fingers and thumbs touching—elbows resting on her knees, listening to the hum of traffic twenty-four floors beneath her. She had recently begun attending yoga classes to help what she'd deemed, *'plugging up her hole-infested center.'* She inhaled and exhaled, trying to concentrate on finding her inner chi. Just as she started to feel the effects of inner peace and calmness, her cell phone, which was placed near the edge of the coffee table and muted, began to vibrate. She opened one eye, stretching her neck to see who was calling. Connie's name displayed on the screen and she knew she'd have to answer.

"Hey Connie, what's up?"

"Hello Ary. G's called a dinner meeting tonight at Cloak & Dagger, 7p.m. sharp and it's mandatory."

"Tonight? Okaaay," she lingered, her brow furling in suspicion. "Who else is invited?"

"There'll be six total," she said, intentionally remaining vague on any specifics.

"Then I'll see him and the *others* tonight, I guess."

"And Ary, I don't think there'll be any valid excuses for not showing up."

"Got it. Thanks." Ary held the phone after disconnecting, thumping it lightly against her temple, wondering if she should try calling G prior to dinner to inform him of her conversation with Marguerite. *I just don't know what to do with this*, she thought. *Could it be a trap for me? Is Marguerite being truthful? This feels like a crime drama I never even auditioned for.*

CHAPTER 82

"HEY Deidra, it's me, Dwayne Hargis," he said, after getting her voicemail. "I'm so sorry but I'll have to take a rain check on our plans tonight. My boss is erupting like a raging volcano and insists on dinner with his management team. So, I'll call you tomorrow and hope you'll still want to talk to me. Goodbye." He hit the end call button, licked his dry lips and decided to go home for the next couple of hours. There was a lot to think about before tonight's meeting. Walking past Ann he said, "I'm out, and this time I'll have *both* cells," he laughed, holding them high above his head.

After making his way uptown in a taxi, he opened the door to his apartment and instantly relaxed. *This feels good*, he thought, kicking off his shoes, slinging his suit coat over a chair, and falling backwards onto his inviting, king-sized bed. "Oh man, am I glad to see you." Spreading his arms in snow angel fashion, he inhaled a long deep breath before exhaling a verbal release. "Whew. You're what I've needed all day."

After twenty minutes, he looked up at the ceiling and thought, *I'm barely back from vacation, haven't had a chance to shoot the breeze with anyone I'd care to share my memorable time away with and already there's commotion at NPI. And this time, it doesn't involve Joseph. I never thought I'd admit it, but somehow I wish he and the 'B' were still here to calm G down. I've never had to do it on my own and this'll certainly be a test—a test I'm not so sure I can pass alone.*

CHAPTER 83

AFTER getting off the train and settling in her car at the commuter parking lot, Deidra checked her phone for any missed calls or voicemails. She'd left it in her handbag and turned it to vibrate while in transit, preferring to sit in the quiet car and ponder her evening with Dwayne. After listening to the message he'd left, all she could say was, "Well that's disappointing." But instead of changing her plans, she called a few friends who lived in the city, determining that it would be less of a hassle to meet on such short notice and invited them to dine. *Why sit home and waste a perfectly beautiful evening when I had my heart set on going out?* she reasoned. *This is, after all, me challenging myself and growing into a better, more fulfilled human being."*

"You're the best," she said, feeling relieved after landing one friend's availability. "And there'll be no arguments, dinner and drinks are on me, and yes, I plan on having more than a few," she joked.

CHAPTER 84

G sat at the head of the elaborately set, round table, dressed in a dark designer suit and perfectly coiffed hair, reminiscent of any number of Godfather scenes. He watched as his staff arrived, one by one, greeting him with a head nod or a light pat on the back or shoulder. Ary was the last to arrive, at 6:59pm. She'd chosen a dark blue, wide striped Basler pantsuit, complimented by a pink silk blouse with a plunging neckline and Alexander Wang suede ankle strap four inch sandals. Her make-up was flawless, complimented by peach colored lipstick and an intentionally messy, windswept hairstyle crowning her face. Looking around at the table of five men, she knew she'd have to be on her 'A' game.

"Good evening G. Gentlemen," she nodded, choosing to take the seat next to Dwayne, even though there was another empty seat closer to her CEO.

As G rose, the others followed suit.

"I've called this meeting," he said, slowly taking his seat, "because I've come to believe that a hostile takeover of NPI has begun."

The men gasped. Ary held a steady gaze.

"And, as all of you who know me well, knows that is not something I would allow to happen. So I've contacted my West Coast allies to find out as much as possible about this firm, The Oil Trust, or as it's better known, T-O-T and its CEO, a Mr. Dave Winters. But so far, nothing unscrupulous about him or his firm has been uncovered. They've been working on small oil and gas contracts for almost two years with an employee base of roughly six to eight and only two principals—Winters and one other guy.

But Winters seems to be the one who's out front for most of their deals and it seems that because they have such a small staff, they outsource anything they can't handle locally. But what I can't understand is why would any reputable firm here or out West trust relative newcomers to handle multi-million dollar contracts? Why would BP, of all the giants, award them this particular contract? I get why they'd want NPI in the loop—to keep T-O-T from fucking up, but is that all? That's the question I'll need all of you to answer within a relatively short period of time."

"What do you consider a 'short period of time,' G?" Dwayne asked.

"Three weeks, tops," he answered brusquely. "The board is expecting a signed agreement between the two firms and an executed contract shortly after that, so that doesn't give us much time at all," he said, gauging the faces around the table. "Look, I know this all sounds suspicious, bizarre even, I agree. But never in my wildest dreams did I think something like this would happen so soon. You always expect, if you're a successful firm to be presented with a buyout, sure—but on your own terms. It's not like we were drowning and needed to be bailed out. No, this came without warning, a complete surprise, more like a shock." He looked over at Ary and said, "You were there, what was your take on the announcement? Did you notice anyone's expressions when it was first made? I'm a true believer that someone's body language can tell you more truth than any lies that come out of their mouths." The men nodded with nonverbal head shaking. Ary took a sip of sparkling water, then looked at Dwayne, whose eyes had only briefly turned away from her while listening to G.

"I need to speak to you in private, G."

The room erupted in loud fits of, *Whaaat? What's going on?*

"Please! Please! Gentlemen, everybody calm down." Only he and Dwayne had kept their composer. A waiter walked into the private space and asked if they were ready to order. G ushered him over, whispering instructions in his ear.

"Listen, I'll need you all, except for Ary, to follow the waiter downstairs to the members only barroom. Drinks of course are on me and I'll call you back up in just a little while."

Ary watched as each man pushed back from the table, looking at her as they began filing out of the room. As Dwayne rose to leave, Ary said, "G, I'd prefer if he stayed, if that's okay with you?"

Pursing his lips, and considering it for a quick second, he said, "Yes, of course. It's fine."

Dwayne looked at G, then Ary, and slowly sat down in his chair. The other men looked back towards the dining room, shaking their heads as another waiter closed the curtained double doors.

"What is it Ary?" he asked, breathing deeply and placing his clasped hands and elbows on the table. "Tell me everything you know."

Dwayne turned his chair slightly towards her, steadying himself for what might be a bombshell, all the while hoping he wouldn't be speciously involved or implicated.

Ary told G about her inexplicable conversation with Marguerite, stressing that she was just as shocked to hear from her as anyone might be after all that had happened.

"The Chairman!" he yelled, pounding his fists on the table, causing a few glasses to tumble to the floor. Ary flinched. Dwayne remained steady. "That fucking bastard! I always knew he hated me, but I figured it was just personal, because of her. And now, to try and take over or destroy NPI? It has to be more to it than the fact that she chose me over of him. That's what we have to unearth. I know for certain he wouldn't jeopardize his place on the board because of a lost relationship. It's not his way of operating. Look, he's an extremely powerful board member, well-liked by most, feared for his ruthlessness by others. I've always had a cordial relationship with him, despite the issues with her. But how did she become involved in this? My understanding from her was that they hadn't spoken to or seen each for years after the breakup, so none of this makes any sense."

Ary and Dwayne noticed that G had only referred to Marguerite as *'she'* or *'her'*. They could both identify with feelings of mistrust and betrayal, and not wanting to have a relationship with someone who'd deliberately hurt you. But this was different. Marguerite was reaching out, trying to help in whatever way she could. Ary rationalized that it must have taken a healthy dose of humility for Marguerite to even call her and ask for help, especially from someone she'd recently considered her mortal female archrival. She knew it was going to take G swallowing his pride and checking his ego at the door if he wanted to get to the bottom of it all and save his company. And she was keenly aware she wouldn't be able to convince him on her on.

"G, I agreed to meet Marguerite next Sunday at two o'clock."

"Where?" he asked, anxiously.

"Uh, I'd rather not say right now."

G's brow furled. Dwayne's eyes widened.

"Why not, Ary?"

"I promised I wouldn't tell anyone, not even you, G. The truth is, she wants you back and she's not sure how to..."

"What!" he interrupted. "That'll happen once hell freezes over!"

"G," Dwayne interrupted. "No matter how you feel about what went down, remember, it wasn't Marguerite who was trying to destroy NPI. For all intents and purposes, she was once your partner. And no matter how much she and I disagreed on *most* things, well, just about *everything*," he laughed, trying to inject some lightness into a heavy conversation, "she believed in your vision for NPI, as we all do. But her belief was deeper than what we felt, G. You were at the center of it all. I truly believe that there was nothing she wouldn't have done for you. And yes, she fucked up with the ethnicity B.S., but Marguerite was dealing with a generation that wasn't so tolerant of his fellowman and their brown or black skin, or in your case Ary, a mixture of black, brown and sweet cream," he said, winking.

"I *beg* your pardon!"

"Look," he continued seriously, "In today's hotbed of racial animosity, who knows what she was going through, especially in an industry that, if we're completely honest G, is not the most tolerant here in the states.

"I see your point Dwayne. But I'm not there yet. I'm not ready to forgive."

"That's understandable. But I think we should let this play out with Ary getting as much information as she can so you'll be able to strategically put all the pieces in place and decide how you want to proceed. G, we all want to do our part in watching NPI eventually take its rightful place at the top, and this is precisely why I'm backing Ary in keeping her promise to meet Marguerite, alone, at an undisclosed location.

Ary couldn't take her eyes off him. Dwayne was confident, eloquent, decisive and convincing. This was the man she'd come to know and respect. It was also the man she'd wished she could freely love. *He was standing up to G, of all people!* she thought, passing on advice and wisdom to a man who up until recently, had only relied on the final words of his two senior executives. He never looked sexier, she thought, with his grey Theory suit and tieless sky blue shirt, opened just beneath the hollow of his neck. She felt her body responding to every word being pushed from his liberal lips. Forcing her attention back to G, she waited for his response.

"Okay. Let's go with that and reconvene with a conference call after your meeting with her."

Ary exhaled, Dwayne turned to her and smiled, and G got up to push a button near the door, summoning a waiter who entered the room immediately.

"Send up two bottles of Cristal, a crystal of Royal Ossestra caviar, and a tray of antipasto. Have the men return as well," he said, sounding like the decisive, confident CEO they both knew and admired.

Ary tried to figure out a way to excuse herself, hoping that Dwayne was entertaining a similar thought. How could she make her intentions known without arousing the suspicions of the others, or G?

As the men paraded back into the dining room, beverages in hand, looking nervously towards Ary and Dwayne, she walked over to G, whispered in his ear and bade everyone a good night, lingering a moment to glance in Dwayne's direction.

"I'll walk you out," he said, accepting her cue. "Excuse me G, I'll be right back."

CHAPTER 85

DWAYNE quickly caught up with her as she stood at the door of the elevator, lightly grabbing her elbow and said, "So you knew all about this? The mysterious meeting with BP—which didn't include me? You were aware that there was a takeover attempt?"

"Were you *not* just in the room?" she countered, watching the elevator door open and close without her. "That's precisely why I asked for you to stay Dwayne. I can't go through another NPI drama by myself. This is getting to be too much. I can't even do my job without some nonsense happening every other week. How are we supposed to make a living or a difference when..."

Before she could finish, Dwayne leaned in, pressing his lips hard against hers, not caring about who might see them.

"Dwayne what are you doing!?" she whispered, pushing him away. "This is neither the time nor place to..."

Wrapping his arm around her waist, he pulled her into his chest. "Meet me at my apartment. Here, take my keys," he ordered, putting them in her hands. "If you don't show up, there'll be no way for me to get in. I'll be there in an hour."

"I, I don't remember your..."

"427 West 96th street, 10th floor, apartment 16. In *one* hour." He turned away before she could object and joined the others for champagne and hors d'oeuvres.

Ary stood there, looking towards the dining room, waiting for him to reappear, tell her that he was only joking. She stared at the keys in her hands then walked the short distance to a door that lead to the stairwell. As she reached the main floor, opening to the large dining room, the maître d' asked if there was something he could do for her. "No, I have to make this decision on my own."

He watched as she made her way through the restaurant and out the exit door. Standing outside near the curb, she checked her watch, waived away two taxis and wasn't bothered by the people angling around her to catch the cabs she'd dismissed. She didn't move. She stood there for a minute or two more, finally deciding to walk an extra city block, hoping for some insight on what to do. As much as her body insisted she needed him, her conscience cautioned her against it. She needed to concentrate on her upcoming meeting with Marguerite. But before she could think another thought, she stepped off the sidewalk and yelled, "Taxi!"

CHAPTER 86

DWAYNE listened as G informed the others on what his next steps for protecting NPI were, but his attention had left with Ary. He thought of her waiting for him at home. Every ten minutes he checked the time on his watch, telling a colleague who'd jokingly asked if he'd had somewhere else he'd rather be, that he was checking for an important email. Dwayne quickly consumed two glasses of champagne and a plate full of anti-pasto and caviar. He declined when G asked if he were ordering a full meal from the menu, explaining that in addition to the work required for NPI, he wanted to check on his parents before it got too late.

"Family first, Dwayne," he said, wishing him a good night.

Trying not to arouse any further suspicions, Dwayne walked around the table, patting each guy on their shoulders. "Hey man, it was good to see you. Enjoy the rest of this delicious food." After all the informal discourse, he walked out of the dining room and into the waiting elevator. "Perfect timing sir," a waiter standing nearby said.

"Yeah, let's hope so."

CHAPTER 87

HE watched as a few cabs passed him by, thinking, *I don't need this racist bullshit tonight.*

A black Town car raced over to the curbside a few minutes later and he jumped in. "Listen, I'm on West 96th Street and I know how much the fare should be, so if you're thinking of trying to jip me, I'll get out right now."

"No sir, not at all," the meterless driver answered. "From here, twenty dollars, flat fee sir. Only twenty dollars."

"Let's go."

As his car angled through traffic, Deidra and her girlfriend were getting out of a cab just a few blocks away. "I was curious about the restaurant he'd offered to take me, but there were no open reservations, so they recommended their sister location," she explained, looking up at the eatery. "I just hope there's enough interesting men and colorful cocktails in here to take my mind off calling him and loudly expressing my disappointment," she laughed.

"In other words, cussing his ass out!" her girlfriend said, laughing and pulling her towards the eatery. "C'mon, let's think of it as a further cleansing of the mind and soul. Besides, who needs *that* man when there's top shelf liquor, good food and hopefully some fine, *available* men waiting inside?!"

"You are *soooo* right!" Deidra giggled. "So let's kick start this rite-of-self-empowerment, my friend!" They locked arms, strutted ten steps in their six-inch heels and walked into the restaurant where a few men waiting for tables with their wives or girlfriends had to be summarily reminded that they were not alone by intense stares, swift tugs on their lapels, and stern whispers.

"This is gonna be *so* much fun!" Deidra whispered to her devilishly smiling companion.

CHAPTER 88

DWAYNE paid his fare and tipped the driver another ten dollars for his honesty. Realizing he'd also given Ary the key to the lobby door, he rushed to catch it as a couple exited. "Hold the door please, hold it! Thanks." Sprinting towards the elevator his heart pounded against his chest, not from lack of exercise, but from want of what he imagined awaited him. *She looked so beautiful tonight,* he thought. *I just can't seem to shake the overwhelming feeling I get whenever she's around. And the added fact that she's a kick-ass business-woman in a male dominated industry just makes her even more attractive.* Stepping aside as a few familiar faces walked out from the elevator and sharing some evening pleasantries, he pushed number 10 on the panel and reminded himself to, *pull it together dude, and don't be so transparent in your feelings for her. She respects strength and power and you my friend have a lock on that shit,* he grinned.

Dwayne walked around to his apartment and rang the door-bell. *This feels strange,* he thought, waiting on the other side of his own door for someone to let him in. He waited a few moments, looked around the hallway when he heard voices then rang it again. *Hmmm, that's weird.*

He tapped the door a few times with his knuckles—still no answer. *What's going on?* Pulling out his cell phone to call her, he realized that he hadn't yet replaced all of his personal contacts from his smashed phone. Unleashing a loud sigh and knocking again, harder this time, he leaned his forehead against the door. *Maybe she's in the shower.* He checked his watch and decided to give her a couple more minutes. He was pacing the hallway when a neighbor, two doors down emerged from an apartment and began walking near him. "Hey Dwayne, how you doing?"

"Good, man. How are you?"

"Great. You okay? Are you locked out?"

"Hope not," he laughed.

Not exactly sure what Dwayne meant, he thought best not to press the issue. "Alright then, enjoy your evening."

"You too," he said, growing more anxious.

Waiting for his neighbor to disappear around the corridor, he pushed his ear against the door, listening for any signs of movement. There were none, not even running water. Now he pounded on the door. *Are you ever gonna learn that she enjoys twisting your fuckin' balls man?* "Damn!" he yelled.

Not sure what to do or where he'd stay tonight, he began walking away, stopping suddenly when he heard a door unlock, and instinctively turning around. Who he saw was Ary, barefoot, standing just over the threshold, wearing only a sheer, gold colored bra and thong, gently swinging a bottle of wine from side to side. His eyes widened. He put his hands in his pockets and strolled towards her with the swagger only certain men possess, stopping at the entrance, meeting her equally penetrating gaze, and said, "Follow me."

CHAPTER 89

DWAYNE walked straight into the bedroom, took off his suit jacket, tossed it onto a 19th Century leather and fabric covered English club chair and turned to face her. She watched as he unbuttoned his shirt, offering to help by placing her hands on top of his. He pushed them away and instead, ordered her to unbutton her bra while still facing him. Drawing her into his arms, she closed her eyes and felt his throbbing manhood against her. Her knees weakened, he held her up, kissing her neck beneath the soft stands of hair resting against her shoulders. He spun her around. She tried turning back—he wouldn't let her. This time, he was in control. Holding onto to her, he caressed her breasts with one hand, unbuckled his belt and unzipped his pants with the other. He listened to her moan as he freed himself from the clothes that restricted their intimate contact. She reached around and held onto his hard, bare buttocks as he grabbed hold of her hands, placing them up and around his neck while he used his fingers to stimulate her. She screamed his name, "Dwayne, take me."

"First tell me that you're mine," he demanded.

"I am, Dwayne, I am."

As her hips swiveled in circular motions, she pressed firmly against his fully erected manhood. His mind soared beyond the confines of his bedroom. Lifting her up by the waist, he lowered them both onto the bed, positioning her onto his torso, where, facing away from him, she glided slowly, back and forth, holding onto his well-developed thighs, leaving traces of heated fluids of desire. He felt his body tremble. She turned to capture the expression on his face and whispered, "Not yet." Rolling onto her knees and tilting her head, she used her glimmering eyes as a guide to ecstasy. Accepting her silent cue, Dwayne entered from behind, thrusting gently at first then harder and deeper as she let out a rapturous moan.

"Yessss Dwaaayne!"

At that moment, she was all that he envisioned in his world. "Ahhhhhh!!!!!!," he yelled, collapsing onto her, careful of his full body weight before rolling onto his back.

After a few moments, she turned over and tapped him on the shoulder, whispering seductively, "My turn."

He smiled, summoned his expended strength, spread apart her long, lithe, shapely legs, and allowed his tongue to take the lead this time. Starting from the center of her glistening breasts, teasing her nipples with passionate kisses and gentle tugs, intensifying her delicate dance of desire, he nudged her legs even further apart with only his forehead and stimulated her womanhood with the skill and precision of a master painter, brushing his tongue up and down, and side to side, watching as her firm belly rose and fell to his expertise.

"Oh, oh, oh, Dwaaayne!" she called out repeatedly, until an intensely passionate eruption prevented any further words. As he rose to meet her, she curled up into his embrace as they both fell silent into the night.

CHAPTER 90

MATTHEW finalized the surprise party plans with the event coordinator, after being convinced to make it a more intimate setting instead of the one hundred people he'd discussed at their first meeting.

"So we're good now, right?" he laughed.

"Yes, finally! And the fact that you managed to keep it a secret from that very nosey man of yours is no small feat, Matthew."

"You're telling me! All he ever says is, '*I hope you're not planning some big birthday bash because I'm not so sure turning sixty is something I want shouted out from the rooftops.*' So, of course I've had to lie a little, which as you know, I'm not very good at."

"No worries. All is well in the world of party planning and a little fibbing just makes it all the more exciting! Oh, there is *one* small detail I need to discuss before I let you go."

"Sure, what's that?"

"I've gotten thirty-eight *yeses out* of the fifty invites so far, which is a great response! However, none of those are from his ex-wife or children."

Matthew sighed, his chin dropping down to his chest in disappointment. "Well, I don't consider that a *small* detail, but we still have a few more days before the RSVP expires right?"

"True."

"So let's not count them out before then. I really hope they make it. It would mean a lot to him, to us, to have them there. It'd be the icing on the cake, so to speak, especially after the meeting we had at Sonya's house in New York. I felt at least she and Marcus were prepared to look past the pain and self-prescribed suffering, and finally focus on the future. But I especially hoped Ary would consider coming. Her father isn't getting any younger, none of us are," he laughed. "And I know there's nothing more he'd want than to have the love, respect and a new relationship with his daughter."

"I so agree with you Matthew. Do you want me to nudge them, just a tiny bit?"

"No. I only want them to come if they're willing. But thank you for all you've done. I know it'll be a memorable occasion for everyone."

CHAPTER 91

SONYA arrived early Saturday evening at the gallery for her showing. She was nervous. It had been some time since she'd had a major event and there were very influential buyers, gallery owners and philanthropists from the art world that had been invited tonight along with a throng of everyday art lovers from the tri-state as well as friends and unknown fans. Sipping on a glass of Perrier Jouet Fleur de Champagne, she walked around the venue with the gallery owner and artistic director, checking lighting; positioning; distance; and placement, making sure nothing had been changed from her initial discussion and walkthrough. Satisfied, she could now just sit back and wait for the exhibition to begin. She waited in the artist's quarters—a spacious room resembling a posh hotel suite. She was delighted to have a floor length mirror where she was able to take another look at her dress, a gift sent by a childhood friend from Harlem who'd moved to Dubai years before it became fashionably overrun by 21st century, oil-rich millionaires and billionaires of the Royal Emirati families. Warm memories conjured up a welcomed smile. The dress was a long sleeved, low back design by Zahair Murad, with a flesh colored bodice, and prints of thin, tree-limb veins covering the silk blue overlay. Her friend wanted her to have something special for tonight's event, something to remember her by, knowing she wouldn't be able to make it to the states due to her own private showing for a member of the Royal family in Ryiadh, Saudi Arabia.

Sonya looked almost ten years younger than her 53 years and as elegant as any red carpet celebrity. She felt a newfound confidence and a sense of empowerment as well as extreme pride in the artistic works she'd created.

As guest began arriving, she peeked out from the room to see if Ary and Marcus had come in. She'd asked that they come early to join her for a special toast to what she'd hoped would be a strong resurgence of her domestic showings, and a successful launching of her global presence. After years of working with the same agency and manager, she was convinced, several months ago that a change was needed. An agency recommendation by her friend in Dubai pushed her creative buttons—insisting she go outside her comfort zone while offering a new perspective on personal growth and expansion and persuading her to dig deeper into her personal life to release the pain she'd experienced, putting it on canvas or in a sculptured piece. Reluctantly, she submitted to the challenge. Her new creations were shockingly bold. She sensed her God-given, inner talents broadening beyond anything she'd attained before or what she'd become known for in New York City circles. As the adrenaline started to flow closer to show time, the door to her private waiting room opened suddenly and Ary walked in with Dwayne at her side. This was her first time meeting him, and aside from the initial surprise of seeing him there, it was alarming how much he reminded her of Bruce. He was tall, dark, handsome and commanded attention as he walked in the room. He was impeccably dressed, wearing a dark blue, Hugo Boss two-button trim fit tuxedo with a contrasting silk notch lapel, a white, single button French cuff shirt and a blue silk bowtie. Reflecting the bright overhead lights were his black patent leather Italian made oxfords.

She held a steady gaze for a moment before turning to her stunningly attired daughter. Ary wore a couture design by Duro Olowu. The gold flared, strapless silhouette, with a full pleated skirt and tulle underlay swathed her petite frame as if it were designed specifically for her. Streaks of bright yellow and muted white lines, peaking from between the folds were interwoven throughout the dress. She'd chosen nude velvet, three-inch, ankle strapped heels by Raye of New York, not only for their style and beauty, but because of the comfort they would afford during an extended evening.

"Hi mom, congratulations!" her smiling daughter said as she walked over for a light hug. You look stunningly beautiful!"

"Thank you, love. So do you and your guest."

"Oh sorry! This is Dwayne Hargis, my brilliant boss who so graciously, and on such short notice, agreed to be my plus-one for this very special occasion."

Sonya extended her hand for him to shake. He instead took hold of her fingertips, lightly kissing the top of her hand.

"It's my pleasure to meet you Mrs. Alexander. And although we quickly made our way through the gallery, Ary pointed out some of your pieces, and may I say, they're as beautiful and impressive as the artist herself."

Sonya smiled. "Thank you Dwayne. I appreciate your kind words." Turning back to Ary, she beamed. "You two look like President Obama and the First Lady hosting a State dinner."

"Thank you, but this is your night mama. And they did a wonderful job in staging the space. But knowing you, most of it was your brainchild!" she laughed. "Marcus isn't here yet, I see."

"Not yet. I thought maybe he was coming with you."

"Nope. I haven't seen or spoken to him since we had breakfast the other day. I'd assumed he would have been here before me. He does live in the city now after all—what, twenty or thirty minutes away by train, right?"

Both Sonya and Dwayne looked at her, detecting a scornful tone.

Sonya's agent knocked at that precise moment summoning her to the crowd of excited guests. Dwayne curved his arms, offering them as a gentlemanly gesture to the ladies and said, "Please, it would be an honor if I could escort two brilliantly talented and beautiful women this evening."

The ladies, taking hold of each arm, emerged into the gallery to a lengthy chorus of '*oh wow,*' '*beautiful,*' '*fabulous,*' and '*what an entrance,*' emanating throughout the space. Sonya tried hard to hold back tears of joy. *If only Marcus were here*, she thought, *this would have indeed been the perfect start to a new beginning.* Dwayne stopped in the middle of the room, first looking over at Sonya, tipping his head as a cue to release his arm, then turning to a smiling Ary who wrapped her free arm even tighter around the one she was already holding onto, leaving Sonya to be formerly introduced to her waiting admirers. As they mingled among the many guests, Dwayne, unaware of Deidra standing on the far side of the room, whispered to Ary how proud he was to have been a part of something so important to both she and her mother, then gently kissed her cheek. Deidra stood there, witnessing it all, frozen in disbelief.

CHAPTER 92

MARCUS left several voicemail messages asking Caroline to call.

Listening to all of them, she'd convinced herself that not answering was the right thing to do until she felt absolutely sure that he loved her for who she was and who he was, independent of being connected through her uncle and certainly not as a way to prove to his father, once and for all that he was a heterosexual man capable of loving and marrying a woman. She'd refused to be a patsy in an Alexander fabrication.

CHAPTER 93

BEGINNING to worry that G still hadn't reached out to him or his firm about the partnership agreement—that he was intentionally procrastinating, trying to ride out the clock by not signing the contract, Dave requested a three-way call between himself, Joseph and Lawrence. He'd wondered if there had been a breech and wanted to get to the bottom of it before anything or anyone was exposed.

"What's up, Dave? I'm here with Lawrence. We got your voicemail. You sounded alarmed."

"'*What's up*' is that he hasn't signed the fucking papers yet and my sources are telling me that he's snooping around, asking questions about T.O.T."

"Did you really think that John G. Gicardi, the consummate businessman was going to enter into a partnership without a thorough screening of the firm he's being forced into? Really, Dave?" Joseph asked, sarcastically, looking over at Lawrence.

"Hell no, I didn't think that. But I also didn't anticipate the Chairman wanting a bigger cut of the deal either."

Joseph's frustration was on full display. "What the hell are you talking about?"

"I got a call from my cousin yesterday telling me that he'd had a conversation with the Chairman about the transaction and that he'd pointed out his retirement next year, wanting to make sure that his '*flow of funds,*' as he likes to refer to it, from T.O.T as well as his other business holdings would be secure with no '*fuck-ups*' until the day he died."

"Dave it's me, Lawrence. Listen, I've known the Chairman for a number of years and to me, that would seem a bit out of character. I mean, this man is no novice when it comes to manipulating substantial deals like this one. If I were you, I'd be wondering who else on your side, family or not, was pressuring the Chairman for a more generous slice of '*prosperity pie.*'"

"Are you insinuating that my cousin is involved in some sort of double dealing? Because if you are…"

"Whoaaa…man, calm down. I'm not implying anything. But think about it, he's all of a sudden demanding more money when he already has more than he'll ever be able to spend in two or three lifetimes! It just doesn't make sense."

"Then who could…?" Dave started, before Joseph interrupted, not being able to hold his tongue any longer.

"Look Dave, when we brought you on board, it was because of your inside connections. Truthfully, we really could have done this shit on our own."

"What the fuck are you saying, Joseph? Are you saying you don't need me or my company now?"

"Hold on gentlemen," Lawrence interrupted, fielding what could have turned into a contentious play. "Let's not let our tempers flare or soaring egos get in the way here. I'm sure there's a simple explanation to this. We agreed that both firms were needed to pull this off. Are we back-peddling on that now because there's been an unexpected bump in the road? This is a partnership, remember? And partnerships require trust, coordination and extraordinary patience."

"Two of which are quickly eroding," Joseph countered.

"Oh, is that right Joseph? Are you saying you don't *trust* me now because I brought up a legitimate concern? And that you're running out of patience with my timing on this project?"

"I don't know what I'm fuckin' saying. But there's one thing I *do* know unequivocally, and that is, this deal will get done, one way or another, the way it was *originally* agreed upon, with *no* mid-season changes in the line-up, with or without you. Do I make myself clear?"

Dave was livid. He wasn't used to anyone talking to him in such a manner and he wasn't about to allow it now. "Lawrence, let me suggest that you have a conversation with your partner about *trust* and *patience* before we go any further and I'll call you back this evening."

Joseph disconnected the call.

"Was that really necessary?" Lawrence asked.

"I'm getting a bad feeling about this Lawrence. I need a moment. Maybe we should reconsider this so-called partnership with this fucking fool."

Lawrence could only stare. He'd trusted Joseph not only for his business savvy, but as a friend he'd known for over a decade. But he also knew this wasn't a deal to walk away from and that right now, whether Joseph was in agreement or not, Dave Winters held the keys to all the doors that needed opening to be able to take their firm to the next level.

"Don't sabotage this Joseph. I know he can be difficult sometimes, even irrational, we knew this going in. But his relationship with the Chairman is crucial to us being able to fund the second phase of our own venture. So no matter what, don't let your feelings about Dave get in the way of what *we're* trying to do here. Like it or not man, we need him and we might just have to play by his rules until this deal is done. And remember, it was *you*, not *me* who was convinced that he'd be a useful addition to this project."

"Yeah, a useful *tool* it turns out." He swallowed hard and conceded. "Listen, I know you're probably right, but this little guy is really working on my nerves, Lawrence. But hey, I understand we need this cash infusion to begin the off-shore drilling. So I'll keep that in mind and visualize it every time we speak with or meet with that obnoxious, pompous, little creep."

"Joseph!"

"Sorry. I meant to say that affable and trustworthy collaborator we've enlisted to assist us in exploring lucrative opportunities."

Lawrence shook his head and said, "I know things are a bit stressful now, but it's all coming to a head and we're sure to benefit from any bullshit we have to endure in the interim."

"Well, let's hope so man. In the meantime we both have serious work to do and a relatively short timeframe to get it done."

"Agreed."

CHAPTER 94

IT had been a memorable, yet exhausting night and all Sonya wanted to do after the celebrations, congratulations, adulations and invitations were over was to go home, enjoy a cup of soothing green tea and relax in her cozy bed. She was grateful to have been provided car service to and from the gallery—a luxury her former agency had never provided without a fuss. As the driver made his way, weaving in and out of New York City traffic and onto the Long Island Expressway towards Brookstone, she found herself smiling, thinking about her daughter and how beautiful she looked and happy she seemed to be on the arm of a handsome man of color. This had been what she'd wanted, always skeptical whenever Ary discussed her 'relationships' with non-black men. Were they only curious about sex with a beautiful black woman, giving in to the stereotypes of a racialized society? Or was she looked upon as a novelty because of her privileged upbringing and uncompromising intelligence? Although she didn't know the extent of Ary and Dwayne's relationship, and dating her boss wasn't something she would have advised for her willful oldest child, she did, however, feel it was better than the past few men Ary had been involved with and had professed her love for. Sonya also knew not to say too much, too soon, simply because doing so in the past seemed to have caused Ary to further dig in her designer heels, just to prove her mother wrong.

A sudden chill crossed over her body as she thought of Marcus. He hadn't shown up or called. She'd expressed her concern to Ary who tried convincing her not to let him ruin her night. *This is all about you, mama,* she'd said. *You haven't had an opening like this in a while. Relish in it. These people have spent a pretty penny to come and support you. Reap the benefits of your hard work. And as always, you make me proud to be the daughter of Sonya Dodd-Alexander,'* she'd finished, combining Sonya's maiden name with the name she had yet to surrender.

I know I shouldn't worry, she thought. *But as a mother, I don't have the luxury of an 'on-off' switch when it comes to my children, grown or not. No responsible parent does. But I also know she's right, even when it's her who's causing my anguish,* she laughed. *So, I'll put it out of my head, if only for tonight and call him tomorrow morning.* Sonya leaned back against the soft leather seat of the limo, exhaled, and closed her eyes. The GPS instructed to driver to take the next exit into the township of Brookstone.

CHAPTER 95

MARCUS sat in the darkness of the family room, waiting for his mother. He was groggy and tired, but knew he had to stay awake. This was a conversation that couldn't wait.

CHAPTER 96

ARY led Dwayne seductively from the elevator down the hallway to her apartment, unraveling and pulling his bowtie, watching as he playfully pretended to pull away, ducking and weaving like Sugar Ray Leonard. After opening the door, she placed her handbag and keys on the table in the foyer and pointed to the tufted chair in the living room. But as he began to sit, she grabbed his broad shoulders, causing him to abruptly stand back up. He was confused—she wasn't. She forcefully pushed him down into the chair, walked over to the four-tiered shelving unit, turned on Robin Thicke's, *'Lost Without You'*, and returned to him, spreading his legs apart. She stood between them, her eyes fixated on his wistful stare and reached behind her back, slowly unzipping her dress. He watched with intensity as it fell seemingly in slow motion down to the carpeted floor exposing her nude, strapless bra, matching bikini panties and thigh-high, flesh colored stockings. Carefully lifting each shapely leg out from her dress, she held up one designer heel, resting it on the edge of the chair, waiting for him to unbuckle and slip it off, and then repeated the ritual with the other. His breathing intensified. Using her strength and training from years of ballet, she lifted her arms above her head, clasping her hands in a praying pose and slowly turned around on her tiptoes, unpinning her hair so that it fell to the rhythm of her movements, coming to rest across her shoulders. She looked down at him, playfully using her eyes to indicate that he should unclasp her bra. With all the patience he could muster, fighting against the natural urges of a man, he rose from the chair, removed her bra with his tongue and teeth, caressed her generous breasts, and waited for further direction. She moaned—he shuttered. As she began swiveling her curvaceous hips to the tune of the music, he nearly tore off his tuxedo jacket and shirt, eager to infuse his burning flesh with hers. She backed away, continuing her provocative dance, relishing in the agony of his desire.

"Tell me how much you want me," she whispered in his ear.

Without a single word, mesmerized by her séduisant danse (seductive dance), he swooped her up into his arms, took her to the bedroom, looked deeply into her eyes and said, "We will never forget this night."

CHAPTER 97

AS the door swung open, Sonya flinched and gasped at the shadow cast off by the light left on at the far end of the foyer. "Oh my God!" she screamed.

"Don't be afraid," he said, it's just me. I turned off the alarm."

"Marcus!" she cried out, her hands placed firmly on her chest." You nearly gave me a heart attack!"

"I'm sorry mama. I probably should have called to let you know I was coming, but I wasn't even sure where I was driving when I got behind the wheel," he said, rising up to greet her with a kiss on each cheek."

"What's wrong? Why didn't you come to the opening? Why are you here, honey?"

He walked around in circles, appearing lost in his childhood home, stopping only to watch his mother who was watching him. He put his hands in his pockets and pulled them out. He licked his lips and brushed over his hair with one hand, then two. He started to speak, halting in mid-sentence, all while Sonya grew increasingly nervous and anxious. And just as she felt forced to break the unbearable silence, he interrupted and said, "Mama, I'm gay."

CHAPTER 98

SONYA'S knees buckled, but she managed to break the fall, holding on to the nearby sofa. She looked over at her son and began to cry. He walked over and held her steady—staring into her eyes he said, "Don't cry mama, don't cry. It's okay."

She leaned into his embrace, silent, her head resting against his chest as a steady flow of tears fell between her designer gown and his black polo shirt. Her shoulders hunched up and down as he rubbed her back and kissed her hair, allowing her to release the pain and sorrow he felt he'd caused, all the while praying there wouldn't be a repeat scene of his announcement to marry Caroline just a few months before. His eyes welled up as he tried hard to prevent any tears from falling.

"Mama, I let something happen tonight," he began, his voice cracking as he tried to explain. "Something I'm sure I could have prevented but chose not to, and I feel ashamed and embarrassed. I couldn't bring myself to face you or Ary at the gallery, which is why I didn't call or show up. It just happened mama—it wasn't planned.

Sonya backed away, leaving only a few inches between them. She looked up at her son, wiped the tears from her eyes and said, "You're my son Marcus, and my love for you is unconditional. I'm not the woman I was thirteen years ago and you're not the man I thought I was marrying. I brought you into this world to live the life of your own choosing and I hope I've learned at this stage of my own life, that once your children are adults, the only thing you can wish and hope for is that they make responsible choices, realizing the impact those choices will have on themselves and anyone else they may get involved with."

As she backed further away and sat down in her favorite chair, the very chair in which he'd caused her to fall into a coma after his marriage announcement, she took a long, deep and thoughtful breath. "Tell her Marcus, be honest. Don't give her false hope. Don't do to her what your father did to us. If you love her, confide in her and hopefully, walk away with your friendship."

Marcus walked closer to his mother and knelt down to the floor alongside her. He searched her eyes and expression. He watched as the tears continued to gently roll down her face and listened to the inflection of her voice, trying to determine if everything she said was how she truly felt. This is not what he'd expected, but then again, he wasn't really sure how she would react. He only knew that he needed to tell someone he could trust. He wanted to feel free of his recent guilt, as confusing as it was. He wanted to know that the most important person in his life at that moment would accept him for *who* and *what* he thought he was. But he also wanted his mother to tell him that at twenty-six years old, he was *'going through a phase'* not a permanent way of life like his father. He wanted her to assure him that maybe this was just curiosity, experimentation, and confusion because of his childhood. But she said none of that. She only listened and offered her support. He wondered if she would tell his sister and father. Ary, he felt, would tell him it was a mistake—that he wasn't responsible for what had happened, that he was more than likely taken advantage of because of his carefree demeanor. And he secretly wished it to be true. He *had* been feeling depressed, lonely and rejected by the only woman he'd ever considered marrying. And he'd spent the evening drinking at a bar for most of the night when the handsome stranger began talking to him.

All he could remember after their hour-long conversation

about music, sports and politics, was that he ended up lying face-up on an oversized sofa in a Soho apartment, staring at a smiling, scantily clad man standing near him, holding a bottle of beer. Marcus panicked, anxiously looking around the unfamiliar space. He wasn't sure what had taken place. He looked down at his pants and saw that they were still on and fully zipped. His shirt however, was untucked and his socks and shoes were scattered near the front door.

Although his memory was still fuzzy, he recalled leaving the bar, hopping into a cab with his bar-room companion and being kissed solidly on the lips in the back seat. But he couldn't remember how they eventually made it up to the apartment or whether they took the elevator, stairs, or even what building it was among the many four, five and six story structures and rows of brownstones. After coming to grips with what he thought had most likely taken place, he grabbed his sports jacket and fled without uttering a word. He ended up leaning against the side of the cold edifice after desperately, and without luck, trying to hail several passing cabs. With his head spinning and his mind in a total state of flux, he flagged down a couple of strangers and begged them to call a Lyft for him—they crossed the street. Finally, a woman and two girlfriends sensing the fear in his voice, offered to make the call. He'd managed to give them his home address and within fifteen minutes was on his way to safety.

Marcus recalled the kiss, and how he hadn't recoiled at the stranger's advances. It reminded him of the locker room kiss when he was in junior high school. He didn't retreat then either. Maybe, he thought, Caroline had sensed what he was afraid to confront. Maybe it was finally time to admit that he shared more in common with his father than he was ever willing to accept. Or maybe, he hoped, this was all a foolish, drunken, nightmare. Marcus considered for a split second, calling his father, but just as quickly dismissed the notion that Bruce would either be sympathetic, pleased or completely indifferent.

"How long have you known, Marcus?" Sonya asked, holding her sons trembling hands.

Looking into her mournful eyes, he said, "Maybe all my life."

CHAPTER 99

THE sun rose with her firmly enwrapped in his arms. It was a familiar and comfortable place, one where at times, she had envisioned the two of them as the years passed. She stared at the veins in his muscular arms and felt safe, even flirting with the idea of becoming a 'couple' in the traditional sense. *What would that feel like again?* she wondered. *How would it affect our working relationship? Could two 'Type A' personalities with enormous ambitions actually coexist under one roof? In the same office? And who would our children be most like? Wow,* she thought. *I'm not so sure I'm ready for that kind of commitment.* As she maneuvered through his loving grip to wake him and enlist his own thoughts, his cell phone rang, putting her questions on hold.

"Babe, your phone."

"Mmmm, good morning," he said, smiling, realizing she was still in his arms.

"Do you want to take it?"

"Yes please."

She reached over to the night table and handed it to him on the third ring. Reluctantly letting go of her, he laid on his back, folding one arm behind his head, but making sure their warm bodies were still touching.

"Hello," he answered, wiping the sleep from his eyes. "What?! Slow down man, slow down. What the hell are you saying?!" he yelled, sitting up abruptly, causing her to shift her cozy position beside him and stare with grave concern.

"Dwayne, what is it? What's going on?"

He turned his back to her, held his forehead in the palm of his hand and inquired somberly, "When did it happen?"

Her eyes grew wide, growing even more alarmed as she leaned over and gently stroked his back.

"Okay, alright, I can be there in a few hours. Try and keep it together. Let him know I'm on my way."

She watched as he stood up, gathered his clothes from the floor and nearby chair and walked out of the bedroom down the narrow hallway, all without saying a word. She waited before going after him, guessing that something must have been terribly wrong in his family. She shuttered when the bathroom door slammed shut and stiffened as his fists pounded against the wall.

She grabbed a silk robe from the armoire, considering all she could do was comfort him—but still uncertain of who, why or what he needed comforting from. Easing the door open, she found him sitting on the edge of the bathtub, his hands covering his face with visible tears streaming down to the floor. He was clearly in pain. She sat next to him and curved her arms around his broad shoulders, resting her head against his throbbing temple.

"I'm here baby. I'm at your side. You're not alone."

He turned to look at her—his eyes filled with sadness, his heart crushed.

"She's gone," he managed through falling tears. "My mother's passed and I never got to say goodbye. She never got the chance to see me because I was too busy working," he said, his eyes shutting tight, his brow furled, his body shaking and his voice barely above a whisper.

"I'm so sorry Dwayne. I didn't know she was ill. Please don't blame yourself for anything," she counseled. "Now isn't the time," unsure of what else to say to lessen the burden. "Let me know what you need and it's done."

This time he would depend on her for strength, unlike when

he discovered her unconscious in bed after taking an overdose of medication after the NPI debacle. He craved her soft touch and comforting words. At that moment he trusted her more than anyone, and so he leaned on her and cried.

CHAPTER 100

MARCUS spent the night in his old bedroom where he laid in the queen-sized bed that had long ago replaced the bunk beds of his childhood and stared at the off-white ceiling. He hadn't slept. His thoughts felt like the pictures he'd seen of busy nighttime highways with red and white car light trails stretching out through the photographer's lens. He felt pulled in a thousand directions, not sure whether he had been violated or submissive. *I'm a grown ass man,* he thought. *How could I have* let *it happen if I wasn't a willing participant? Who in their right freakin' mind would believe that? Was I drugged? What the fuck did I do? My pants were still on, but his weren't. Am I still trying to run away from what happened to me more than a decade ago or the conversation I heard between daddy and Matthew?* Marcus tossed, turned and punched several pillows. Although he was tired, he knew he wouldn't be able to force his brain to consent or his eyes to close. He also felt that he'd already divulged more than his mother could possibly bear, but he still needed to talk to someone, so he called his sister.

CHAPTER 101

ARY sat on a stool at the kitchen counter using her tablet to check on flights for Dwayne. Finding reservations for this afternoon or evening to West Virginia from one of the New York City airports, proved challenging. Deep into her search, she was startled by her ringing phone. Rushing over to retrieve it from her handbag in the living room, she wondered who would be calling so early.

"Hi Marcus," she said, seeing his name on the screen. "What the hell happened to you last night knucklehead? Mama was so disappointed, she wanted to…"

"Ary wait. I have to tell you something," he interrupted.

"Huh? What is it?! Is mama okay?!" she panicked.

"Yeah, she's fine. Well, I think she is."

"I'm not in the mood for games Marcus. What's going on?" she demanded, growing annoyed with his ambiguity.

"It's not mama this time Ary, it's me. I think I'm gay."

"What did you say?" she asked, baffled, stunned and jointly confused, hoping she'd misunderstood him.

"You heard me Ary. Something happened the other night, or I let it happen, I'm not so sure anymore and now I have to face the fact that I'm gay."

"Are you crazy?!" she yelled. "This isn't something to joke about. No one just *turns* gay! Have you seriously lost your mind? What the hell are you talking about? Where are you, Marcus? Are you home?"

"Will you please let me explain before insulting me and talking to me like I'm some helpless child?" he shouted. "I'm at mama's and I told her last night and..."

"You're where? At mama's? And you *told* her? Oh my God! What the fuck are you trying to do to her...*again!!!* Remember Marcus, you were the one who almost killed her just a few months ago and now you decide, over the course of a few days after whatever the hell happened, that you're gay and then think it's okay to tell her about your little *'outing'* ! You're an idiot Marcus. I can't believe this shit, I..."

"Why did I think you'd be compassionate? Why!!!" he yelled. "You embody all that Bruce Alexander ever was. You're without feelings for anyone but your own selfish ass, Ary!"

"You wait one damn minute Marcus. You're the one who failed to show up to what was one of mama's most important openings and then you mysteriously appear at home and tell her about a little sex fantasy you decided to have instead! Give me a fucking break about being selfish! I'm coming out to the Island and you'd better be there when I arrive. We need to talk."

Marcus abruptly hung up and cursed himself for calling.

Sonya called him from the bottom of the staircase after hearing a round of expletives. "Marcus, are you alright? I'm making breakfast. Won't you come down and join me?"

Marcus stared at the slightly opened door and said, "No thank you mama. I'm leaving."

CHAPTER 102

NO longer able to concentrate on the task of finding a flight, she raced to her bedroom, breezing right past him with no acknowledgment or updates on his trip. She rustled through her closet choosing a pair of skinny leg blue jeans and a red, v-neck, hi-lo sweater. He watched as she hurried out of the room, down the hallway and into the bathroom, quickly closing the door.

He waited there, trying to interpret what was happening. *Maybe she found a flight and she's rushing to get dressed.* She *had* offered to drive him home to save precious time. But it seemed that her entire demeanor had gone from caring and reassurance to cold and dismissive. He walked down to the bathroom and tried opening the door. It was locked.

"Ary," he called, knocking lightly. "What's going on? Were you able to find a flight for me?" He heard the sound of running water and knocked again, forcefully. "Hey, did you have any luck? We need to get going. Remember, I still have to go home and pack."

The door swung open, causing him to stumble inside. She was fully dressed and twisting her hair up into a ponytail.

"Dwayne, I'm sorry but I have a family situation that I have to deal with right now," she explained, squeezing past him. "I wasn't able to find a flight for you, but I'm sure you'll be able to get something today or tonight. I know there must be an airline that flies frequently to Virginia from JFK, LaGuardia or Newark."

He was shocked. His muscles grew tense as he recovered from his near fall with the veins in his head bulging. The only words he could muster were a defiant, "*West Virginia*, not Virginia. It's Greenbrier, West Virginia!!!"

Watching in astonishment as she hurried around the apartment, choosing a pair of flats from her wooden shoe rack and a New York Yankees baseball cap from the top shelf of her closet, he felt as though he was in a dream. *What's happening? Did I miss something in-between the bedroom and bathroom? Did I say something to piss her off?*

As she made her way through the living room, collecting her handbag and keys, she turned to him and said, "Don't worry about me, just make sure you close the door when you leave. I'll call you later to check on whether you were able to fly out. Oh and please extend my condolences to your family." And with those last words, she walked out the front door of her apartment, down the hallway and into the elevator. Dwayne stood in the center of the living room speechless, grappling for something to say, shout or punch. But he had no words, his voice was hoarse from sorrow and he'd been taught long ago by his parents to never hit a lady. But this was one of those times where he questioned their valued advice. Feeling brute rage, he decided the safest thing to do was to just leave. So he returned to the bedroom to get his wallet and keys left sitting on a small, round, basswood and marble table in the corner near the window. He noticed the cursive letters, '*SA*' engraved near the edge on top and realized it must have been one of her mother's creations. Dwayne walked into the kitchen, opened a cabinet drawer and pulled out a steak knife. Returning to the bedroom, he carved his own initials in the tabletop and avowed with chilling indifference, "Here's something to remember me by." His anger had reached a level of unrecognizable fervor.

CHAPTER 103

MAYBE *I was born to be unhappy,* she thought, speeding carelessly through narrow side streets as she made her way to the George Washington Bridge. *I don't know of anyone who goes through this much shit!* "It's like living your life on a perpetual merry-go-round with no way off!" she screamed, not caring if any nearby cars could see or hear her outburst. *Marcus has to grow up. I can't keep fixing everything. It's like he has no concept of his actions when it comes to what he says or does to mama. Why doesn't he ever confide in daddy? They did just have a family reunion. I thought everything was all sorted out!*

But before any further thoughts could go unanswered, her phone rang.

"Oh God! I really don't need this right now," she said, after looking at the caller's name display on the car console screen. "Shit!"

"Hello?"

"I'm going to need to move our meeting up to this afternoon. Something's come up and we don't have the luxury of time."

"What are you saying Marguerite? I thought we'd agreed to meet on Sunday. Isn't that what we'd discussed the other day?"

"Look Ary, I'm not the one calling the shots on G's takedown and I have no control over when or whether the schedule of destruction changes. So either you're still willing to help or you're not. You need to let me know right now because…"

"I have an unexpected family emergency," she tried explaining. "I'm on my way out to Long Island right now to…"

"Then I'll take that as a 'no,'" she interrupted.

"That's *not* what I said," she answered, irritably. "Where should I meet you?"

"The Victorian Restaurant on 86th and Lexington Avenue at three-thirty. I'll be sitting at a table in the back of the restaurant wearing a Carolina Herrera black floral dress and gray Louboutin lace up pumps. Don't be late. If you're not there by three-forty, I'll assume you're not coming."

"Don't worry, I'll be there," she confirmed, feeling beads of sweat forming on her forehead. *She's getting ready to divulge this nefarious operation to destroy G's company, but yet she has time to describe her designer attire,* she thought. *That's takes a special kind of vanity.* All of a sudden her thoughts turned to Dwayne.

I just left him there with no way to get back to the City! Geez Ary, when it comes to your family, you drop everything and immediately put blinders and headphones on. His mother just died and you walked out on him after promising you'd be there! I can't do this. I have to go back. Marguerite and Marcus will just have to wait. She took the first exit off the bridge and u-turned around to cross back to her apartment. Once she got off the elevator and made her way down and around the corridor, she noticed her door was slightly opened. Her heart pounded against her chest at the thought of someone inside. She hesitated before going in, wondering if she should call security downstairs. "Dwayne, are you still here?" she asked, slowly pushing the door wide open. "Dwayne?"

As she stepped inside, pausing just over the threshold, she scanned the space for anything that seemed out of place. Against her better judgment she walked through to the bedroom, checking the closet, armoire, and underneath the bed. She then walked down to the bathroom, sliding the shower curtain aside to look in the tub. Satisfied that no one was there, she checked her jewelry case on the dresser and determined that nothing was missing. *He must have mistakenly left it open when he left,* she surmised. Suddenly, from the corner of her eye she noticed the sculptured table her mother had given her as a 21st birthday gift, and the steak knife protruding out of it. "Oh my God!" she screamed, running out of the room and out of the apartment. She was terrified and still shaking when she reached the security officer's station in the lobby, tearfully explaining what she'd seen.

"Okay, I'll go up and have a look. I'm sure whoever was there is gone by now," he said, trying to reassure her. "I'll call the police once I check it out and you can fill out a report with all the details you have."

"Should I go with you? I don't know if I can go back up there!" she said, tears rolling down her cheeks.

"You can either stay here or wait outside your door in the hallway while I check it out."

"Ok, I'll go with you and wait outside." Ary followed him into the elevator and up to the 24th floor, but instead of remaining outside her apartment, she went inside, walking closely behind him as he inspected each room.

"It doesn't look like any forced entry," he said, examining the front door lock and frame. "Are you sure you didn't mistakenly leave it open? Sometimes we're in such a hurry we think it's closed when…"

"No, I've never done that," she made clear, feeling the sting of his accusation.

"We'll, we've all made mistakes," he confessed, walking into her bedroom. "I mean, even I…"

"I know what I did, and I didn't leave my door opened or unlocked or plunge a knife into my…"

But before she could finish her statement, she noticed the initials, '*DH*' carved right next to Sonya's on the table.

"Ughhh!," she gasped, clasping her hands over her mouth.

"What is it?" he asked, spinning around to see the horror written over her flushed face.

"I think I know who did this," she admitted, slowly lowering down to the bed, fixating on the 8-inch knife.

"Ma'am, do you want me to call the police?"

"No," she said, almost whispering. "It was my fault. I'm responsible for this."

"Excuse me?" he asked, shaking his clearly confused head.

"I hurt someone deeply and he lashed out," she explained, looking up at him.

"Well, I'm not gonna pretend to know what you're talking about. But before I leave, is there anything else you need me to do? Are you gonna be alright?"

"Yes, thank you. You can go now. I'm sorry I bothered you. I apologize for overreacting."

"Hey listen, no need for apologies. This is what I'm here for, okay. But if I could suggest one thing?"

"Sure, of course," she said, reaching for a tissue on the night-stand near her bed and getting up to follow him out.

"You might want to get some new friends," he proposed, stopping near the front door. "Preferably ones that express their anger or prove their point in less destructive ways."

"I'll take that into consideration," she said, forcing a grin.

Ary leaned against the door after shutting and locking it. Her stomach roiled from a nauseating migraine. Checking her watch, she remembered the meeting with Marguerite and expelled a deep sigh. All thoughts of apologizing to Dwayne were no longer being considered. Right now she didn't care how he made it back home or whether he was able to book a flight to Greenbrier or anywhere near it. As in the past, she figured somehow or way, she'd be able to make it right again.

CHAPTER 104

MARGUERITE arrived at the restaurant a few minutes early and ordered a vesper martini. "I'll have it stirred, straight up, with a twist," she instructed the waiter.

"May I offer you one of our special appetizers?"

"No you may not," she said, defiantly. "This is business, not social and certainly not special."

"Of course, madam. I'll be right back with your drink."

Marguerite's stare followed him as he walked away, tapping her freshly pedicured nail on the table. She stretched her neck to scan the space once more, making sure she hadn't missed anyone she may have known or someone that might have spotted her when she entered. Growing anxious, she checked her watch—it was 3:25pm. This would be the first time she'd seen Ary since her astonishing removal from NPI and her feelings for the rising star were as entrenched today as they'd been the day they'd laid eyes on one another in the decorative hallways of her former lover's company. Marguerite wondered how she'd begin the conversation. Her first thoughts were to treat Ary the way she'd treated her as her superior at the firm, with disdain and indifference. But that was no longer the case and she was no longer employed. She felt that by entrusting Ary with information that might save G and his company would also put her in a better light not only with her former partner and lover, but also in the eyes of other, non-corrupt players in the industry. So this meeting would be multi-pronged and therefore would require her to be on her best behavior, as challenging as that would be.

"Your drink, madam. Will there be anything else?"

"I'll have a Malibu Cocktail," Ary ordered, standing behind him, surprising both he and Marguerite. "And right on time I might add," she indicated, pointing to her watch and moving to the side as the waiter pulled out the empty chair for her.

"Will you be ordering lunch, madam?"

"No she won't," Marguerite answered before Ary could even open her mouth. "Just bring her the drink please!"

"I'd love to see what's on the menu this afternoon," she said, savoring Marguerite's appalled expression."

"Yes ma'am. I'll be right back."

"You look lovely and rested," she said, slightly grinning. "But then again, I guess that's what a little '*time off*' will do for you, wouldn't you agree?"

Marguerite was incensed and the fact that the effects of her drink had not sufficiently traveled through her bloodstream only added to her fury. "I'll let that slide for now, *Artimus*," she shot back with a dose of familiar derision.

"Okay, so now that we've reconnected and gotten the cynicism out of the way, what gives?" Ary inquired. "How am I supposed to save NPI?"

"Let's get something straight right here and now," Marguerite insisted, leaning across the table. "No one said anything about *you* saving NPI okay? If anyone is going to be credited with exposing the iniquitous business being carried out by the bad seeds in this industry, it'll be *me*. Do I make myself clear?" She sat back in her chair, took a long sip from her cocktail and continued without allowing Ary to respond. "No matter what G may think of me right now, I know deep in my heart he still loves me and believes I'd do anything for him. And the truth about this entire calamitous situation will become clearer in the coming days."

Ary felt unsettled by Marguerite's tone and the staid expression etched on her face, thinking, *The fact that she actually believes*

G would be willing to take her back is questionable at best. She thought back to their initial conversation on the phone when Marguerite admitted that, '*Right now, you're the only one that he trusts. So I have no other choice but to confide in you,'* she remembered. *So I may have been* shocked *by her call, but I do remember what she said to me.*

The women ordered a second round of drinks, but this time Ary insisted on having a turkey and avocado wrap to help her remain focused. Reluctantly, Marguerite ordered a walnut and cranberry arugula salad, still determined not to spend any more time with Ary than she felt absolutely necessary.

CHAPTER 105

DWAYNE arrived home in a Lyft still infuriated, but trying hard not to let it interfere with all that he needed to do before leaving. During the ride home, he was able to find an 8:00pm flight and book it out of LaGuardia for more money than he'd ever spent on a domestic flight to West Virginia. He'd also called his father to reassure him that he would indeed be home tonight to lessen the burden of saying goodbye. He'd entrusted his youngest brother Darrell to smooth things over for he and Dion before he arrived, not wanting any acrimony to get in the way of all they'd need to accomplish.

After rushing up to his apartment, grabbing a large suitcase, and packing far too many clothes, not sure of how long he'd be away, his thoughts turned back to Ary. *Jesus man, how could you have done that to her table? A work of art by her mother! And no matter what* she *did, as nuts as she makes me, she didn't deserve that. I know how her family pulls at her emotional strings and I get it, so does mine, but there comes a time when you have to stand up and say, 'enough,' I'm an adult with my own life to live and that doesn't mean I care any less for any of you. But I really don't think she'll ever be able to pull far enough away to stand up on her own. I think they feed off of each other...and not in a healthy way,* he tried reasoning. *And I shouldn't have left her door opened, that was some stupid, childish, bullshit. I should call to make sure she's okay.*

He looked in his closet and determined that the three suits he'd packed would suffice during his time in Greenbrier, along with four pairs of slacks, six button downs, three polo shirts, boxer shorts and eight pairs of socks. He looked over at his designer shoe collection and thought better of wearing a pair of five-hundred dollar Santoni Wingtips, and instead opted for two pairs of oxfords and a pair of dress shoes from one of his favorite designers, Guinean-born, Armando Cabral. As he made his way down to the lobby to wait for the airport car service he'd arranged earlier, his cell phone rang, interrupting any further thoughts of wardrobe or Ary.

"Uh Oh," he said, recognizing the caller, hesitating, trying to decide if this was a conversation he was willing to have. "Hey Deidra, how are you? Look," he said quickly, not giving her a chance to answer, trying to offset any potential hostile conversation she may have wanted to engage in. "I'm on my way to West Virginia. My mom passed away unexpectedly and I'm trying to get to my family as quickly as I can."

"Oh my God! I'm so sorry to hear that Dwayne, I really am. If there's anything you need please, let me know," she offered, deciding not to chide him after hearing his news.

Wow, he thought, *those were almost the exact same words I heard from 'Dr. Jeckel-ette and 'Ms. Hyde-from-my-real-feelings.'*

"I appreciate that Deidra, I do. But I'll be fine. My family needs me and that's all I can think of right now. I'll be in touch when I get back, okay?"

"Sure, of course. Have a safe flight and call me if you need someone to talk too."

"I will thanks. Goodbye," he said, walking through the lobby doors and into the waiting limousine. Sitting back in his seat he let out a much needed sigh. *I can't believe what's happening right now,* he thought. *It feels like a fucking dream or nightmare. I'm heading home to Greenbrier to bury my mother, and after the funeral and goodbyes, I'll come back to New York having one less parent. Did I really do all that I could have for them or was Dion right when he said sending money was no substitute for being there? They always told me to go out and make a name for myself, and that's exactly what I did. But did I lose who I was underneath the façade of being successful? Was I really embarrassed of my background as my brother has accused me of so often, or was I constantly trying to make my folks proud so they could brag to their friends about their boy 'up east' as they'd say. I hope you know how much I loved you mom and will always love and cherish your memory.* Tears began trickling down his cheeks. *I feel like I don't even have time to grieve, mom. I'm still in shock from Dion's call. I thought I'd be able to make it home to see you and surprise ya'll with a new bedroom set. I know pop's had said you didn't need it, but I saw that bed the last time I was home and the mattress had seen better days and nights. I shouldn't have let him talk me out of replacing it, joking that he liked the squeaking noise it made 'cause it reminded him of how, in his younger days he could even make a bed sing when ya'll got busy,* he laughed, *which always made me throw up a little in my mouth at the thought of it,* he smiled, remembering how his mother would always punch his father on his shoulder, reminding him that although their sons were adults, some things should never be discussed in front of them. His dad however, would continue with, *"Woman, do you know the last time that bed has seen any real action?"* To which she would dutifully reply, *"No dear, when?"*

"Every year when I flip over that darn mattress." And they would both laugh.

Dwayne's parents loved each other and always wanted the best for their sons. Although they came to rely on him more than the others, they never made a difference or showed favoritism towards any one of them and for that Dwayne admired and loved them even more. He felt that as the oldest and most successful, it was up to him, as his parents grew older and their health began to fail, to help his younger siblings financially and continue to encourage them to pursue their secondary education. His words held more sway with Darrell, the youngest of the trio. Dion resented what he'd termed his big brother's 'meddling' in his decisions. He'd always said school wasn't for everybody and it '*definitely*' wasn't for him. But he'd also come to resent the fact that he wasn't able to help his parents financially and repay them for all they'd done and sacrificed for their children, like his older brother had. So he decided to remain at the family home and help in whatever way he could around the house, to which Dwayne had argued, was never enough.

Dwayne paid for a caretaker to come once a week to look after his ailing parents—never knowing that his father cut the visits down to once a month, citing that the privacy in his own home was being violated by this unwelcomed stranger. His argument to his wife was that he was still physically able to care for the two of them—when in reality his health was failing just as rapidly as hers.

"It's United Airlines, Terminal B."

The driver pulled into the drop-off lane reserved for taxis and limousines and popped open the trunk. He placed the large piece of luggage on the curbside and just as he was heading back towards the driver's side of his car Dwayne tapped him on the shoulder, reached in his wallet and included an extra $25 dollars to the $65 dollar fare.

"Thanks for taking some of the pressure off this trip, man."

"Thank you sir and enjoy your time away" he said, routinely.

Dwayne stood there for a second and thought of explaining his reason for traveling, but quickly decided against it. Instead he responded, "Thank you. Enjoy your evening."

CHAPTER 106

DARIAS didn't want to face a new week at the office without having a clear sense of what the next moves of the Chairman and his sideshow of dedicated minions would be. He wasn't satisfied to sit by and let the old ways of business continue as Julian had suggested, especially in light of the Chairman's obvious and sudden contempt for him. Although their relationship was never one of private golf club vacations together or summer invites to the Chairman's domestic or international estate, he'd left that up to Julian and the others, never thinking it would have any lasting effect on company transactions, decisions or relationships. He was confident in his acumen and solid reputation among the other board members. But he couldn't help thinking about the remark the Chairman made in reference to his vacation with Ary, and felt his blood simmering all over again. He wanted to get to the bottom of the T.O.T deal, and learn as much as he could about Dave Winters.

He'd convinced himself that none of this had anything to do with his friendship with G or his admiration for the accomplishments of NPI or how he felt about Ary. It had, in his mind, everything to do with protecting his executive position, his integrity and his belief that BP was still the righteous company he'd worked for and believed in for more than eight years. Flipping through his list of contacts on his smartphone, he stopped at Marguerite Armstead. *She should know something,* he thought. *Just because she's out at NPI doesn't mean she's out of the loop or isn't fielding offers from some of the best in the industry who still value not only her expertise, but her well-placed connections.* Darias tapped the call button and waited.

"What took you so long?" she asked, answering on the first ring.

CHAPTER 107

"MARGUERITE, it's good to hear your voice," he said, almost relieved. "How've you been?"

"My dear Darias," she said, cynically. "If you really meant that, I would not, just now, be hearing from you. But I'll forgive you darling. So aside from all that, let's discuss the reason for your call."

He knew he was in no position to argue or negotiate with his former lover and was quickly reminded of her *'no-nonsense'* way of handling business and any crises she'd faced. She was, after all, the reason he'd worked for BP by reaching out to her connections years ago.

"Let me tell you first of all how devastated I was and still am by G relegating me to the hidden corners of an expansive walk-in closet—like a second-hand Chanel bag, which, as you know, I would never possess, except of course if it were authentically vintage."

"Of course not," he said, masking his sarcasm, instantly reminded of her portentous nature as one of several reasons for their breakup.

"I was also humiliated because of all the gossip circling the industry. I had to literally see a therapist to keep from harming myself and killing him!" she admitted. "I'd dedicated my life to his company and to the man who told me in no uncertain terms that NPI was his *first love*, not me, *N-P-I*!" she shouted. He briefly removed the phone from his ear.

"But I put up with him because of love, respect and the belief that one day NPI would be larger and more profitable than any of the others. That's how engrossed I was, Darias. I became so blinded that I lost who *I* was. All I thought about was how to lift him up in this dogged industry. I couldn't separate…"

"Marguerite," he interrupted, "I don't understand. We both always knew G was capable of taking his company to the next level alone, and stopping anyone that got in his way. And we both also know that he's a good guy, well, I guess you know that better than anyone else. But here's the thing. G's been accused in the past of being, well, arrogant."

"G?" she interrupted.

"Let me finish. That's not to say that he's not deserving of a little arrogance. I look at him as a stealth bomber; sleek, smooth, focused and hard to affect. But if anything or anyone stands in the way of him accomplishing his goals, there would be hell to pay. And look, I'll be honest with you Marguerite. I don't claim to know all that went down with you, Joseph and Dwayne, or even Ary. But what I do know is that it's more than just questionable activities happening right now, which could not only mean hefty fines, bad publicity and lawsuits, this could quite possibly lead to jail time and corporate restructuring on a massive scale, including job losses whether you were involved or not."

Marguerite listened to every word. She weighed if and how Darias could be useful in exposing the Chairman without her suffering any further damage, and also helping to smooth things over with the man she still adored. She explained all that she knew about the Chairman's plans and the mysterious man who called her with updates to prepare her for the function she'd be responsible for in the takedown. She told him about her meeting with Ary and the task she'd entrusted her with—that of convincing G that there was indeed a plan to ultimately sabotage NPI so that T.O.T could amass a complete take-over, forcing G to forfeit the entire contract, risking his rock-solid reputation in the industry.

She went on to say that they'd scheduled one more dinner so that she could relay the final details of the proposed *'partnership'* and any subsequent actions she'd require of her after meeting with the Chairman, allowing G a small window of potential prevention.

"So here's where you'd come in," she started, revealing and explaining every furtive detail he'd need to grasp in order to expose and undermine the Chairman and T.O.T. "You do understand that if this blows up in our faces, we're done? All of us!"

"I know, I just told you…never mind. What I can't believe is that this shit is happening again, with NPI at the center of it. But right is right, and I can't just stand by knowing what improprieties are taking place in front of my own eyes and do nothing. That's not who I am, Marguerite."

"Oh, I know. That's what I've always admired about you Darias, your kind heart and deep introspection. And it's also why I knew you'd be calling."

They talked for another forty minutes with Marguerite divulging her plan to stall the Chairman, and how she would try to get him to arrange a meeting between her and the man she'd deemed the 'mysterious one.' They discussed their next moves together, both agreeing that it had to be implemented as soon as possible. Marguerite insisted that her name or imprint be concealed at all costs and that no one ever suspect she had initially agreed to the takedown or played a role in its defense. He agreed and was prepared to face any resulting consequence.

CHAPTER 108

DWAYNE stood solemnly beside his father and two brothers. The tears fell silently down his face as he tried hard not to break down completely. He knew he had to be strong for his family, especially his frail, but proud father, himself battling coal workers' pneumoconiosis, otherwise known as black lung disease, from his years of working in the mines to supplement his income. He'd looked around the church as he walked in and was amazed at all the mourners there to pay their respects to a woman whose quiet strength had held his family together for over thirty-five years, even when she had to do it alone when his dad was off working at the shipyards in Richmond for months at a time. His wife had also held down two jobs in her earlier years while raising their sons and teaching bible study at the only black church in Greenbrier County. She had been pestered for years by rumors of the temptations men face being away from their wives and girlfriends for long stretches of time, but she decided long ago that if he wanted to be unfaithful to her and the kids, it wouldn't have taken almost 300 miles away or the cover of a tanker ship to do it. There were women in Greenbrier County who'd had their eyes on her man years before when he was a cook in the Navy and subsequently after he'd decided to stay on and work in Richmond. They struggled even with the two of them working, but managed to stay off state assistance as a source of pride when the boys were young to the chagrin of others who were struggling from layoffs, alcoholism, drug addiction, extramarital affairs, death or a combination of all five. She would always tell her children that no matter what happens, "*The Lord will see to us. We gon' be alright.*" And although her husband never discussed his time in Richmond or his work at the shipyards, he always took pride in bringing home his paycheck, right before the new school year, just in time to buy two new outfits for each boy and a new pair of shoes at the only department store in Greenbrier County.

Dwayne stared at the open casket his father had insisted on having, and thought of all the financial struggles his mother had gone through during her own childhood. But he felt extreme pride in being the oldest son of Levi and Gracie Hargis. No matter what anyone thought of his family, they were always taught that love, respect and pride was what mattered most.

Suddenly, his attention was interrupted by the faint sound of a child's cry. He turned and looked toward the pews a few rows back. It was Jaden, his five and a half year old son, sitting there with his mother, the woman Dwayne had labeled more than four years prior, a common whore, and who'd told him, only the day before that she wasn't bringing him to the service because she would feel out of place and ridiculed by his entire family. His chin fell to his chest as he excused himself, maneuvering behind his father and brothers, walking three rows back to bring him to sit with his family. Dwayne held onto him, holding his little shoulders and telling him everything would be alright. He kissed the top of his curly head and held his hand. "I know how you feel son, I miss her too. And I promise you right here and in her presence, I'll be a better father." With his tiny eyes looking up at the man he knew only during brief summer vacations and by the elaborate gifts he'd received for Christmas and on birthdays, through his tears, he answered, "Thanks papa, I'd really like that."

CHAPTER 109

ARY called Marcus from home to continue the conversation they'd had a few days before. She reiterated that they should meet, but this time, sounding composed and less combative.

"Marcus I'm sorry for yelling at you the other day but you surely understand why, don't you?" she asked, before continuing her explanation. "Just think about it for a moment. It's almost like losing daddy all over again on *Thanksgiving* of all holidays, when you're supposed to be offering thanks for your family, and for all you have—not revealing your plans of destroying everything they ever believed in."

"Hold on, Ary, this is nothing like that. I didn't plan on this happening. I don't even really know *how* it happened. Hell, if I'm being honest with myself, maybe I was just giving in to what I think daddy always thought of me. And now that I've had a few days to reflect on it, I really think I might have been drugged."

"What?!"

"I mean. I don't recall everything that happened. I just remember drinking to the point where I'd accepted a drink from a guy I'd been talking to about sports and other shit and the next thing I know, I'm in a cab and we're locking lips."

"Ewwww Marcus! I don't know if I want to hear anymore."

"Well, you were the one who said she was coming out to mama's house threatening me to stay put because we needed to 'talk,' and according to mama, you never even showed up."

"Hey mister, don't give me that shit. Mama told me you left without warning. She said she'd made breakfast for the two of you and you just left without any explanation. So don't try and be a saint. It won't fly with me."

"Okay, so now what, Ms. *Perfect* daughter. How can we fix this? I'm more confused than ever before. I still have the same feelings I've always had for Caroline and I *don't* have the urge to go out and find myself an eligible bachelor."

"First off, as I've always believed and said, you don't just all of a sudden become gay. It's not a choice and it's certainly not something to be flippant about or take lightly. You either come to accept that you've always been gay, like daddy, or you're just curious to know what it'd be like to have sex with someone of your own gender. It's that simple, Marcus."

"No the hell it's not, Ary. It's not '*that simple.*' Sometimes I wonder if you have amnesia or D.I.D."

"What the hell is D.I.D?"

"Dissociative Identity Disorder. It used to be called multiple personality disorder. I know you're not stupid 'cause you finished at the top of all your *damn* classes. But I guess just because you're book smart doesn't mean you're filled with common virtuosity. Look, I'm not gonna spend my time rehashing all the hurt we've all gone through because of daddy's revelation and choices. But I *will* admit that you give good advice when you're not yelling or being sarcastic or treating me like some imbecile."

"Don't say that Marcus. I know you're not an imbecile. A stubborn, boneheaded, knucklehead maybe, but never an imbecile," she laughed. "After all, not everyone knows what D.I.D. means or can go through what we've gone through and come out relatively unscathed, right?"

Marcus could only shake his head, realizing that his sister would always put blinders on when it came to upholding and defending the integrity of her family.

"Yep, you're right sis. Not everyone could withstand the challenges of being an Alexander."

Ary suggested Marcus seek therapy to help resolve his sexual identity issues. As much as she'd wanted to help and advise him, they both decided that this was something that needed professional expertise. They also agreed, like Sonya, that he needed to be honest with Caroline and allow her make the decision whether or not to stick by his side.

"So now what Marcus? What else can I do to help? Do you want me to try and find this guy that's caused your confusion and possibly find out if we can bring charges against him for drugging you?"

"Ary," Marcus said, frantically. "I just noticed that a few of my credit cards are missing."

"What do you mean? How?"

"From my wallet, my Visa and American Express aren't in their usual slots."

"And you're just now realizing this Marcus? Do you think that guy took them? Don't you check your statements? Who doesn't check their wallet and notice empty slots?"

"I don't know, I can't answer all your damn questions, Sherlock. But I'm guessing my drunken playboy playmate had something to do with it."

"That's not funny."

"Well, I can either laugh or cry, or call the card companies to see what kind of financial damage he did to my accounts."

"Alright. And in the meantime I'll call a friend of mine whose wife is a new prosecutor somewhere downtown to see if there's anything we can do. I think this might qualify as fraud."

"Ya think?" he said, chuckling. "Hey sis thanks. I love you, even though at times you drive me bat-shit crazy."

"I know you do 'lil brother. I love you too and I promise you we'll get to the bottom of this. No matter how we fuss and fight sometimes Marcus, I always remember them telling us that…"

"Yeah, I know, *'we're all we have.'*"

"I'll call you later."

"Okay sis. Catch you later."

After ending the call, Ary slid further down into her most recent furniture purchase, an antique, muted yellow, wingchair commanding center stage in the living room, and found comfort in its velvet embrace. She thought about how Marcus' problem was one more unforeseen crisis to add to her growing list. *I know you probably hate me Dwayne, and you'd have every right to. But right now, at this moment in my life, I need your strength and guidance more than you could ever realize.*

CHAPTER 110

JOSEPH couldn't shake the uneasy feeling he had about Dave Winters and decided it would be a futile effort to try and convince Lawrence otherwise. He felt that they'd both worked too hard and had risked too much to let someone he'd only known for less than a year, but who had won the trust of his partner, hold so much power with so much at stake. He decided to place a call from home to their investor in San Diego and request a meeting. He knew there would be pushback, because this was a silent partner and he'd always insisted on *funding* high growth ventures, not having direct contact with them or their operations. He was content to stay out of the limelight while reaping vast profits from his investments.

CHAPTER 111

"HELLO?"

"Hey, it's Joseph Larsen. I know you'd rather remain under the radar and I respect that, but there's something going on that might very well cost all of us millions of dollars and I thought you'd want to know."

"You've got my attention."

Joseph went on to describe his anxious feelings about Dave Winters and his ongoing fidelity to the project as it was initially proposed. He reiterated his understanding of the immense fallout this might create and whether continued funding would be made available and the long-term credibility of his firm with his partner, Lawrence. But he felt compelled, especially with the hundreds of millions of dollars at stake to make the 'angel investor' aware of his troubling intuitions.

"Look, I don't want to come off as some frightened little girl, and Lawrence doesn't seem to believe that Dave is anything other than honest and willing to make this happen, but I've gotta tell you, when I have a hunch about something, it's usually dead on, and right now, I'd stake my reputation on it."

Listening to Joseph prompted anger and anxiety from the investor who'd trusted both he and Lawrence to bring in whomever they thought would be essential in helping to make this deal a reality. Now it seems Joseph was equivocating. This was not what he'd expected for the amount of money he was advancing.

"Joseph, I've invested heavily in this venture because out of all the souls I've ever dealt with in the industry who *might* have been capable of pulling this off, I had more than just blind faith that it would have been you and Finney. You have a track record like no one I've seen in decades, aside from your former mentor, the infamous, John G. Gicardi. And now you're calling me to say that you've run into a brick wall and…"

"Now hold on. That is *not* what I said at all. I'm just…"

"You're just what?" he said, cutting him off, with little tolerance for listening to any further explanation. "I don't take kindly to anyone informing me that I'm about to forfeit a shitload of money. So whatever the issue is with Mr. Winters, you should nip that shit in the bud and do what you've all agreed to do. Oh, and one last thing before I end this call. There's another person involved in this transaction, a woman on the East Coast that was recommended by the Chairman. He was confident that because of her long-term relationship with Gicardi, and from what I was told, messy breakup, that she'd be a perfect stooge for passing along information on what he may do if he becomes aware of, or gets tipped off to what's about to happen. I hear she was known to even finish his sentences during meetings. That's how in-sync they were. So I agreed that she would be useful."

"Are you fucking kidding me?!" Joseph shouted. "You're referring to Marguerite Armstead?"

"I have no idea what her name is, but I'm assuming she's the one. I tend not to delve into infinitesimal details," he said, smirking. "She's been given instructions from the Chairman's contact on what needs to get done from the perspective of motivating anyone that might be thinking of exposing this operation on the BP side to think twice before going down that road."

Joseph was shocked and incensed. Why wasn't he or Lawrence informed about Marguerite's involvement? He'd admitted that the two of them had had a rocky relationship at best during their time together at NPI, and he'd known the intimate details of her relationship, breakup and subsequent friendship with Darias, whom he despised. But to hear this now, at this stage of the project was infuriating. He could envision his company and the operation blowing up in their faces and ruining all that they'd poured into it over the course of the last three years. And he wondered who the Chairman had put in place to steer a notoriously stubborn Marguerite Armstead. This was quickly developing into his worst nightmare.

"How, may I ask, is she supposed to do that? Her name is mud right now around town! What bona fides does she have? I'm sorry, but what the hell is happening? So someone is calling a person they may have little knowledge of, giving her instructions and information on what she should be doing next for this, this multi-million project that you yourself have a *significant* financial interest in and *you* don't even know her? And you're taking the word of a, pardon the expression, out of shape, out of touch, geriatric, two steps away from full-on dementia oil executive, who's clinging on to his last breath of power on the board advising you of who would be an essential '*stooge*'? Well here's a newsflash—they used to date!—they were lovers—she left *him* for *G*!!! Why the fuck would she want to destroy the man I'm sure she's still in love with? The Chairman hates to lose and he'd do anything to get her back if only for the sake of throwing it in G's face! Oh my God, she's fucking helping to quarterback this game and you're all too fucking blind to see it!!! Oh my freakin' God!!!"

"Get a grip Larsen, you sound like you're having a nervous breakdown! You also need to locate a fucking course correction and straighten this shit out. Look, I don't customarily use such foul language and the fact that I have to engage in such litany, quite frankly, is unsettling and triggering second thoughts, which is *not* something I'm known for having. So here's the way this is going to play out. You're going to get this potential train wreck back on its track; stick with the deadline to get the contracts signed; ensure that the first round of funding from BP is in my bank account by the agreed upon date, and I'll match that with the funds needed for you, Lawrence and Dave to expand the first phase by hiring the folks needed to kick-start the off-shore drilling project earlier than what anyone expects. That way we get a head start on those commercial contracts before any competitors can pull together a team of competent drillers. And as I said to you previously Larsen, if this thing is as successful as I expect it to be, we'll all stand to increase our collective wealth threefold. And after it's all done, I can disappear again until the next profit making venture comes along that piques my interest, whether that be with your growing firm or someone else's. And for future reference, there will be no further phone calls until either you or Lawrence calls to inform me that it's done and we can all be on our merry way, understand?"

Joseph bristled at his condescension, but didn't want to fuel anymore speculation and decided to end the conversation with no further questions, requests, suggestions or theories.

"Understood. Listen, I'm probably on edge because of looming deadlines and the fact that I'm a perfectionist when it comes to everything going according to schedule, with *no surprises*," he said, caustically. "I apologize for wasting your time."

"Goodbye Joseph."

"Goodbye."

Out of sheer frustration, he pounded his fist onto the slate kitchen countertop. "Ahhhhh fuck!!!"

CHAPTER 112

DWAYNE convinced Jaden's mother to let him spend the next few days with him at his childhood home. Through his loss, he'd finally begun to realize that all of the frustrations he'd felt and the mistakes he'd made with her had been perpetrated for far too long on his child. And over the course of time, his own mother had tried to explain that although Jaden had been conceived through love but born from lies and deception, it should never have interfered with the miracle and gift of life. She'd always stressed that Dwayne should have been more involved. She would say, *"Even tho' you didn't get to see yo' daddy as much as I'd liked, he was always present in y'alls lives through his strength and faith. And he was respected and loved not only by me, but by so many people in the county who admired him for doing what he had to do to take care of his family. And that's the kind of love and respect we expect you boys to pass down to your own children."*

Precious time, he felt, had been lost on his doggedness, embarrassment, vindictiveness and unadulterated hatred of Jaden's mother. His emotions ran from guilt to pride as he stared at his child, running and playing around the house, from room to room, more familiar than Dwayne had been in recent years, playing with the children of first, second and third cousins who'd come back to the Hargis home to reminisce and console. He could see the resemblance of himself and his own father in his son. *The strong jaw line, the focused stare, the athletic legs and big hands, even at such a young age were all Hargis traits*, he thought. The only major difference was his skin tone. While the Hargis men's complexion tended to slant towards silky shades of ebony, the kind women find irresistibly easy to fawn over, his son's lightly tanned skin was foreign and exotic, prompting strangers to ask, *"What is he?"* and *"Is his father from Greenbrier?"* Code for: "Is he black or some mixture of another minority?" To which Jaden's mother would callously answer, *"He's human and the rest is none of yo' damn business."*

Dwayne contemplated bringing his son back to New York and putting him in a private school now that his own mother would no longer be the positive presence in his young life. She'd babysat from the time he was born; sometimes having to take him with her while she worked in the homes of strangers when Jaden's mother would leave him without warning. She'd also take him to church every Sunday to fill his young mind with the *'good word.'* She made sure to instill the Hargis family values in him during those times she had him, which was more frequently than Dwayne ever knew because even though Jaden's mother was no longer in the business of prostitution, Mrs. Hargis felt that her long hours as a cocktail waitress at the 'Coalminer's Retreat' was no way to raise a child.

How would it affect my lifestyle, my insane work schedule, and my personal interests? he wondered. *Would she even let me take him? Would he even want to live with me in an environment so vastly different from Greenbrier—away from his friends and family? And would it be fair to him? Maybe I'm being selfish or just overcome with grief and guilt for being an absentee dad.* Dwayne thought of broaching the subject with his father, but just as quickly abandoned the idea after catching a glimpse of him sitting in one of the twin, dark gray cushioned rockers in the living room, a Christmas gift he'd sent several years ago, surrounded by family, friends and acquaintances, but unable to shake the feeling of loneliness while suffering the reality of an irreplaceable loss.

No, he thought. *I can't take him away from his family. I don't know how much longer pops is gonna be here and I'm sure Darrell isn't gonna stick around for much longer either, and they're who he knows. It's up to me to be more of a presence in my son's life whether that means me coming down here more often or him visiting for the entire summer and not just for two or three weeks at a time. I need to step up and stop pretending I've been doing the right thing by sending a check every month. I'm always talking about how much I love my family, when here it is, I don't even know my son's favorite color, favorite book, dinosaur or sports team. I don't know how I'm gonna do it, but I have to try and figure out how to be a better father.*

CHAPTER 113

JUST as his roaming thoughts were beginning to square, his cell phone rang.

"What the hell?" he winced, after seeing the caller's name on the screen.

"Ary look, I'm down here with my family and I really don't have time to listen to you yelling at me or offering some feign explanation about why you did what you did or do what you do. I just don't have the time or the will to hear it. One thing I will do though is apologize for leaving your door open—that was unforgivable as well as ruining your bedroom table. I'll pay whatever it cost to get it refinished. You know, I could go on for hours just recounting the foolishness we always find ourselves in, but I won't. I have my family, including my son with me and I hope to God it's not too late to make up for all the hurt I've caused them."

"May I come in?"

"Excuse me?"

"I'm outside in a cab."

"You're what?! Where?!"

"I felt terrible for leaving you like I did and I saw the hurt and pain I caused by, quite frankly, abandoning you when you were most vulnerable," she tried explaining. "Dwayne, I'm sorry. I know my words can't possibly make up for my behavior but they're all I have. I'm asking your forgiveness in what I'm certain is the most sorrowful moment of your life. Please let me make it up to you somehow. You know my family makes me crazy and I haven't yet learned how to say *'no'*, even when it's to my own detriment. I also know what it is to lose a parent, or who I thought was a parent, and I can tell you that the anguish is never far from your mind and rarely, if ever, completely mended. Believe me Dwayne, you may not be able to see it right now or even be willing to forgive me, and I'd have to accept that, but I promised I'd be here for you and I jumped through a thousand hoops to make good on that vow."

She nervously stepped out of the cab holding onto the strap of her tote bag.

"And not that I'm complaining, but I literally paid a king's ransom to find a flight that could only get me as close as Roanoke Regional Airport in Virginia, then hired that nice gentleman," she pointed, hoping he could see for himself, "to drive me the other 100 miles to Greenbrier, and whose meter is still running—in case you told me to leave. But as much as it would hurt, I'd understand any decision you feel you'd need to make." She stood there, in the middle of the narrow, dusty, country road, exhausted, but fashionably dressed in Tracy Reese and Layla-Joy Williams with her eyes fixed on the front entrance of the house, anxiously awaiting his decision. Her racing heart and trembling hands, unsteady at the thought of rejection and having to find a hotel until she could arrange a flight back home, were all in contrast to what her emotions had prompted her to do.

With the phone up to his ear, he walked slowly through the kitchen and living room and over towards the front screen door and saw her standing there. His mind told him to lock it, back away, slam the wooden door shut, and return to his family scattered throughout the house. But he couldn't. His innermost desires dominated his better judgment and lead him to walk outside, down the porch steps, over the freshly cut grass and into her arms. She let her prized Gregory Sylvia bag fall to the ground and held onto him with every viable muscle in her petite frame. "I'm sorry, Dwayne. I'm so sorry I hurt you," she managed through falling tears.

"Shut up, don't talk," he whispered in her ear. "Don't say a word." He mourned for the loss of his mother and wept for the years he'd never be able to recover in his young son's life. He cried because of the comforting confusion he felt in her embrace but was able to say, after several minutes of silence, "Come inside, I want you to meet my son."

"I'd be honored." she said, still holding onto him.

"But I guess we should let the taxi dude go, huh?" he suggested, through a faint laugh. "I'm sure he'd prefer to be picking up other fares rather than watching this reality-show scene." he finished.

"I agree," she smiled, reluctantly loosening her embrace to bend down and retrieve her bag.

"Wait over on the sidewalk while I pay him," he instructed, checking his back pants pocket for his wallet.

"Oh Dwayne," she called, "my luggage is in the trunk."

He turned to look as she walked away. *Luggage?* he thought. *How long does she plan on staying?* 'Okay, I've got it." Dwayne walked over to the driver's side window and said, half-jokingly, "Am I gonna need to mortgage my parent's house for this fare?"

CHAPTER 114

SONYA deliberated for hours. *Should I call him? What'll he say? Or should I wait until I see him and discuss it in person? Is it even my place to bring it up?* But before she could answer her own thoughts, she found herself dialing his number.

"Hello Bruce, how are you? How's Matthew?"

"Sonya, hello, I'm good. Busy as always and so is Matthew. It's nice to hear from you. As a matter of fact, I'll be traveling to New York in a couple of weeks and wanted to know if you'd like to have dinner with me on the last Friday of my trip? I can either come out to the Island or meet you in the city, whichever is easiest for you."

She was taken aback at his offer, still trying to adjust to their newfound '*friendship*.' For a moment, it almost felt like an old acquaintance asking her out on a date—it felt nice and flattering. But the reality was, this was her ex-husband, the man who'd waited for years to reveal his true self and had chosen to live the rest of his life with another man at the expense of his family's deeply rooted anguish in order to pursue his own path to happiness. As difficult as it had been for years, she desperately wanted to move on and hoped their meeting in Brookstone was the first step. She hadn't planned on seeing him until her trip out to San Diego for his surprise birthday party, but maybe, she felt, this would be a better time to discuss Marcus' revelation.

"I'd like that," she answered, smiling. "There's a restaurant in the city I've been eager to try, but I didn't want to go alone."

"Then it's settled. All of my meetings that day should be

wrapped up by five and I can meet you there any time after that. Just text or call me with the details."

"Okay, I will."

"Oh, I'm sorry, Sonya. I started babbling about my trip before you could tell me the reason for your call."

"No, no, it's fine. It was just a friendly hello, that's all, nothing more."

"I appreciate that, I really do. It means a lot to us to have your friendship, Sonya. Well, at least yours and Marcus'. I think it's going to take Ary some additional time, based on her reaction at the house. I just hope she doesn't wait until it's too late."

"Too late? What do you mean, Bruce? Why '*too late*?"

"Nothing, it's nothing. Forget I said it," he admonished, authoritatively, immediately taking her back to his obstinate ways. "So I'll check back with you in a week just to confirm. Have a good evening, Sonya."

"Yes, you too." She reclined against the brown and gold, satin striped settee, imported from Pakistan after a family vacation—her eyes spanning the spacious bedroom like a visitor at a realtor's open house. *Although I've replaced* most *of the furniture, including the king-sized bed and matching dressers, somehow I'm still finding it difficult to fully replace the feelings I once had for him.* Sonya retrieved her cup of green tea from a Cameroon mango-wood table, and reminisced for just a short while about happier times before drifting off to sleep.

CHAPTER 115

"ARE you seriously suggesting that I'm involved in some kind of sinister behavior to destroy NPI and G? Have *you* lost *your* mind Joseph? I have absolutely no idea what you're talking about or who you're insinuating I'm in cahoots with. And I caution you to leave me out of your conspiracy theories. I have no interest, whatsoever in collaborating with you on anything ever again," she finished, referencing their collusion in Dwayne's firing.

"I didn't call to bullshit with you Marguerite. You of all people should know I have neither the time nor the interest in that. But what I will tell you is this—I know who your contact is," he lied, trying to elicit a name from her."

"What did you just say?"

"You heard me. I know who he is and he told me the role you're playing in this, '*little production*.'"

She was astounded and conflicted.

"So here's the deal Marguerite. Tell me what you know, and how they're compensating you for your information?"

Marguerite knew her cover was blown and had to decide within seconds how to salvage her plan. "Ok Joseph. I'll tell you this much. I *have* been in touch with a man who calls me to get information about G, but he's never revealed his name or how to reach him. It's strictly a one-way communications portal. My compensation in this is a financial bonus from the Chairman, who himself keeps his involvement close to the vest. The only reason I agreed to this was because of how G treated me and the fact that he promised to destroy my reputation in the industry so that I'd never be able to work again, at least not in New York," she said, adding the lie to throw him off. "But I've had a change of heart and I'm not so sure I want any more to do with this. The scope of it seems to be growing outside the realm of a lover's quarrel and I don't want to end up on the front page of the Times, the Daily News, or the Oil Industry Review. I'm also not sure who else is involved, but I'm guessing from your unwelcomed phone call and frenetic tone, you just might have a considerable role. So listen, whatever other information you thought I could provide, I'm sorry, that's it, that's all I know. And I don't want to know anymore than I know right now or even how you've inserted yourself into this. I'm going to call the Chairman and tell him I'm done and collect the fee I've been promised. No more phone calls or instructions from my elusive contact and no more unwanted and unwarranted calls from you either. My hands are clean from now on and I never want G to know that I was involved in whatever happens from this point on."

"Oh really? You think that's all it takes to wash your dainty little mulatto hands of all this? A phone call to the Chairman? Well let me hip you to a bit of reality Marguerite Armstead—you're dead wrong. You and I both know G isn't gonna let this happen without a cogent fight from his full legal team, to say the least. And believe me, the Chairman doesn't want that to happen. That's why he wants this little business deal to go through as smoothly and as expeditiously as possible and…"

"And what, Joseph? Are you going to snitch to G? I can tell you that he wants nothing to do with you ever again and wouldn't take kindly to you trying to contact him for *any* reason. That's what I *do* know and I'm 100 percent certain of that."

"Here's what I need you to do," he said, roundly ignoring her threats.

After years of futile exchanges with Joseph in NPI's boardroom, and quickly sensing that her argument had nowhere else to go, she conceded. "What's that? And before you answer, keep in mind I don't owe you a *damn* thing."

"Oh, you'll owe me plenty and lose even more if you think you can back out of this with no repercussions."

"What-do-you-want?" she asked, gritting her teeth in defeat.

"That's more like it. That's what I want to hear," he scoffed. "You're going to tell the Chairman that his boy Dave Winters is trying to squeeze out a bigger cut than what was originally agreed to and that Winters' cousin contacted Woolfolk to try and convince him to join them in their long-term, lucrative, drilling plans, effectively sabotaging the original deal concocted by the Chairman."

"What? Who the hell is Dave Winters and his cousin? And how significant would any conversations between Darias and this guy be to the Chairman?"

"Listen carefully, Marguerite. It's Winters' company that's partnering with NPI for the BP project. Only I'm certain Winters won't be satisfied with just a partnership, he'll eventually want control of the entire project and try to figure out a way to cut loose any additional baggage."

"Okay. So I know something about a partnership deal but I wasn't clued in on the company specifics or its players. How deeply is Darias involved in all this?" she asked, secretly trying to gather as much information from Joseph as she'd need for her own investigative plans.

"It'd be foolish to think he didn't know in advance that the awarded contract was a shared venture, but I'm not convinced he knows much about Winters. The Chairman keeps that relationship under tight wraps and has given strict instructions to other board members to follow suit. And as long as he has a controlling interest along with the last two sons of BPs founders, no one would be willing to challenge him. And, my dear former colleague, let's not pretend you don't know how Darias feels about the Chairman and vice versa. It's no secret to anyone."

"So all you need from me is to make the Chairman aware that this Dave Winters is trying to stiff him for more control, along with his cousin? What about the man that calls me for information on G? Do I let him know as well?"

"No. And from now on, I don't want you accepting his calls. I'm sure you've given him all he needs to know."

"How do you know that?"

"I don't. But I'm willing to bet that you won't be hearing from him as much as you may have in the past," he said, contemplating his next move out loud.

"Alright Joseph. Now I *am* curious to know the extent of your involvement? You don't do anything without profiting from it. What have you been promised? And by whom? What's your cut?"

"All I'll tell you is that I've been offered a stake in Winters' company," he said, telling a half-truth. "But that's before I found out his business principles weren't up to my high standards. And since he has such a close relationship with the Chairman, it would be hard for me to try and sway his mind about the deal. So that's where you come in. That's what I need you to do. I know he'd listen to you if you suddenly informed him that based on your own reliable sources, Winters was no longer a safe bet or satisfied with the initial offer. Then let them quibble over the details. And by the time Winters finds out who told the Chairman anything, I can stop whatever bleeding that would come out of it."

"That's it. That's all you want me to do?"

"That and keep your damn mouth shut about this discussion. But come to think of it, I don't really have to remind you to keep a secret now, do I?" he said, laughing. "I think we all know how good you are at that."

It took all she had not to curse him out and remind him of his own transgressions.

"I'll contact you on Wednesday. That should give you enough time to talk to the Chairman, convince him in your cunning little way that Dave Winters is a fraud and then I'll take over from there. Oh, and if I were you, if you haven't yet collected your snitch fees, I'd do that sooner rather than later. Don't let me down, Marguerite or I'll have to spill the beans on your involvement and we don't want that to be the case now, do we?" he asked, releasing a sinister chuckle.

She hung up the phone, waited two minutes and called Darias.

CHAPTER 116

MARCUS decided to take a walk in Central Park. There were thoughts, decisions and questions running through his mind and he didn't want to tackle any of them from home. It was a bright, beautiful morning and the park had not yet begun to host the countless tourists and New Yorkers who delighted in the sights, sounds, and wildlife that made up the more than 150 year-old landmark. He entered on the East side at Sheep Meadow, making his way to Bethesda Terrace and the Fountain where he stopped and laughed, remembering how as children he and Ary would race around the cascading waters synchronized to the sounds of a small orchestra playing classical music, and the throngs of park visitors, including his parents, relishing in the gratuitous summertime City gifts. He walked past Loeb's Boat House, stopping to reminisce the countless times his family had hosted out of town family and friends who'd wanted to experience every trap of tourism the city had to offer. Having grown up in a house filled with artistic beauty, today's destination was to sit near the Obelisk on the Great Lawn, with a spectacular view of the Metropolitan Museum of Art. He'd felt a sense of serenity and protection in museums, and the MET in particular, with its large, small and persistently thought provoking exhibits, from all things prehistoric to contemporary, had no rival in his mind. Even having traveled the world with his family, visiting the museums of France, Italy, and one of his architectural favorites as a teenager, The Royal Museum for Central Africa in Belgium, a beautiful massive space, notwithstanding its role in the brutal colonization of the Congo, which was thoroughly explained to him by his parents, was still no match for the MET.

He sat on a park bench facing the museum as time passed from morning to afternoon. Not until his stomach signaled its desperate need for nourishment was he willing to leave. As he stood up and turned to collect his backpack, he bumped into a woman about to take his place on the bench.

"Oh, sorry, I didn't see you. I guess I'm still lost in thought about...well, so many things."

"It's okay. No worries. I'm just glad to find an empty spot. I tried sitting on the steps of the museum out front but it became so crowded, so quickly, and I just wanted a bit of solitude."

Marcus couldn't take his eyes from this woman who was taking the time to offer an explanation to a question he hadn't even asked.

"Well, I'd like to say that I knew you were coming and saved this seat just for you, but I can't lie to a beautiful woman whose name I don't yet know," he said, offering an infectious smile.

"I'm Deidra Scott, lover of art and all things New York," she said, offering her hand.

"It's my pleasure, Deidra Scott. I'm Marcus Alexander, also lover of art and *most* things New York," he laughed. "There are *some* things about the city I can do without," he said, accepting her soft hand.

"Oh yeah?! I find that hard to believe. You must not be a native New Yorker," she said, returning a smile.

"I've always considered myself a native, having grown up on Long Island with at least one parent from the City. That should be an automatic qualifier, right?"

"Wait while I Google it," she laughed, pretending to check her phone. "Why, yes it does!"

He was intrigued by her sense of humor.

"I also grew up on the Island, but now that I'm starting a new job in the City, I want to rediscover all the spaces and places we New Yorkers take for granted."

"I like that," he said, still smiling. "Do you mind if I sit back down for a few minutes, I don't want to intrude on your solitude, but all of a sudden, I don't feel ready to leave just yet."

She smiled. "Not at all, I'd welcome the company. Oh, and tell me Marcus, what'd you mean exactly about not being able to *lie* to a *beautiful* woman whose name you don't know? You wouldn't fib to me now that you know *my* name, would you?"

The two strangers laughed and talked for more than an hour, recounting their experiences in the city and their travels abroad before Deidra made the connection between Marcus and his mother.

"Wait, you're the son of '*Sonya Alexander*,' the famous New York artist, whose very works I have in my home, and, I'm embarrassed to say, sometimes didn't pay my rent on time because I had to acquire them before someone else snatched them up *and* did not go clothes shopping for months at a time because of how her works touched my heart and the fact that I knew their value would only increase over time. You're *that* Sonya Alexander's son?" she asked, half laughing, half serious, and fully out of breath.

"Wow! You almost make *me* feel famous!" he laughed. "But yep, that's my mom, and I must admit, she is *awesomely* talented."

"She's more than just a talent to me Marcus. Especially being an African-American woman in the artist-sphere. I've followed her showings here in the City and on the Island. I've read about her travels and the inspiration she derives from those experiences. Needless to say, I'm an art nerd with no real aptitude of my own. I minored in art history at St. Johns University in Queens and always felt later in life that, even though I wasn't much of a painter, there would have been something for me to do in that world. But after school, like most new grads, I knew I had to make money if I wanted my own life and independence, and I did enjoy science, so I went back to school to become a nurse, which, don't get me wrong has been wonderfully satisfying, but also a highly stressful career. But in doing that work I've come to realize the sheer brevity of life and the fact that there are so many other things I want to pursue before my time is over. So, in lieu of getting the chance to say this to your mother, I'm honored and proud to be a supporter of such artistic brilliance."

Marcus was struck by her honesty and openness. The pride of being an Alexander at that moment was something he hadn't felt in a while. It felt surreal to be talking to someone who was such a fan and admirer of his mother. Although he and Ary had attended countless showings with her, they'd never had the opportunity to engage in deep, thoughtful conversations with her guests who were there to meet the artist, not her children. He looked at his Apple watch and said, "I haven't eaten all morning and my body is gonna collapse if I skip lunch too, and there's a really good spot just a few blocks out of the park. Would you like to join me, or at least make sure I get there before passing out, you being a nurse and all?" he joked.

"I'd be delighted to monitor your endurance before discharging you out into the cold, cruel world, Mr. Alexander," she said, standing up and reaching for his hands. As they walked through the park and onto 5th Avenue, Marcus' internal struggles were at least, for the moment, cast aside.

CHAPTER 117

DWAYNE packed up his clothes and reluctantly said goodbye to his father and brothers. He'd gotten a call from G inquiring about his return. *'I hate to intrude Dwayne, especially at a time like this, but I wanted to get a sense of when you'd be returning to the office? And listen, once everything here is back on track, I don't mind if you take a few extra days to see to whatever family matters requires your attention.'* He took that as a direct order to get his ass back to work and help G save his company. He walked down the hallway to his old bedroom and kissed his son lightly on his head, causing him to turn over, struggling to open his big green eyes. "Jaden, I have to leave. I have to get back to New York. Your mom's gonna be here to pick you up in a few hours. I've left something for you with grandpa, so don't forget to ask him for it before you leave, okay? He can be forgetful sometimes," he laughed. "But it's important that you get it, understand?"

"Yes papa," he said, wiping away the sleep and crust from his weary eyes. "When will I see you again, papa?"

"Very soon son. Now go back to sleep. You've played hard during these last few days with all your new and old cousins, so I know you must be tired, but I'll need you to help your uncles look after grandpa until I can come back. I love you Jaden," he said, trying desperately not to cry.

"I love you too papa," he said, pulling the covers over his head and falling quickly back to sleep.

He called Ary who was staying at his cousin's house. They had graciously extended an invitation for her to stay there instead of traveling into town to stay at the Greenbrier Holiday Inn, to which she was eternally grateful.

"Hey, it's me. I'll be there in about an hour. I know that doesn't give you much time to pack but I got a call from G and he wants me back there *'A-sap'*. One of my cousins agreed to take us to the airport and he'll be here soon and then we'll swing by to pick you up and be on our way. The plane leaves at 12:30 and I already called to make sure you could get on the flight with me and paid the difference in fare to change your ticket."

She'd been up for more than two hours after having received a similar call from G, who had no idea she was in West Virginia with Dwayne, telling her she needed to be in his office by four o'clock today for an urgent meeting, and a text message from Marguerite reminding her of their eight o'clock dinner for solidifying their plans. She'd already made calls to the airline for a flight out and luckily it happened to be the same one Dwayne had already booked.

"Good morning. I'm already packed. I received the same request, well, it was more like an order from G, and was getting ready to call you when my cell rang. I'll be waiting downstairs."

"Ok, I'll see you soon."

"Alright. Oh, Dwayne, I want to thank your relatives for being so kind in offering to house a total stranger at such a heartbreaking time," she said, hoping he'd volunteer a suggestion.

"Hey, don't worry about it. They wouldn't expect anything from you. It was a heartfelt offer."

"I know but…"

"That's it. No more talk about it. Just be ready when I get there."

Dwayne knocked on his father's door, hugged him goodbye and handed him a large manila envelope with Jaden's name written across the face of it.

"Give him this pops. It's the key to my apartment and this letter. I know he's too young to read and comprehend it, but as time goes by, he will."

Ary reached for her handbag to see what cash she'd brought and pulled out two, one-hundred dollar bills, two fifties and three twenties. She placed the hundreds, twenties and one fifty dollar bill underneath the doily of a lamp sitting on top of the chest of drawers and wondered if there might be an ATM within walking distance—quickly remembering that she hadn't even seen a supermarket as her driver drove off the paved roads of the one lane highway onto the dusty path leading to the Hargis' home. "Well, this is all the cash I have. Maybe I can send a check once I return home. I hope they know how appreciative I am for opening up their home to me at a moment's notice," she said to herself, packing the last of her outfits. After lightly knocking on the bedroom door of her hosts, she peeked in and expressed her gratitude, complimented them on the closeness of the family and headed downstairs to wait for Dwayne. Within the hour, they were off to Greenbrier Valley Airport and on their way back to facing an unwelcomed reality.

CHAPTER 118

"YES Darias, we have to meet tonight. Time is running out. And before you know it, we'll all get screwed. I spoke to Joseph Larsen and he's involved in this somehow—surprise, surprise, and I'm sure he stands to make a ton of money if we stand by and do nothing."

"What?! I should have known Larsen had his dirty hands in this. Okay, where and what time?"

"Trattoria Molino on 48th and 1st at 9pm sharp, I only have an hour and don't be late. You know…"

"Yes Marguerite, we all know how you feel about punctuality. But let me just tell you this, I'm done with anymore NPI entanglements. I don't owe any allegiance to anyone or any company other than BP—who pays me generously to bring in *legitimate* business and make sure things run smoothly. I surely never signed up for any of this bullshit."

"None of us did. I'll see you tonight."

CHAPTER 119

ARY and Dwayne rushed through the airport and straight through security. Dwayne had upgraded their tickets to first class so they'd be able to sit together and strategize for their meeting with G. She told him about her conversations with Marguerite and suggested he be at the restaurant tonight. At first he resisted, explaining that he didn't want to jeopardize any plans Marguerite may have made and also the fact that she hated him and had been Joseph's co-conspirator in his firing. But ultimately, she convinced him to go and request a table near the back. She'd make sure her table was close by, even if she had to insist on changing it from the one Marguerite had already reserved. Dwayne suggested she record the conversation in case this escalated well beyond their capabilities.

"That's a great idea, I hadn't thought of it."

"Yeah, but just make sure you don't say anything to incriminate yourself. It's getting harder and harder to know who to trust in this industry and I'm growing tired of it, despite the money. I'm not so sure it's worth it if this is something that happens on a quarterly basis."

"I know. But I really don't think it's the norm, Dwayne. I realize the more money you make the more risks you encounter, but it's not like we're being set up for the downfall. We're just helping G save his company. We can always work for another firm if things don't work out at NPI."

He could only stare at her, realizing that underneath the tough exterior she worked so hard to present, she was still very naïve when it came to everyday common sense. He attributed it to her privileged upbringing and at that moment, felt even more protective.

"Ary listen to me. This is serious, and if it doesn't pan out the way we want it to, our careers just might be *finished* in this sector. No matter what you may think, they *can* and *will* pull the strings they need to try and ruin us. Remember, we're still just two African-Americans operating in a world of whiteness. We're not over in the Middle East where our footing might be a bit more stable," he explained, using a deeper and more solemn tone. "So as much as I'd like to believe we're '*helping G out of another bind*,' I'm more concerned about *our* futures," he ended, gazing into her gleaming hazel eyes.

Ary placed her hand over his on the armrest and leaned over to kiss him. She stopped a flight attendant coming down the aisle and asked for two vodka martinis, straight up. "I'm not sure that's what you would have ordered Dwayne, but it seemed right to me," she said, revealing a nervous smile.

CHAPTER 120

MARCUS and Deidra spent hours at the restaurant talking and laughing about their childhoods, traveling and their changing career plans. She recounted how she'd gone to Sonya's opening in the Village and was even more captivated by her new works and displays than ever before. He avoided any lingering conversations about it, explaining that he was under the weather and regrettably had to miss it.

Marcus couldn't remember the last time he'd laughed so much, feeling at ease with their unremitting tête-à-tête.

"Deidra, I know this may sound weird but here goes. I felt like I was in a crisis just a few hours ago, and please don't ask me to go into detail. But then, as fate would have it, you showed up and here we are, having lunch and laughing like old friends, and I mean 'old' in a beautifully young way," he laughed. "Thank you for walking into my life. You'll never understand how much this means to me."

She wondered what he could have meant, but refrained from prying. "Thank *you* Marcus. I was feeling a little glum myself. I'd just ended a relationship and thought I was on the verge of beginning a new one when I realized his heart wasn't ready to let go of someone his mind was trying to forget. So I appreciate having met you. And it felt good to laugh. Maybe we'll see each other again."

"How about tonight?" he blurted out, "If that's not too presumptuous of me. I'd love to take you out to dinner at a little place in Harlem where the food is incredible and afterwards we can make our way down to Times Square, pretend to be out-of-towners looking up at skyscrapers like aliens from another galaxy, take unrelenting and annoying selfies and then listen to people whisper, or not, saying with scorn, 'Tourists! They should all be rounded up and shipped off to some distant land…like New Jersey,'" he ended, laughing.

"Hey hey, careful! I have friends and relatives in Jersey! And besides, I don't think we'd need to ship them—it's not *that* far away, we can just put them on the Path train, wink-wink!" she laughed in return.

"Boy, you really are a New Yorker!" he teased.

"Guilty! And Marcus, I'd love to join you tonight."

"Let's meet at eight o'clock, if's that good for you."

"Eight it is."

"I'll text you the details."

They talked and laughed for another ten minutes before saying goodbye.

CHAPTER 121

G continued to check in with his contacts on the West Coast to gather any additional information on T.O.T, but there was little more than what he'd already been told. He found it almost unfathomable that such a small, relatively unknown oil firm would even be in the running for such an important contract and no one question its validity. "It has to be someone on the inside pushing for... Idiot!!!" he said, thumping the side of his head multiple times after it suddenly became crystal clear in his mind. "That must be the reason she wants to meet with Ary, to pass along any demands she may have. Well, it's not going to work. You'll have to do better than that to try and ruin me Marguerite and I'd think you'd know better than to take me for a fool, lying down while you and your gang of degenerates tries to destroy me."

G called Ary's cell but it went straight to voicemail. *Damn it!* "Ary it's G. Try to get here before four o'clock today, ideally by three or three-thirty. I think I know how to head this thing off before any meetings you've scheduled with Marguerite. Call to let me know you received this message."

Ary and Dwayne were jumping into a cab outside of LaGuardia airport, and it was impossible to hear her phone ringing. But as they got underway on the Van Wyck expressway, she noticed he'd called.

"Oh no!" she said, after listening.

"What is it? What's the matter?" he asked, trying to keep his eyes from closing. His time in Greenbrier had included a number of sleepless nights.

"G's had some kind of revelation and now he wants me in the office before four. What should I make of it?"

"Nothing. Don't change your plans with Marguerite, and if he doesn't know you're meeting her tonight, don't tell him. See what he knows and maybe use it for leverage if she becomes all, well, '*Margueritie*'," he said, infusing a bit of levity in his effort to keep her calm and himself awake. "Do you want me to come early, to be there with you?"

"No, he only asked for me. I'll see you at his four o'clock meeting, and besides you have to get ready for whatever goes down tonight at dinner, remember?"

"Hey don't worry about me. I'm not the one known for not showing up at places," he said, remembering how he'd asked for her help only a few short months ago during his meeting with Joseph.

"Okay, alright mister. Let's not resuscitate a dead horse. I'll admit I may have screwed up, just a little…"

"A little?!" he shouted.

"Dwayne!"

"Sorry. And by the way, how the hell do you '*resuscitate a dead horse*?" he grinned.

"I thought that was an actual maxim," she said, playfully punching his arm.

"No, no it's not lady. Just leave it to me when it comes to clever truisms." They both enjoyed a much needed chuckle.

CHAPTER 122

G paced his office, looking out the windows onto 5th Avenue on the East side, with views of the East River. On the West side there were cargo ships, cruise lines and water taxis all sharing the lanes of the mighty Hudson. He'd given instructions to Connie to usher Ary in immediately, even if he was on a call. At precisely 3 o'clock, Ary arrived and was escorted in. Inwardly, she could feel her anxiety surfacing, but her outward appearance showed no signs of mental strain.

"G, I'm sorry I couldn't get here sooner, I was actually working off-site this morning, preparing the Kendall Oil extension contract for your approval," she feigned.

"What? Oh, yeah, that's fine. Listen, you haven't met with Marguerite have you?"

"No, not yet," she lied, trying to remain vague. "I'm waiting for her to confirm. Why do you ask?"

"Because I'm pretty certain about what she may be proposing."

"Huh? I mean, what were you thinking?"

"Before the Chairman took on the role of Lord and Master of BP when the founder died, I'd heard that not only did he want to prevent me from winning any BP contracts, he wanted to destroy my company. But I've always had people on the inside to keep me informed of his next moves—people like Darias Woolfolk and Julian Dorchak. But now, after the chaos and shakeup here at NPI, I'm certain he felt this would be the perfect time to use her to get to me. It all makes perfect sense Ary, and I guess I was too caught up in the intricacies of it to see the big picture unfolding right before my very eyes."

She stared at the coldness and intensity in his eyes before answering. "You're right G." She looked at her watch, it was 3:20pm and she was sorry that she'd insisted on Dwayne coming at four. She hoped that by some miracle he would show up earlier after thinking about what he'd said regarding the two of them being involved in a world of white conspiracy, and the only ones coming out losers. She felt nauseous.

"It's okay Connie, he's expecting me," Dwayne cautioned, holding up his hand as he walked right past G's assistant and into his office. "I hope you don't mind G, but I came straight from the airport knowing how important this was," he lied. "Oh, excuse me. I didn't see you Ary. I apologize for barging in on your meeting."

"I'm sorry sir," Connie said, poking her head around the half opened door. "Would you like me to reschedule Mr. Hargis?" she inquired, squinting pointedly at Dwayne. "I'll check your calendar for available times tomorrow if you'd like."

Visibly annoyed by her questions, G insisted, "No, no, it's fine, it's okay. Close the door on your way out, please!"

Ary breathed a deep sigh of relief, looking over at Dwayne and mouthing the words, '*Thank you.*'

"Dwayne, first let me say how very sorry I am for the loss of your mother. And listen, whatever you might need—the use of my private jet, or one of my homes for your father or family members should they need to, or just want to get away. Anything, just ask."

"Thank you G, I appreciate that, I really do," he said, sincerely. But he couldn't help but think of the fact that G had called to '*request*' that he immediately get back to the office on the first plane out of West Virginia when he barely had time to bury his mother. "And I'll certainly extend the invitation to my family, but right now, it's important to prevent any further fraudulent actions against NPI. We're family," he said, turning to look at Ary with a subtle wink.

G, looked at Dwayne with the eyes of a proud father, and walked over to him, placing both hands on his shoulders and said, "You will never know how much that means to me." Turning to Ary, he said, "Now, let's all put our heads together and strategize."

CHAPTER 123

AFTER returning home from what he'd described as a tranquil morning and an incredible afternoon with Deidra, Marcus prepared for his evening out. The neurons in his brain were firing faster than his thoughts could keep pace. *What about Caroline? What about the fact that he'd told his mother he was gay, or was it that he was bisexual, involuntarily drugged or just confused? Was he really interested in her as a woman or was he merely trying to mask his ongoing pain, insecurity and doubt?* But even with all the unrelenting questions, he felt excited and eager to see her again. He went online and made reservations at one of his favorite Ethiopian restaurants in Harlem, then sorted through his closet for the perfect ensemble. Quickly determining that Ralph Lauren would impress tonight, he chose a striped blue and white button-down, a gold-button navy blazer, and a pair of straight-leg, cotton tan chinos. Andrew Marc brown leather lace-ups would suffice as his footwear choice. With his wardrobe decision finalized, he walked just outside the bedroom to his single-person sized bathroom and jumped into a steamy shower. Marcus adjusted the jets on the showerhead to a vigorous pulse, allowing the water to beat his back like a heavy-handed masseuse. He turned from side to side, front to back, leaning forwards and backwards, washing and conditioning his closely cropped hair, turning the temperature from hot to warm to cool every few minutes. He could feel the stress draining with the soapy water and hear the Caribbean drumbeat blasting from the MP3 player sitting dangerously near the edge of the sink, helping to ease his mind. But what he couldn't hear was his cell phone ringing several times in the bedroom. Caroline had come to a final decision and she wanted to set up a meeting to tell him face-to-face. She needed to see him, not hear his voicemail. So she hung up without leaving a message, deciding to try later in the evening.

Marcus wrapped a towel around his slender, but toned waist and headed for the bedroom. Checking his cell he noticed her call, but decided instead to text Deidra, confirming their evening plans.

CHAPTER 124

ARY and Dwayne walked separately out of G's suite. He returned to his office, she left for home. She wasn't feeling well and wanted to take a few hours to try and recover before meeting Marguerite. She called for a Lyft and was on her way within fifteen minutes.

She'd convinced herself that this would absolutely be the final time to get involved in what seemed to be *'business as usual'* in the hardnosed game that oilmen seemed to delight in. *I took this job to make money, knowing there would be challenges—but damn!* she swore, *this is like a fucking James Bond movie and I'm playing the part of the femme fatale without all the Hollywood perks or a cute little orange, Halle Berry bikini. This shit stops tonight though. Maybe mama was right all along. Maybe..."*

But before she could conclude her thoughts, her phone beeped a text message. The sender's information was blocked.

"I know you have a dinner meeting with Marguerite tonight because you have G's best interest at heart. But tread lightly—this is well above your pay grade."

"Oh my God! What the hell? Who is this? Who has my phone number?" Her heartbeat sped up to keep pace with her thoughts, racing faster than she could even process. "I don't know what to do!" she screamed. "This isn't my fight!" She scrolled through her contacts until she came to Darias' personal number and pushed the call button. It rang several times before his voicemail answered. "Please Darias, I need you! I know you're furious with me and you have every right to be, but please, please call me back!"

CHAPTER 125

DWAYNE'S feelings were vacillating from resentment for having to leave his family sooner than he'd planned, to concern for Ary's health, after noticing her complexion go from the tanned glow of her recent travels to a visible pallid as they stood near each other in G's office. He'd also sensed her uncharacteristic apprehension about tonight's meeting with Marguerite. But right now exhaustion was invading his body and demanded he rest. He laid his head down over his folded arms on the desk, hoping to silence the dizzying thoughts and lessen his mounting tension. Not leaving anything to chance, he set the alarm on his Apple watch for seven o'clock. Tonight, he knew there was no room for error.

CHAPTER 126

MARCUS arrived at Massawa, a chic Ethiopian eatery Harlemites frequented every hour it was open, making it hard for those outside the neighborhood to garner what had become a coveted reservation. But Marcus knew the chef, they were old college friends from NYU, and although they'd gone their separate ways, pursuing different career paths, once the restaurant launched on Harlem's Restaurant Row, to great fanfare and reviews, and Marcus found out his friend was the master chef, he'd been able to get in just by mentioning his name.

Seated at a table near the window, anxiously awaiting Deidra's arrival, he summoned a familiar waiter and asked for his usual—Tangueray with a twist of lime. He fidgeted with his shirt collar; unbuttoned and buttoned his blazer several times, and even repositioned the table to a slight angle, switching chairs, just so he wouldn't miss her entrance.

The waiter brought his drink and asked if he wanted to order an appetizer while waiting for his guest. "No man, I'll wait for my date. But don't be a stranger cause my stomach's likely to object," he joked. And just moments later, he saw her, getting out of a cab. S*he's beautiful,* he thought, e*ven more than this afternoon.* Marcus stood up as the hostess brought her to the table.

"Thank you for coming," he said, slightly grinning and leaning over to kiss her right cheek."

"You're welcome Marcus," she said, returning a smile and taking her seat. "Did you think I wouldn't show up? We had such a wonderful time earlier and I couldn't think of a more perfect way to end my evening."

Marcus sat down, his eyes trained on hers as his head filled with thoughts and feelings of sexual orientation confusion, his love for Caroline and confession to his mother and sister. *How can* this *be happening? I still love the woman I proposed too, but this is so different. Am I straight or gay? I have no desire to be with another man, none whatsoever! Was I just drunk, drugged, taken advantage of and robbed all in one night? Even so, I can't undo what I did and I'm not exactly sure what it is I did in the first place.*

Only Deidra's question stilled the one-man debate in his mind. "You look lost in thought Marcus. Is something wrong?"

"No. Everything feels right. Forgive me for staring, if I was, but it all just became clear."

She tilted her head and pursed her full, rouge colored lips and asked, "What became clear? Is it anything you'd like to share?"

Just as he'd begun to formulate an answer, his cell phone beeped a text message. He'd left it lying on the table near his folded arm, but out of Deidre's immediate view. Glancing quickly, he saw that it was from Bruce. *Hey son, I'll be in NY in a few weeks. Would love to get together for lunch or dinner. Love, Dad.*

"Uh, no, not now anyway," he grimaced, quickly putting the phone in the breast pocket of his blazer. "But this I will share with you," he teased, quickly changing his tone, as well as the direction of the conversation. "The mild lamb is their specialty. It's cooked to perfection in a thick, well-seasoned, spicy sauce. And because I know the chef personally, we'll get a larger portion than just these regular folks in here," he laughed. "And if you find that it's way too much to handle in just one sitting, don't worry. I'm hoping we'll have the chance to finish any leftovers together."

Deidra was captivated, perplexed, curious, humored and uncomfortably flattered by his presumption. And as much as she'd wanted to press him for an answer to her earlier questions, she thought it best to leave it alone. "Hmmmm," she pondered, scanning the menu, "So the lamb, huh?"

"You *cannot* go wrong with the lamb," he insisted.

"I'll have the chicken."

"Hey! What the…?! And after my impassioned testimonial? Oh okay, I see what you did there, young lady. You got me." They laughed in unison.

CHAPTER 127

ARY had taken two Dramamine pills once she'd returned home, trying to alleviate the nauseous feeling she'd felt in G's office and the fear and uneasiness from the anonymous text. So far it hadn't worked, and the time had come to meet Marguerite. Instead of driving, she called a car service. She checked her hair and clothes one last time in front of the floor length mirror in her bedroom, slipped on her favorite pair of comfortably stylish, Kate Spade black and white ankle strap, three inch pumps, grabbed her matching handbag and headed down to the lobby to wait for her driver's text. She stood near the large glass door to get a better angle of the arriving Towne car and contemplated calling Darias again. But before she could follow through, she noticed the car climbing the circular driveway and she walked out the door to meet him. Settling in, she took a deep breath and reminded herself that after this final meeting with Marguerite, she'd inform G of the information she was able to obtain and be done with it. *Let the chips fall where they may*, she thought. And before any further reflections could take shape, her cell phone rang.

"Oh! Thank you for calling me! I…"

"Ary listen, I don't appreciate it when someone takes me for a fool and you apparently don't understand that," his tone, harsh and unfamiliar.

"I completely understand and I would never have reached out to you if I didn't think this was terrifyingly important."

"What are you talking about?"

"I received a threatening text from someone suggesting that I was in over my head with what's happening between NPI and BP. Darias, I didn't ask for this, I swear. It's like a dreadful nightmare of what just happened and here I am again, right at the center of it all," she explained, her tone rising with each explanation.

"Slow down," he said, exasperatingly, "Tell me what's going on."

She recounted her conversations with Marguerite but stopped short of divulging tonight's dinner plans.

The driver pulled up to the curbside of the restaurant, looked back at her through the rearview mirror and announced their arrival. She put her index finger up to her lips to silence him and continued talking. He sighed and pointed to his watch; a not so subtle way of urging her to get out of his car. She ignored him.

"Would you be willing to meet me tonight, after nine o'clock? I have commitments up until that time. I really need you," she pleaded, her voice quivering.

He thought about his own nine o'clock meeting with Marguerite and hesitated. "Uhhh, alright. Meet me at my place around ten. If I'm late, tell the doorman you're my guest and he'll take you to one of the private guest waiting rooms. I'm sure one of them will be available at that time and I'll stop and get you once I arrive home."

"Thank you."

"Don't be so quick to thank me Ary. I'm not trying to rescue your ass again. I'd like to be able to just do my job without anymore of these unnecessary interruptions."

"Yes Darias, I understand. I'll see you tonight." Ary reached in her handbag and pulled out three twenty dollar bills, reaching across the seat to give the driver. "I'm sorry. I hope this makes up for the extra time." He accepted the money without saying a word. She stepped out of the car, one long slender leg at a time, tugged at her skirt, stood on the sidewalk for a few seconds, watching as male passersby ogled at her beauty, and with a renewed burst of confidence walked into Trattoria Molino, announcing her arrival to the host.

CHAPTER 128

"I'M meeting Ms. Armstead."

"Oh yes. Please follow me," he said, leading Ary through the well-appointed eatery towards a table near the back where she noticed Marguerite on her cell phone, quickly ending the call after seeing her approaching, and placing it face down near her clutch on the table.

"Your waiter will be over in just a moment ladies. Thank you for being our guest tonight."

As the host walked away, Ary moved the chair to sit directly across from her former foe. Marguerite, examining her from head to toe asked, "Are you alone like I *told* you to be?"

Ary's immediate thought was to say: *Believe me, you're fucking lucky I even showed up. I want this to end as quickly as you do.* But letting her better judgment prevail, she said, "You mean, like you *asked* me to be? Yes, of course. Why would I jeopardize anything at this point?"

"Alright good. So listen, this has to happen within the next couple of days, or it'll be too late to do anything about it and then we'll all come out looking like complete assholes or far worse."

Ary's expression depicted her astonishment before uttering a word. She frowned, pulled back and cocked her head before asking, "*We'll* all come out looking like assholes? I *didn't* or *haven't* yet agreed to *do* anything except listen to you try and figure out a way to help G save his company. So please, I would ask that you *not* cast those aspersions onto me."

Marguerite's rose-colored cheeks turned a fiery red. Never in her wildest imagination would she think she'd be relying on any female to facilitate a reconciliation with her former lover, or help in rescuing his company—especially Ary Alexander. She conferred all that she knew up to this point about the Chairman's latest deeds and his sketchy relationship with Dave Winters.

Ary interrupted. "But what about the repercussions of deceiving the firm you're entrusted with protecting? What about the liability of crossing the line between deception and outright fraud? Doesn't anybody think about any of that?" she asked, genuinely concerned.

"Oh my dear little innocent apprentice," Marguerite mocked. "The money to be gained from any transaction of this magnitude far outweighs the fines or proverbial slaps on the wrist from the F.E.R.C. This is the big leagues sweetheart, and if you're going to play the game, you'll need to become more sagacious when it comes to the ways of how we, in the oil business, operate. And while you're at it, grow a thicker skin. No one gives a *shit* about what's right, it's all about growing your bottom line. Haven't you learned anything from your so-called *'relationships'* at NPI and whatever other *'little'* companies you've worked for?" she asked, smiling contemptuously.

"Waiter!" Ary called, turning away. "Bring me a Sazerac cocktail, no ice, and quickly."

"I'll have a Blackberry Gin & Tonic," Marguerite said, coolly, trying to determine whether Ary would be up to the final task.

"Of course ladies. And have you had a chance to look over the menu for appetizers or dinner?"

"No! And we won't be needing it," Marguerite answered.

Without taking her eyes from Marguerite, Ary motioned for the waiter to lean down, saying, "I'll have *whatever* the special is tonight," she countered. And just as he'd begun to walk away, she tugged on his shirtsleeve and whispered, "As long as that special is a shrimp salad, and I'll trust your choice for a calorie friendly side," she winked. Marguerite could only glower at her nemesis.

"Can we *please* continue our conversation or do you have any other requests for the help?"

The Help?! The Filipino waiter looked at Marguerite with scorn and thought, *I'm sure we've been called a lot of different things, but being called 'the help' to our faces by a dinner guest? That's rich. I'll have to add that one to our book of insults...snobby bitch!*

Ary was mortified. She looked at her watch and said, "Just tell me what else I need to know and do. I have to leave by nine o'clock."

"So do I," Marguerite answered, flipping her cell phone over.

Ary looked around to see if Dwayne had discreetly arrived. She even made an excuse before her meal arrived to go outside for air because of a contrived bronchial disorder. She tried calling him. He never answered. She knew she'd be on her own. She also knew G would be relying on her to furnish him with any additional information she'd uncover from Marguerite, helping to prevent any further machinations of NPIs takeover attempt. Then she remembered that she hadn't recorded a single word of their conversation as Dwayne had suggested. "Damn! What now?"

She steadied her nerves, walked back inside, sat down, planted a vicious stare towards a skeptical Marguerite and said, "I'll do it."

CHAPTER 129

DEIDRA excused herself for a visit to the ladies room. Marcus called the 'W' hotel. He knew the cost for a same night reservation would be exorbitant, but he didn't care. This was something he wanted to do—felt he had to do. His only hope was that she would agree to go. His heart convinced him that there was definitely male-female chemistry between them—his conscious pushed him to prove it.

CHAPTER 130

"ALRIGHT then, everything's settled. And as much as I'd like to continue this convivial conversation and delight in your beguiling presence, I have other more pressing obligations this evening," Marguerite offered, in her signature cynicism.

"Worker!" she called, lifting her delicate index finger. "I mean, waiter!" she corrected, after watching Ary's eyes widen in revulsion. "I'd forgotten how you might take offense to that, seeing as though this *was* once your *'profession,'* she recalled, remembering the time Ary lied about working as a waitress at the Four Seasons before accepting the position at NPI, feigning how difficult the job could be because of unreasonably demanding customers.

Idiot! Ary thought.

"Why don't you get a, what do you call it, a *'doggy bag'* for your leftover salad. I'm sure you must know *someone*, an acquaintance or family member who could use a healthy meal from a highly regarded restaurant."

"No thank you, Marguerite," she said, standing up and reaching for her handbag. "I just hope that while they're dumping it in the trash, they don't mistakenly throw you out with it. Enjoy the rest of your evening."

Black fucking bitch! Marguerite thought. *I don't ever want to see her again after this, ever!*

Walking through the restaurant towards the exit, she took one last sweeping look to see if somehow, she'd missed him. Taking a deep breath, she lifted her head and proceeded out the door, standing on the sidewalk, contemplating whether to go to Dwayne's apartment and confront him for being a 'no-show' before going to Darias' or risk an awkward meeting at the office. She looked at her watch. It was 8:50pm. She hailed a cab and said, "427 West 96th street, and hurry."

As the taxi blended into traffic, Darias' driver dropped him off in front of the restaurant where Marguerite, still fuming from her self-imposed dependence on Ary, had consumed her second Blackberry Gin & Tonic.

"What?" he asked, pointing to his watch after noticing the fury written over her face and the smell of alcohol escaping her breath, "I'm right on time."

CHAPTER 131

"MARCUS believe me, this is *not* something I do with any kind of frequency," she said nervously as they entered the hotel suite.

"Shhhh," he cautioned, leading her to the bedroom of the luxurious space. "I promise you won't regret it." Stopping and turning to face her, he continued. "I'm hoping this'll be the first of our lasting time together."

Marcus closed his eyes and kissed her soft, shimmering lips. He placed one hand just at the nape of her neck, the other around her thirty–two inch waist, pulling their willing bodies into a deep embrace, whispering, "I think you're what I've been waiting for, for far too long."

Her heartbeat sped up to meet the pace of raw emotion. She removed his sports coat, slowly, letting it fall down to the carpeted floor beneath him, unbuttoning his shirt without taking her eyes from his gaze. She rose up in her heels to match his slender stature, softly kissing behind his ear. Inwardly, he shivered, outwardly he longed for what the night might promise. Deidra lowered herself seductively onto the soft, king-sized bed, kicked off her heels and reached for his hands. He willingly took hold, but instead of joining her, whisked her up into his long, lean, strong arms and carried her over to the window of their fifty-second story suite. Pushing open the curtains that revealed the glowing city lights, shining from surrounding buildings and shadows cast by the muted stars above, he positioned himself against the sturdy glass, pulled her close and began the heated ritual of slowly undressing her, sensually kissing her round breasts, squeezing and manipulating her pear-shaped butt. He leaned down to remove her panties using his heated tongue and teeth. She moaned in ecstasy, he groaned in disbelief. Every emotion he thought had been lost flooded his mind and body. After examining her nakedness, he pushed her back, gently, inches apart, and began undressing himself, stabilizing his stance against the window. He lifted her up, placing her femininity over his fully erected manhood. Her arms clung tightly around his neck as he helped direct her swaying frame, up and down, up and down, concealing and exposing his bulging erection and exhibiting the strength and finesse he'd worked hard to achieve. Their brown eyes met as she rose and fell to his sexually throbbing exercise. As he lowered her sweetly scented body to her feet, he led her to the pile of feather-filled pillows on the bed, laying her down gently while kissing her eyelids. He whispered, "The rest of the night is for you."

Marcus pushed her arms above her head, tracing the outline of her sultry, feminine physique with the tips of his fingers as he slowly began exploring every inch of her burning body, tracing the cusp of her breasts with soft, teasing kisses, before gently spreading her legs apart. Using only the tip of his tongue, he traveled down to her womanhood, inducing the natural reflexes of her hips to rock from side to side, moaning his name, imploring him to bring her to ultimate ecstasy. He climbed on top of her, thrusting deep and hard, igniting the full force of passion and desire until they both collapsed into a poetic finale.

CHAPTER 132

ARY pushed the buzzer several times. She felt anxious, annoyed and betrayed. *Why did he lie?* she wondered. She'd trusted him. Was he trying to retaliate against her for not showing up at his dinner with Joseph?

"Yeah? Who is it?" he asked after getting up from his warm bed and walking unsteadily through the living room to the buzzer near the front door. He was still worn from days of family stress, strain, travel and work.

"It's me Dwayne. Buzz me in please."

"Ary?! What are you doing here?"

"I'd like to find out why you never came to the restaurant tonight after promising me you would," she yelled, causing residents and visitors alike to stop and stare. Lowering her voice after realizing the small spectacle she was causing, she continued. "And I don't think the vestibule is the proper venue to have this discussion."

Oh shit!, he said, realizing he'd silenced the alarm on his watch, forgetting about his meeting with her and heading straight home from the office. *I guess there'll be hell to pay for this,* he thought.

He decided to try and explain why he wasn't there and hopefully be able to move forward with whatever plans she'd propose. But instead of ringing his doorbell, she knocked, hard, several times. He looked up towards the ceiling and thought, *I have a feeling I'm gonna be calling on you tonight, Lord. So, please answer when you hear my voice.* He inhaled deeply before opening the door.

"Hey Ary, first let me apologize for…"

"How could you?" she interrupted. "You left me there all alone with her, with no one to back me up!"

"I know and I'm really sorry. I'd set my alarm after making a few client calls, but I guess I was more tired than I'd even realized. So again, I'm sorry. Can we discuss it now?" he said, wiping the sleep from his drowsy eyes.

She stood just over the threshold, glaring, considering whether she would accept his explanation or continue the argument she was prepared to have. She could see the weariness in his eyes, face and posture and watched as he staggered slowly over to his leather recliner, collapsing into it.

"Are you drunk?"

"What?! No I'm not drunk. I'm tired Ary. My mother just passed away and I'm trying to do right by my son. There are a ton of decisions I need to make for my ailing father and the expenses he's facing, along with helping out at least one of my brothers. I have a stressful job. I'm either in a relationship or I don't know what you call this. And on top of all that, I've been roped into some type of espionage going on between BP and NPI," he rattled off. "So no, I'm not '*drunk*,'" he said, mimicking her. "I'm just fucking sick and tired of all the bullshit that seems to surround you and those people."

Her eyes bore into his as she stepped further into the apartment. She was fuming. "Really! Bullshit? *Those* people? Let me make something crystal clear to you Dwayne Hargis. If it weren't for me, we'd end up in the exact same situation we found ourselves in weeks ago. Were it not for me putting *myself* and *my* job on the line, both of us just might end up in a line of unemployment!" she screamed. "Do you actually think I chose NPI for *these* types of challenges?" her tone escalating with every word. "You think *you're* the only one with family issues?! My brother just announced he's gay! The reason? He got drunk, drugged, kissed, attacked and robbed by a man in the back of a New York City taxi!" she screamed, exaggerating on the exact details. "How am I supposed to fix *that*? How?!" she shouted.

Dwayne watched as she fell apart. And before he could prevent any further breakdown, she walked directly in front of him to continue her tirade.

"And now my mother, whose spent half her life in misery over my father, a man who decided years ago that his family wasn't worth the time, nor deserving of the respect to just sit us down and explain his reasons for leaving, has asked me and my bemused little brother to accompany her to his surprise birthday party—in San Diego!"

"A man," she said, "who felt it was perfectly logical to wait for his wife to finish slaving over a hot stove, preparing our traditional Thanksgiving dinner, a time we'd always spent at home, together, celebrating and giving thanks for our many blessings, to tell her, after she'd set the table with china he'd actually told her years prior, way before me or my brother were even born, was too expensive, then ended up surprising her on her birthday after his first international business trip to China by buying it, and having it engraved with *'I'll love you forever'* on the bottom of each piece. That very same china sat on the dining room table, holding the special meal she'd cooked all by herself, and this, he decided, was the perfect time to toast us with, *'I'm leaving all of you, for a man!'*"

With tears spilling down her cheeks, she continued. "And now I'm supposed to fly out to fucking California for a 'family celebration' with his and Matthew's relatives and then just sit back and wait until he does something else to break her, no, break *our* hearts, and start the process all over again!" she screamed. "I-can't-do-it!!!" she cried, emphasizing each word. "I can't do *that*, I can't do *NPI* and I can't handle a relationship that's going to constantly check me, correct me, or depend on me for things I may not be capable of giving!" She fell to her knees, covering her eyes. Her body trembled from the private grief she'd relentlessly tried to conceal but had always been apparent to him.

He rose from his seat to sit beside her, taking her in his arms and giving her a safe place to heal. "You're not alone Ary, you're not. I'm here now and will always be here, no matter what happens between us," he said, as she wept uncontrollably. "No one can do all the things you're trying to do, and it shouldn't be expected of you, it's not fair," he suggested, pulling her in closer. "I'm asking you to let me take the burden. I'll handle G and NPI. I'll work with Darias and we'll sort this out. You shouldn't have to get involved. I'll even talk to Marguerite. And forgive me if it's not my place, but it's not up to you to '*fix*' your family or anybody else for that matter, not even us."

She leaned back, looking up into his pleading eyes and said, "I want so much to believe you. I want so much to care more than I do, but Dwayne, sometimes I don't even know who or what I'm fighting for. Sometimes I feel like he stole a part of me that can't be replaced. That's why I wanted to take my own life, just to get rid of the pain. I feel so broken." Her tears were unending. She didn't know how to make them stop until her cell phone beeped a frantic text: *Ary if you can, meet me at my place ASAP.*

She looked at her watch. It was nine-forty-five. Wiping her eyes with her shirt sleeve, she wrestled from his embrace, stood up, turned away without saying a word and walked towards the door.

"Where're you going?" he asked, confounded by her unexpected reaction.

"I have to leave Dwayne," she said, wiping away the last of her tears. "It's important that I at least see this through. I'm..."

"Wait a minute," he said, walking over to her. "What were we just talking about? Is it me that's crazy? You get some mysterious text and then you have to suddenly make a mad dash out of here! What gives, Ary? And be up front with me woman. What-the-fuck-gives?!" he asked, stressing every word.

Sensing his mounting anger, she decided leaving was the best thing to do. "I'll call you tonight, I promise." After she closed the door, Dwayne looked around for anything to throw, settling on a gold clock given to him by G for his first NPI contract award and pitched it at the front door, shattering glass and gold fragments all over the floor. He walked around the chaos and over to his minibar, poured a tall glass of Kentucky Bourbon, fell back into his recliner and yelled, "What is this freakin' hold she has over me!?"

CHAPTER 133

"OF course Matthew, don't be silly, we'll be there. I'll call the kids and be in touch once we land."

"Thank you Sonya. I know it would mean the world to him knowing that *all* his family was by his side."

"We want to be there for you too, Matthew. Believe me, I know the stress it causes when you stand to lose someone you love." Although she didn't mean it the way it slipped through her lips, Matthew paused and frowned. He wondered if her words were intentional, her way of getting back at him when he was most vulnerable.

"Alright Sonya, we'll speak soon," he said, eager to end the conversation, his tone changing from the quiet strength she'd come to recently know to a curt, dismissive tenor that made her wince.

After hanging up, Sonya called Marcus, relaying the information she'd just gotten from Matthew, stressing that he should coordinate with Ary and book their flights together, as soon as possible. He assured his mother that he would and not to worry and that he'd email her the details once their plans were secured.

"Oh mom, where're we staying? Should I find a hotel for us?"

"I didn't even ask, Marcus. But to be on the safe side, yes, please book a suite near the airport so we can all stay together. I'll reimburse you for the charges once we get there."

"Ary and I will split it mama. You don't need to worry about that."

"I appreciate that honey, but I don't know how long I'll be there, so I may need the room after you and your sister leave."

"I'll call Ary to see what timeframes work for her," he offered. "I love you mama, for being there for all of us, especially with all that you've gone through. You are my lifelong hero. Thank you," he ended, tears unexpectedly trickling from his eyes.

"I love you too, baby. That's what moms are for."

After hanging up, Marcus called Ary to give her the news about their father. He wasn't expecting her reaction. She'd reminded him that she had no plans to attend Bruce's surprise birthday party and was sure that Matthew and '*whoever else*' would be enough to take care of him in his time of need. Marcus was livid. Ary warned him not tell Sonya, she didn't want to upset her. She tried to explain what she was going through at work and that she was too stressed to try and pretend that they were one big caring family again. '*Don't call me about him anymore, Marcus! He wasn't there for us when it mattered most,*' she'd screamed. '*I'll call mama once everything is figured out, whatever figured out means,*' she ended.

"Doesn't family mean *anything* to you anymore!!!!" he yelled. But it was too late—she'd made her decision long ago to punish Bruce for her enduring pain.

CHAPTER 134

"I know who texted you," he said, meeting her as she walked through the door of his opulent penthouse.

"What? Who was it?!"

"I made a phone call to a friend on the West coast, whose name I can't divulge right now, but he knows all about T.O.T and Dave Winters, the firm that's partnering with NPI."

"I know who they are," she said, impatiently, "Please tell me who it was?"

"It was that shit bag, Joseph Larsen."

"Oh my God, not again!" she said, covering her mouth."

"He knows you've somehow been looped into this thing and he's just trying to frighten you. I also had dinner with someone tonight who corroborated it," he continued, watching as she paced around the room, placing one hand on her slender waist, the other on her forehead.

"Look Ary, honestly, I initially wanted you off the account because of what happened between us in Greece, but after thinking about it, that would put me in the same league as Larsen, and that is *not* who I am or ever will be. So I don't want to see you getting hurt by any of this and my suggestion would be to just stop whatever it is you're doing and cease communicating with anyone else involved and leave it up to me, G and the others to expose what could very well be construed as a mass level of corporate fraud."

She couldn't take her eyes from him and wondered if he was telling the truth or was this just another scheme brewing that would eventually leave her at risk of losing everything.

"I've been meeting with Marguerite," she began, "and as much as we're polar opposites, I believe her." She recounted all that she'd been told by Marguerite and was expected to carry out. "I don't want to go through another episode with NPI where I either have to voluntarily quit my job or stand a real chance of being fired. But it seems so selfish, if not irresponsible not to act when you know there are people or forces out there trying to destroy not only your livelihood, but quite possibly those of other NPI employees. I also believe in G and the company he's built and I don't want to abandon him when I could very well have done something to help salvage it in some small way."

His head flooded with thoughts of helping her uncover a solution to the latest NPI debacle, to their recent international rendezvous, to her coldheartedly ditching him for Dwayne, to this moment, standing five feet away from him in his home. His heart throbbed, but he was careful not to let her notice.

"Here's the deal, Ary. I've reached out to G tonight to let him know what I've learned, which in and of itself is enough to earn me more enemies than *I'm* even comfortable with in the industry, and we've begun to flesh out what we think is the most effective way to expose the reprehensible players in this latest production. More than likely there'll be some top heads rolling and I really don't think it's a good idea for you or your name to be associated with any of it," he explained, moving closer and embracing her shoulders.

"Are you inferring that only *men* can shed light on alleged corruption, Darias?" meeting his stare, forcefully disengaging his embrace and backing away.

"Of course not, don't be silly. But what I *am* saying is, more than likely there *will* be repercussions and it might be easier for me to find another job than it would be for you if things get…"

"Stop right there!" she cautioned. "Please don't patronize me or lessen what my capabilities are, which by the way, have already been tested and proven in just a short time. And, I might add, executed flawlessly!"

"With my help!" he shouted. "That was all because of the information I gave you!" he tried reasoning with her. "Look Ary, this isn't a game. And let's not pretend here that you did what you did alone! You'd only been with NPI for what, a few short months when all that shit took place? Come on now, be realistic. This is the oil business and I'm sure you've figured out that in this country, forgive my candor, it's run predominately by men who look strikingly like me, not black, brown, or multi-ethnic females, no matter how attractive they may be."

"That's enough!" she screamed. "You say it isn't a game, but every other week it seems like there's some type of contest being perpetrated. Or maybe it's not so much a con-test, as it is a good-old-boys con-game," she said, sarcastically. "But you know what, you're right. Maybe I am, once again, getting in over my pretty little head in this strange sport of rich, white, oilmen. And, as you say, you and G have it all under control. So I'll step aside like an obedient little woman and let the smart '*men-folk*' handle it," she said, bristling with anger.

"Ary, listen to me…" he tried to finish, grabbing her again.

"No! Let go of me! I get it," she said, breaking away. "That's all I needed to hear. Maybe Dwayne was right, yet again!"

The mere mention of Dwayne's name caused an involuntary jolt throughout his body. Grabbing the door handle, she forcefully swung it open, causing it to bounce against the foyer wall and tear a hole in the imported silk wallpapered covering. She raced into the private elevator.

"Goddammit Ary, Don't go!" he pleaded, chasing after her. "Why do you constantly feel like you have to prove that you're better than any man at anything, why?!" he yelled, through the closing door.

She pounded the *'open door'* button, composed herself, stood in the middle of the elevator and said, "Because I am."

CHAPTER 135

AFTER leaving his apartment, she asked the doorman to hail a cab for her. Not immediately sure of where she was going, or what she needed to do, she only knew she had to do something, anything, whether it was to truly try and prevent any further takeover attempts or prove to anyone who doubted her that she actually could.

She instructed the driver to drive around the Upper East Side of Manhattan until she could figure out where she wanted to go. After twenty minutes of slow cruising, they passed the 'Blu on Park' restaurant and bar on 79th and Park, a pre-war building, reminiscent of a 1920s-era brownstone. "Stop there!" she said, tapping on the partition. "Just stop at the corner, please."

She walked up to the maître d' and greeted him with a forced smile. "Hello, I don't have a reservation and I know it's late, but is it possible for me to get a much needed cocktail?"

He looked at his watch, looked at her and winked. "Follow me young lady. If you don't mind sitting at the bar, I think we just might be able to accommodate you."

"I don't mind. Thank you so much."

He led her to the end of the bar, away from a few men whose focus was in tall glasses of brown or clear concoctions. "Let me know if you need anything else," he offered, tapping the counter to alert the bartender before heading back to his station. Ary took a seat on the non-descript, but comfortable bar stool and asked the bartender for his recommendation.

"Well, normally I'd recommend our special, the 'Blu Ribbon,' but for you," he leaned in, whispering, "I think something with a splash of champagne would be more fitting," he winked.

After a few minutes he returned with a pale flute holding a colorful blend.

"Oh wow." she said, softly, after taking a cautious sip. "This is delicious. What is it?"

"A Golden Sparkler, for a shining beauty," he flirted. "Salud!"

She didn't know how much in need of a compliment she was until he offered it. Her nerves were beginning to settle. As she surveyed the elegant space, she noticed three men sitting at a nearby table. Their dinner plates were being removed by the wait staff when she overheard one of the men discussing an upcoming contract. *Do people* ever *stop discussing business,* she thought, checking her own phone for any missed messages. *I guess not,* she half-laughed, surprising herself that she even had the strength. She turned slightly to get a better look at the trio sending her clutch and phone falling from her lap onto the floor.

"Oh no!" she screeched, hopping off her barstool.

"Hey Winters," one of the men quickly ordered, "Help the beauty with her bag, I'd do it but I might not be able to get back up!" he laughed.

She stopped dead in her tracks, looked up and replayed the words in her head, *'Hey Winters. Did he say Winters?* Her heart felt as though it had shut down, along with every other muscle in her body.

Nearing the bar, he leaned down and said, "No no, allow me. The Chairman has spoken," he winked. "There you go," he offered, pretending to dust them off. "Just like new."

"Thank you," she managed, taking the items from him while discreetly shielding her face, hoping he hadn't recognized her. *Oh my God, is that really him?* She hadn't seen him since the meeting at

BP when he rushed around the boardroom after being introduced by the CEO.

Checking to make sure nothing had fallen out, she reached for her compact powder case, covertly pretending to refresh her makeup as she looked at the men through the tiny mirror. Any further doubts she had about his identity were negated after recognizing the 'Chairman' as *BPs Chairman.* Her hands began shaking as she forced her mind to reset. *Think Ary, think.* She noticed Winters had inadvertently swiped her camera on, and remembering what Dwayne had suggested she do in her meeting with Marguerite, took this as a second opportunity. While pretending to take selfies, holding up her cocktail and smiling in several celebrity-style poses, she pushed the record button, hoping to capture all three men in the picture and anything useful they might say. She got much more.

As they stood up to leave, the Chairman grabbed the third man by his shoulder and said, "Listen, it's like I said before, don't ever doubt Larsen. No matter what you may think of him personally, his eye is always on the money and this time is no different except that he's on our side with T.O.T." He reached for his suit coat on the back of his chair and said to Winters, "What's the new name I gave his dying company again?"

"*No Pun Intended*," Winters laughed.

The Chairman laughed so hard it triggered an asthma attack. The two men growing concerned, leaned over to pat his back asking, "Are you okay, Chairman?"

"Ca-ca-couldn't be bet-better," he stumbled.

Ary's mouth dropped open. '*No Pun Intended,*' NPI? She felt her body stiffen. She was afraid to move, to breath, or even blink.

"Oh and Chairman," Winters said, "His former fling is playing hard to reach all of a sudden. Should I read anything into it?"

"No. I think we've gotten more than enough information out

of her. But I on the other hand received some very disturbing news from her the other day, which leads me to having a bone to pick with you and your cousin here." Both men exchanged puzzling stares. "But that's something I'd rather not discuss right now," he said, with a sudden rigidity overshadowing his bombastic face.

She was stunned and checked to make sure her phone was still recording. She waited until all three exited the restaurant and could no longer see them before asking for her check, and questioning the bartender.

"Excuse me," she said nervously, her hand still shaking as she handed him her credit card. "I didn't want to inject myself into an uninvited conversation, but I was just wondering if you knew any of the gentlemen who were sitting at that table."

"Oh yeah, they call the big guy the 'Chairman.' Serves on a ton of corporate boards and likes to come here 'cause not a lot of other '*one-percenters*' in the City have discovered us yet," he laughed. "That's probably why he prefers doing his business deals here—gets a jump on the competition, I'd guess."

"I'm sure," she agreed.

"And the other two?" she pressed.

"Not sure about the talkative one, never seen him before. But I think the shy one is related to the Chairman somehow. Never says much, seems to just listen and agree. But I'm sure when you have that kind of money and power, anything you say is worth listening to right?" he smiled.

"I'd say so," she said, forcing a soft grin. "Well, I'd better get home. It's been a really trying day."

"You need me to call a car service for you, sweetheart?"

"No, but thank you. I can take it from here."

She left a $20 cash tip, hopped off the barstool and walked outside to hail a passing cab.

"Fort Lee, New Jersey, please."

CHAPTER 136

AFTER arriving home, all she could initially do was pace from the living room to the kitchen to the bedroom, listening to and looking at the shaky video of the men at the restaurant and trying to decide whether or not to call Dwayne, Darias, G or all three. She concluded that Dwayne and Darias were more than likely still incensed, so she counted them out. *Maybe I just need to sleep on it, figure it out in the morning. I'm not even sure if it's the right time to tell G who I saw and what I heard. Marguerite did say she wanted to be the one to expose it all, but what do I have to lose by beating her to it? What can she or anyone do to me, really?* She climbed into bed.

Tossing and turning for more than an hour prompted her to brew a pot of chamomile tea, hoping the blend would have a relaxing effect. It proved futile.

She went from her bed to the living room couch several times, hauling a light blanket and two pillows with each trip. Looking at the clock on the DVR, displaying 3:30 in vivid blue numbers, she finally surrendered to the fact that the sun would rise before her eyes would close and decided the only thing that might help to truly calm her nerves and her competing thoughts was a slow, hot shower. Pinning up her feathery locks, she walked to the bathroom, grabbed her shower cap from the back of the doorknob, switched the shower jets to *massage* and stepped inside. *Yes, this is what I needed,* she thought, as the beads of pulsating water rained down on her soft skin.

As the tension faded from her body she thought of Dwayne and their time in Greece—sharing a romantic soak in the tub and making love on the balcony of his suite as the majestic sun rose over Mount Lykavittos on their last day. Her eyes sprung open and she pushed the faucet knob to the off position. Grabbing a towel from the ring, she hurried back to her bedroom, dripping and drying herself as she searched for her cell phone and instructed Siri to '*call Dwayne*'.

CHAPTER 137

"HEL...hello," he answered from a deep sleep.

"Dwayne it's me, don't hang up. I've figured out how to..."

"Ary?!" he interrupted.

"Yes, it's me, Ary. Dwayne, I've got..."

"What time is it?" he asked, rifling for his watch on the nightstand in the darkened room. "Three fifty-five? In the morning? Are you crazy?" he yelled, sitting straight up.

"No, I'm not. I just wanted to tell you what I found out last night or this morning, I don't even know anymore, but I think I have enough information to stop the takeover, and..."

"And what, Ary? And you want me to help? Or do you just need my advice? Let me put it to you this way Ary Alexander, I'm done. I've had it with you, NPI and all the fucking nonsense that constantly surrounds *all* of you. It's no longer worth it for me Ary. I don't give a shit anymore. I'm not trying to save a company I don't own or a woman who's not mine. So do what you have to do, what you feel is right and good luck with it," he finished, disconnecting the call and pitching the phone across the room. "Ahhhh, shit!"

CHAPTER 138

ARY stared at the phone as she felt her heart sinking. Although she was more alert than ever, she struggled to keep her eyes opened and her tears from falling. Trying desperately to stave off hyperventilating, she inhaled and exhaled several times then scrolled through her contacts until she got to G.

"G, it's Ary. I know it's early but I have some information I think you'd need to help in your investigation. Can we meet in your office in an hour?" she asked indifferently, not allowing him a chance to object to the early morning call.

"I'll be there."

CHAPTER 139

G called Darias and Julian, asking that they meet him at NPI. He didn't tell them he'd spoken to Ary or what the meeting was about, only that it was urgent.

The men arrived minutes before her and began discussing all they'd been able to unearth, and assumed that G must have uncovered even more.

As she approached his suite she'd heard voices other than G's, and wondered for a moment, if she were being set up.

They were shocked when the door to G's office slowly opened.

She walked in without acknowledging the other two men and spoke directly to G. "I think what you'll hear will prove useful in your investigation." She handed him a documented timeline of her meetings and conversations with Marguerite, laid her phone on his desk and hit 'play video'. "This is all I can do G. I also hope you come to understand that Marguerite is not your enemy. Although she and I have *almost* nothing in common, the one thing we do share is a solid belief in this company and the utmost respect for you and your vision. And G, she still loves you, but because you weren't willing to forgive her or listen when tried to tell you what was going on, she decided to enlist my help, which I'm sure you must realize, was extremely difficult for her to do."

G didn't say a word. He needed to process all that she'd just revealed. All three men sat there, staring at the video and listening to the brief recording, all while trying not to gape at the young beauty, even at this early hour. She turned to Darias who'd tried unsuccessfully avoiding eye contact. "You told me once that I would never have to face anything I wasn't prepared to handle. I hope this proves it and you'll come to understand that I'm quite adept at playing a woman's game in a man's world."

She smoothed her hands over her lightweight sweater and down her skinny jeans, picked up her phone, sent the video to G's email and turned towards the door to leave.

"Ary," G called after her, "This is incredibly valuable. How can I thank you…again?"

With all the strength and courage she could muster so early in the morning, she looked at him and said, "Pray for my family."

The men looked at each other, not knowing how or if they should respond. She walked out before they could decide.

CHAPTER 140

THE authorities arrived at his home at 5:00am; he was still asleep wrapped in the arms of his latest paramour. The doorbell chimed a beautiful Mozart Violin Concerto No. 3 in G major, followed by a quick succession of fist banging. "What the hell is going on?" he asked, looking around for answers. "Who the fuck is knocking on my door at this hour?" His young guest rolled over at his outbursts, startled.

"What is it Chairman? I didn't hear anything."

He walked over to the security monitor and saw a half dozen men dressed in blue jackets with the letters *'FBI'* on the front. At that moment, the loud knocking was accompanied by male voices shouting, "F-B-I. You're under arrest for fraudulent activity, misuse of private funds and investor fraud. We can do this the easy way or the hard way, it's up to you Mr. Floyd."

"What the fuck?" he yelled, fumbling for his silk robe. "FBI? Fraud?" He quickly made his way down the long hallway and through the wide foyer, tripping in and out of his monogrammed slippers. "What did I do?" he asked, nearing the entryway. "This has to be a mistake." he said, opening the door.

At that moment, two men rushed in, roughly spinning the seventy-two year old around and handcuffing him as he yelled, "You're hurting me! How dare you! Let go of me! I want to call my attorney!" But no matter how long and hard he protested they ignored his pleas and rushed past him, racing into several rooms, sprinting past his overnight guest as she looked on in horror, naked and in disbelief.

"I didn't do anything," she screamed. "I'm innocent. I don't really know him and he couldn't even get it up without those pills over there," she pointed towards the nightstand. The men looked through closets, drawers, file cabinets and locked desks, breaking them opened with what looked like small battering rams. They were determined to find and confiscate every piece of evidence needed to help prove their case. The Chairman was eventually allowed to dress in the pants and shirt he'd thrown over a bedroom chair before engaging in a night of Viagra-filled promiscuity, but was ultimately led in disgrace to a waiting car wearing his bedroom slippers.

"Don't worry Chairman," one of the officers said to him as his head was lowered into the car, "You won't be lonely. A few of your friends will be joining you shortly."

CHAPTER 141

JOSEPH and Lawrence were on their way to Saudi Arabia after having been tipped off before the raid, hoping to ride out the storm while they communicated with their attorneys—eight thousand miles away.

CHAPTER 142

SONYA reached for his clenched fists. She'd asked Matthew for a moment alone, to which he'd readily complied, urging her to take all the time she'd need.

"My heart is broken," she said, looking down at him. "I have never stopped loving you. For all the years you've been out of my life, there was a part of me who could never let go." The thoughts running through her head were like the rushing San Diego River cascading over the falls into an ocean of confusion. His six foot stature, his steadfast, oftentimes misplaced confidence, *which was not lost on their daughter,* she thought, and his commanding presence were still visible in the man lying in the sterile bed. But she couldn't dismiss his patent flaws—his transgressions, his stubbornness and of course, his ultimate infidelity.

Marcus knocked on the door of the private room, wrapping his arms around his heartbroken mother. She tried to smile through her reddened eyes.

"Is she here?"

He paused before answering, remembering what Ary had told him. "No mama, not yet."

CHAPTER 143

ARY stared out the window of the Boeing 767. With more than 300 passengers on board, she'd never felt so alone. She regretted not flying to San Diego with Sonya and Marcus two days earlier and declining Matthew's invitation to her father's surprise birthday party more than three weeks ago and could only hope that time would prove her wrong. The tears began rolling down her face shortly after takeoff and had not ceased an hour later. Her stubborn morning headache had refused to leave even after taking way more Advil than was recommended and she'd concluded that it was equal punishment for her dogged resistance to fully accepting the inevitability of life's changes, to partly blaming Dwayne for not supporting her when she felt she'd needed him more than ever before.

Her eyes fixated on the fluffy clouds, still pink from the morning sun. She wanted to acknowledge how beautiful they were but couldn't find the words. Her heart felt as though it required instructions to continue beating. Without warning, a poem her mother had recited to her and Marcus when they were children came at just the right moment: *God'll make a way, take a little time to pray, just a minute out your day, doesn't matter what you say.*

She closed her eyes and recited it over and over until the flight attendant, who'd asked several times earlier, stopped at her seat and inquired again if there was anything she'd needed—a glass of wine or something stronger—a meal more appetizing than was offered in coach—a warm blanket or a cold towel. And like each time before, Ary could only look up and shake her head '*no*.' Not even the turbulence could shake her sorrow. All she wanted to do was get to her family. Her mind was flooded with all that she'd done for NPI and Dwayne during the past month, in their times of need—now neither was there for her. '*Family first*' she kept hearing in her head and occasionally repeated out loud, causing the female passenger sitting across from her to look over with curiosity and questionable unease. *That's what G said,* she thought again, '*Family first*'.

CHAPTER 144

"LADIES and gentlemen the captain has put on the seat belt sign indicating that we've begun our descent into San Diego International Airport. Please pull up your trays and put your seat-backs in their upright position. In just a few minutes we'll begin making our final walk through the cabin."

Descent and *final* were the only two words Ary heard over the intercom. They described her feelings perfectly. High winds caused the mighty jet to sway from side to side as it approached the runway, causing her to question her own strength against much lesser forces. *Why do I always feel that it's my responsibility to fix everything?* she questioned. *Will I ever be in a position to just let go of the pain that seems to come second nature to me? Sometimes I wish he and Marcus had never found me and let me drift off into the next world.*

The captain apologized for the rough landing, thanked his passengers for their patience and wished them all a continued safe journey to their final destinations. The flight attendants reminded them to remain in their seats until the jet pulled safely up to the gate. Ary ignored all of it, removing her seatbelt and standing up to reach for her carryon in the overhead bin until the same attendant who'd sensed her grief, rushed over to her. "I'll take care of that Ms. Alexander. Please, for your own safety, sit down and buckle your seatbelt. I'm sure whoever's waiting for you will still be there by the time we reach the jet way."

Ary's reddened eyes, already swollen from expending more tears than she'd ever thought possible in the span of a six hour, cross country flight, were beginning to burn. Reluctantly complying, she listlessly fell back into her seat, looked up at the attendant and asked, "Have you ever experienced the loss of your family and people you love, over and over and over again and were finally forced to come to grips with it?" The attendant took the empty seat across from her to the chagrin of the female passenger who'd kept a watchful eye on Ary for most of the flight.

"No Ms. Alexander, I haven't and I'm so sorry. But for your own protection, you must remain seated and buckled." Ary couldn't respond with words, she didn't need to. Her face, body and demeanor told a better story than what could ever have been said verbally at that moment.

CHAPTER 145

WALKING zombie-like through the terminal and down to the ground transportation hub, she inquired at the information booth about a taxi to her destination.

"You won't need to take a taxi," he offered, startling her from behind.

As she turned to see who it was, her heart cried because her tears had been exhausted.